Hollow Court

THE LOCHLANN DECEPTION
BOOK ONE

ROBIN D. MAHLE
ELLE MADISON

We dedicate this to Baby Lera, the accidental lovechild of Davin and Galina who was nixed in the first version of the story.
We know you guys don't miss her, but we do.
If we're quiet enough, we can still hear her gentle coos.

How do I win this war alone?
It's like I'm fighting with a ghost
We're two battleships that always miss
But we can't admit
This is the fear of letting go

— RUELLE

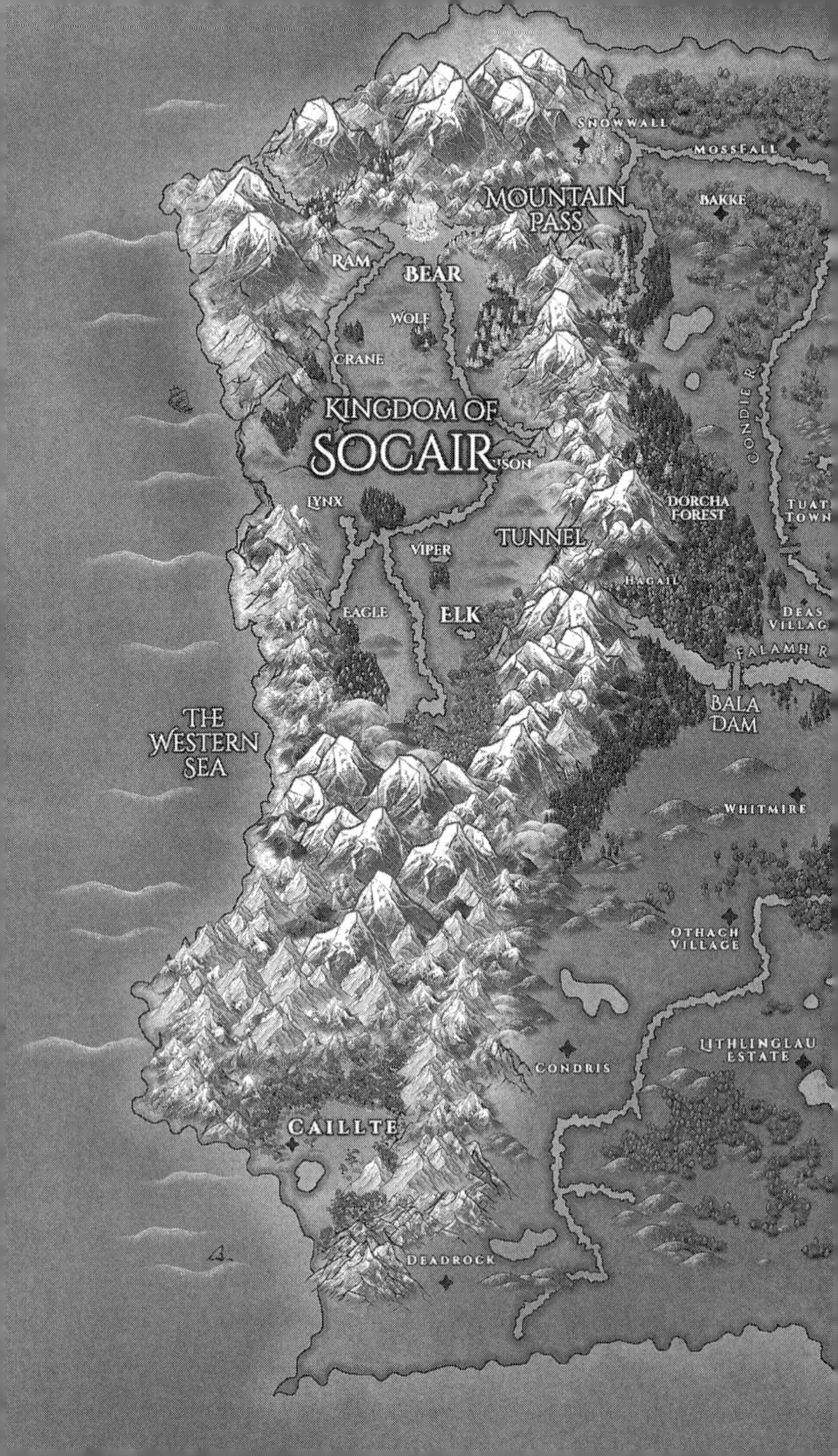
SNOWWALL
MOSSFALL
BAKKE
MOUNTAIN PASS
RAM
BEAR
WOLF
CRANE
KINGDOM OF SOCAIR
LYNX
TUNNEL
VIPER
CONDIE R
DORCHA FOREST
HAGAIL
EAGLE
ELK
FALAMH R
BALA DAM
THE WESTERN SEA
WHITMIRE
OTHACH VILLAGE
LITHLINGLAU ESTATE
CONDRIS
CAILLTE
DEADROCK

THE LOCHLANN REALM

OAKENWELL

ROSS

NGDOM OF
CHLANN

CHRIDHE

NIRUS

GONAND

KINGDOM OF
RIONN

N

THE
EASTERN
SEA

THE
ISLES

ECH

TISAS

HASLA
VILLAGE

RIVERWELL

DRY ROCK

MIDSIDE
BAY

ND

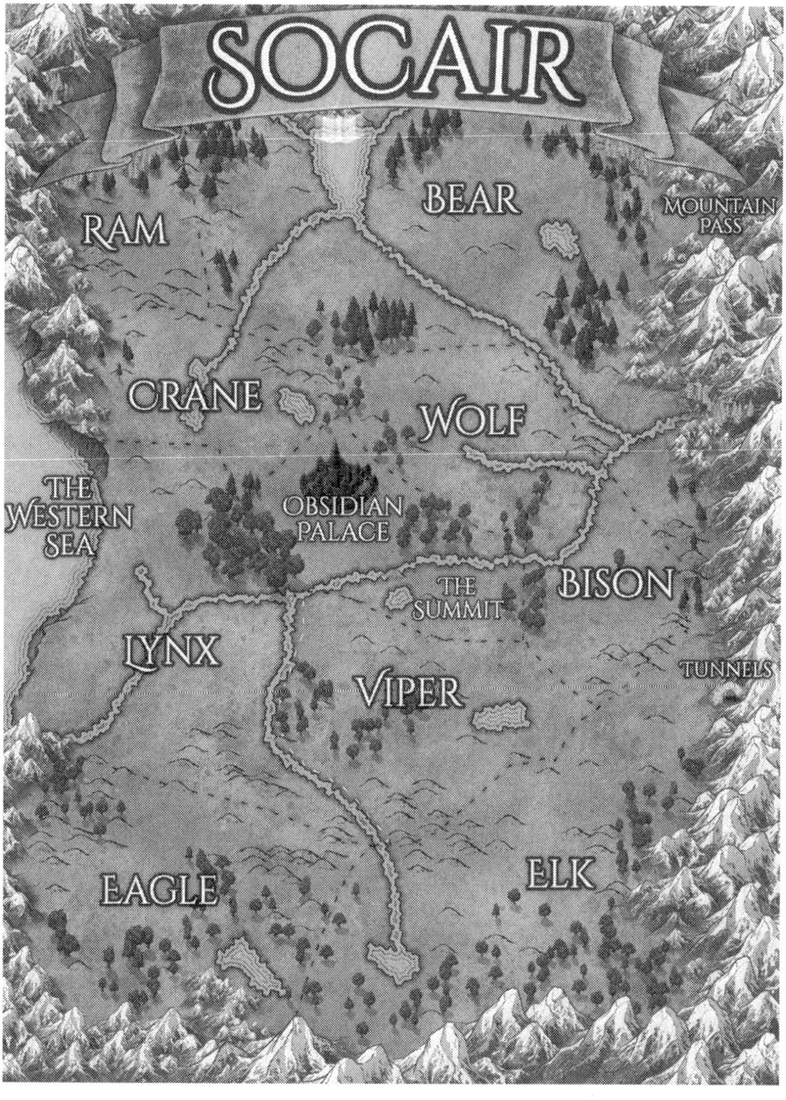

SOCAIR

BEAR
MOUNTAIN PASS
RAM
CRANE
WOLF
THE WESTERN SEA
OBSIDIAN PALACE
BISON
THE SUMMIT
LYNX
TUNNELS
VIPER
EAGLE
ELK

The Life Debt

DAVIN

A Year and a Half Ago

In the year since my best friend died, I had spent more time than I should have imagining what my own death might look like.

Not one time had I pictured it here, on a frigid rooftop in an enemy kingdom, miles away from the people I loved. The kingdom of Socair truly was the gift that kept on giving.

Where Mac had died saving a good family from a house fire, I would die in the noble pursuit of bedding beautiful courtiers.

So we were both heroes, in our own way.

I let out a delirious chuckle as another fist met my abdomen. One of the men holding me hissed something in Socairan, and my mind roughly translated it. He was telling his friends to hurry if they were going to end it before they got caught.

My heartbeat thundered in my ears, slower than it should

have been, and I fought against the soldiers who were pinning me down.

The next blow was a targeted strike at my head, and blinding pain exploded from the point of contact. I had to hand it to the beefy, stuffy lords of our neighbors. They were nothing if not capable.

My vision swam, and I spat out a mouthful of blood before I could speak.

"See, now, if you could put even half this much effort into your bedroom skills, perhaps dear Mariana wouldn't have felt the need to seek company elsewhere."

My assailant's face went flat with rage, and he reared his fist back again before a creaking noise interrupted him.

The men froze.

"I thought you said no one came up here," one of them hissed in his guttural Socairan dialect.

Then another person spoke from behind me, softer and more reserved.

"There you are." The feminine voice was familiar, though I couldn't quite place it.

Any hope I had for salvation fled as quickly as it had come. I had never seen a Socairan woman so much as politely contradict the men in the room, let alone intervene.

"What can we do for you, My Lady?" one of the soldiers inquired, a clear dismissal in his tone.

Lady? What was a lady doing on an icy rooftop in the middle of the night?

"My uncle is looking for you," she responded. "Shall I direct him here?"

Her tone was so neutral, it was impossible to say whether she was being helpful or delivering a threat.

That's when I put the pieces together.

Lady Galina. Perfect, pristine, demure, Socairan Lady Galina.

Her uncle was the duke of the clan, and arseling extraordinaire. He likely would not appreciate the Lochlannian captive —excuse me, *guest*—being harmed on his watch, if only for the political implications.

The men were quick to respond, assuring her there was no need to fetch the duke. They fled after a series of threats not to tell anyone, like I wanted to go running my mouth about the time I got the stars-blasted-hell beaten out of me.

Silence followed in their wake, all but the sound of my harsh, ragged breathing and my chattering teeth. It would appear that I wasn't going to die after all.

Well, unless I froze to death. I needed to move.

The moon swam in and out of focus, and my eyes fell closed for what couldn't have been more than a second. Only it must have been, because a shadow fell over me.

I groaned. *Have they come to finish the job?*

But it was only *her*. The typical, boring lady I was beginning to suspect perhaps wasn't. Why was she here?

"Come to revel in my pain?" I asked her in the common tongue.

No sense in giving away how much Socairan I knew.

This was really the only logical explanation since she had never even glanced in my general direction.

"You're a *laskipaa*," she responded, her fingers prodding along the back of my skull.

I couldn't really deny being an idiot right now, so I didn't try.

"Was your uncle really looking for them?" I asked, my words slurring.

Even under the hazy night sky, her expression was easy to read. It was more or less a repeat of her previous statement.

Of course, Sir Mikhail hadn't needed those soldiers coincidentally right now. So she had lied, rather quickly and quite well...and for my sake.

Why?

I must have said the word aloud because she let out a sigh in a single white puff of air.

"Tensions are high enough without you dying," she muttered, her voice only faintly accented. "Now, I need you to stand. I can't carry you back to your rooms, and you'll freeze to death out here."

Had I ever heard her string so many words together before?

I dipped my chin in assent, waiting until I was standing on shaky feet, half supported by her before I spoke again.

"Thank you," I said, closing my eyes against the stars that swam in my vision. "I owe you my life."

"Those are serious words here," she cautioned.

"I mean it. I owe you a..." I tried to think past the pounding in my head, casting about for the term. "A life debt."

She scoffed. "I'm sure I'll be demanding a great many things from a Lochlannian guard."

That struck me as unreasonably funny under the circumstances.

Of course, she didn't know how seriously she could take my vow. Lady Galina thought I was their captive princess's guard, rather than Rowan's cousin. Certainly not the marquess of the largest holdings in Lochlann.

And I couldn't very well tell her the truth. My cousin was in plenty of danger without word getting out that she had lied to their precious, omnipotent dukes.

I let out a low chuckle, and Galina gave me that look again—the one that said I was an idiot.

Her pale blue eyes glinted silver in the moonlight, ethereal and fathomless, like the fabled lakes from the isles of the fae. It was probably just my burgeoning concussion that made me feel like I was falling into them.

I meant to tease her, but my response came out low and earnest, the three words falling softer than the snow around us.

"You never know."

ONE
Galina

Present Day

THERE WAS NO ESCAPING NOW.

I had done everything in my power to avoid Davin's farewell ball. Well, technically, it was a ball for all three of the visiting Lochlannian royals, but I had no reason to avoid his cousins.

Whereas I would just as soon have gone the rest of my life without ever again seeing the smirk Davin hid all of his lies behind.

My stomach churned with nausea, but I didn't know if it was from the carriage jolting in the wind, the wintergreen scent wafting from Alexei, or this inevitable encounter.

The charms on my bracelet clinked together in a gentle melody as I rubbed my fingers back and forth across the chain, lingering on the wolf's head that Alexei had gifted me the day our betrothal was finalized. It was as menacing as the man at my side, with wild eyes and an open maw of sharp teeth. Quite the contrast to the other, more delicate charms I had collected through the years.

"Stop fidgeting, Galina." Alexei's tone was frigid, but his

hand was warm where it covered mine, searing into me like a brand.

I didn't jerk away. I knew better than that.

"Apologies, My Lord." I cast him a demure look through my lashes, reaching up to smooth a strand of his chestnut hair. "I'm only nervous, taking so much time away from our wedding plans."

Storms bless my lifetime of etiquette training for the smooth delivery of that bald-faced lie.

If there was something I wanted to do less than see Davin again, even less than sit in this carriage next to my bastard of a betrothed, it was think about our ever-looming nuptials.

Besides, most of the planning was being done in his clan, not mine.

It seemed to placate him, though, the reminder that he would soon own me more thoroughly than he already did. His massive shoulders relaxed, and his large, calloused fingers threaded through mine, his thumb rubbing the edge of the wolf charm.

My insides twisted at the sign of affection, but I forced a quick smile before turning my face to stare out the window once more.

Just over the hills in the distance, the Obsidian Palace slowly came into view. Black spires gleamed in ominous contrast to the pale overcast sky. Only six months ago, this area had been filled to the brim with the *Besklanovvy*, bands of those who had been cast from their clans. Then our new Lochlannian queen had conscripted a horde of them into her personal army, effectively siphoning them from the unclaimed land.

It was a shame, really. I might have welcomed an attack from the Unclanned right about now to get out of this ball. Out of this carriage. Away from Alexei.

At least he was going back home after this. I would get a solid month's reprieve before I had to deal with him again.

Every day, for the rest of my life.

My father cleared his throat from his spot across from us, his gaze flitting to where Alexei's hand was still entwined in mine. My mother sat demurely next to him, though I wondered if I imagined the barest hint of disapproval in her eyes as well.

For me? Or for Alexei?

Perhaps I was only seeing what I wanted to see.

It didn't matter, anyway. Neither of them could contradict my uncle's orders.

He was the duke of Clan Ram, a position that allowed him absolute authority in Ram territory. Even the monarchs had no jurisdiction over who he wanted his own family to marry. It was considered a clan issue, one the dukes had carefully excluded from the ruling contract.

"The wedding will be here before you know it, *Malishka*." My father's words were bland, but they almost sounded like a warning to my ears, tempered with his favorite endearment.

Baby girl.

Before I could dwell on it, the carriage slowed to a stop. My heart beat a furious staccato, bile rising in my throat.

There went my last chance to hurl myself under the wheels.

If I vomited before we reached the castle, could I escape tonight's ball?

Would it be worth Alexei's anger to try?

"Honestly, Galina, I know long carriage rides upset your stomach." My mother's tone was gently chiding, but she stole a glance at Alexei, who was carefully scrutinizing me. "But you look as though you're going to an execution rather than a ball."

I bit back a curse, fixing my features into something more appropriate. Only Davin could make me forget myself this way.

It was ridiculous when I knew that our every interaction

had been a lie, ridiculous the way I couldn't quite banish his voice from my head.

You've never even considered wanting more?

Though every word of it had been a manipulation, his question echoed with each footstep I took out of the carriage, steered by Alexei's firm grip.

Had I ever thought about wanting more for myself?

Not then. Not really.

But lately...lately, it was all I thought about.

TWO
Davin

The Socairans looked happier than I had ever seen them.

My first holiday into their esteemed kingdom had been under markedly worse circumstances, but even this trip had seen mostly stern faces and disapproving looks. Until now.

"If I had known all it would take to make them so ecstatic was to finally leave, I'd have done it weeks ago," I commented to my cousins in an undertone.

The four of us stood slightly apart from the crowd of elegantly attired courtiers in the ballroom, enjoying a rare moment of reprieve from the constant politicking that had plagued our lives since we arrived.

Rowan scoffed and rolled her eyes, a move that—as their queen—was probably less than appropriate. I loved her for it, though some of her people were clearly still coming around.

It was hard to believe that less than two years ago, we were captives of this kingdom, and now my best friend and cousin was their queen. I wondered who the turn of events had been more shocking for, her or the stodgy citizens she ruled over.

"You wouldn't have left me so soon after you got here," she argued.

"True enough," I admitted, grinning down at her.

She was short enough that from my vantage point, I could mostly see the top of her black, spiky crown and the crimson curls entwined with it.

Besides, as much as I generally despised dear old Socair, I wasn't exactly thrilled to be returning to Lochlann. Or rather, I wasn't thrilled about what I was going home to.

Especially not after the letter I had received just this morning, the one informing me that a formal challenge had been issued against my birthright.

There was nothing I could do about it now, though, so I tried to focus on my last night with Rowan instead.

My cousin Gwyn echoed those thoughts.

"Remind me why we're spending our last night together with a bunch of stuffy Socairans?" she complained, tucking a wayward auburn curl behind her ear.

"Because otherwise we can't pretend to our parents that this trip was to build stronger relations," Gallagher told her.

To the untrained eye, the twins were nearly mirror images of the other, though Gallagher was a bit taller and broader. Even their faint smattering of freckles fell into nearly identical patterns on their tan cheeks.

"Speak for yourselves," I said, arching an eyebrow mockingly. "Row and I have been working."

Though a large reason for the rather arduous journey through the mountains had been to see my favorite cousin, it had also been to gently scale back on the trade agreement we had established. Winter was just around the corner, and Lochlann's food stores were vast, but they weren't limitless.

I had been tasked to represent our kingdom in those negotiations, and the twins had come along for moral support, or more likely, the party.

"We're here to...help build relations with the Socairans." Gwyn made a face as she said it, looking around at the people in question with thinly veiled distaste.

Gallagher snorted softly. "I'm sure Davin has had enough Socairan relations for all of us."

I put a hand on my chest in mock offense.

"I'll have you know I was quite chaste this trip." Truthfully, I hadn't even been tempted, but I wasn't about to tell them that.

Then they might ask why, and I didn't want to think about how that explanation would go.

Because the courtiers here remind me of someone I never want to think about again.

At least it didn't look like Galina would be here.

I would go this entire trip without seeing her at all. Which was for the best, obviously.

No sooner had the thought crossed my mind than a servant announced the approaching of a new carriage. I bit back a curse.

Like I had summoned her with my thoughts, I knew who it was going to be before Rowan even opened her mouth to say, "Oh, that must be Galina."

Her tone was light and airy, like she wasn't actively making my life worse with her proclamation. Of course, Rowan didn't know about my history with the darling of Clan Ram. No one did.

Any humor I had found in my cousins' banter dissipated, my stomach dropping like an anvil.

"Isn't it a bit late for anyone to be coming for the ball?" I asked in the most casual voice I could manage, gesturing around the crowded room.

Since the Obsidian Palace was a solid day's ride from the nearest estate, everyone else had arrived earlier today or even last night.

"She got caught up with wedding plans," Rowan said distractedly, breaking off when her husband subtly waved her over to his conversation with the duke of Clan Lynx.

Right. Galina's upcoming nuptials.

Her wedding had been the talk of the court since we got here, and I had tried like hell every day to ignore it.

Gallagher eyed me, his features just a hair too innocent. "Didn't you two know each other from your time at Clan Ram?"

And Elk, but I wasn't about to clarify that for him.

This was my most discerning cousin's favorite game. The *lightly comment on something until he got information out of you* game. It worked best with his accomplice, and here she came, of course, ready to back him up.

"Well, they must have, Twinsy. He was held as a captive guest at her estate for, what was it?" She pretended to ponder. "Six weeks?"

"Three," I corrected, nearly admitting there had been another five in Elk before forcibly clamping my lips shut.

Their twin smirks grew even more devious. I had known better than to play into them.

"So three weeks in the same court with her. I suppose you will at least have been...friendly?" Gal baited.

"You know how the courtiers here are," I hedged.

"Not as well as you do, apparently," Gwyn muttered, taking a long sip of her sparkling beet juice before wincing.

I resolved to ignore them more effectively after that.

Fortunately, Rowan showed up to take the conversation elsewhere. Unfortunately, she appeared to be ushering us away from our chosen corner.

Instead of allowing us to converse with the other punctual courtiers, she guided us toward the main doors to greet her newly arrived guests.

With a sigh, I followed her to the door, wondering if Galina was half as unhappy about seeing me again as I was her. Did she regret the way things had ended, now that she knew who I was?

She must have put it together by now.

Galina was many things, but stupid was never one of them.

For all that I spent the entire walk to the front doors steeling myself to face her presence, I was still not prepared when she glided into the Great Hall.

I wasn't sure what I had expected. That she would look different, somehow, in light of everything that had happened between us.

Perhaps she did, at that.

Thinner, at least, the angles of her cheekbones sharper. Otherwise, she stood tall and lithe and graceful as ever, her golden hair braided up flawlessly, not a single thread out of place on her ornately brocaded skirts. Her unnaturally perfect features were carved into flawless Socairan demureness as she took in her surroundings.

Her father made introductions for himself and his wife, his familiar crystal-blue eyes narrowing slightly as he greeted me. We had never met. In spite of my extended stay as a political prisoner last year, Galina's parents hadn't been at Castle Ram when I was there.

Still, he appeared to recognize me all the same.

Then it was Galina's turn—or rather, Lord Alexei's turn—to introduce them both.

Galina was only a few inches shorter than I was, but his massive form dwarfed hers, and that of most of the people in this room, muscles bulging from beneath his gray-and-white jacket.

"I am Lord Alexei, nephew to the duke of Clan Wolf, and this is my betrothed, Lady Galina of Clan Ram." His grip on her arm was possessive and territorial as he introduced her to me like we had never met.

Whether he knew about my history with his betrothed and was being a passive-aggressive bastard, or he was just another controlling Socairan arsehat, I couldn't tell.

If I hadn't known before that Galina was none too thrilled

with the prospect of seeing me, I would have figured it out by the way she pointedly avoided looking in my direction, greeting the other three first.

Finally, she turned her icy blue gaze on me.

Not a hint of emotion shone from their depths, and her bland expression didn't falter.

"Lord Alexei," I greeted after my cousins took their turn. "And Lady Galina. Lovely to see you again."

I managed to deliver that line without a trace of sarcasm.

Alexei's expression darkened before Galina reached up to rub her hand over his arm. She whispered something into his ear, and his shoulders relaxed slightly as he glanced down at her with greed in his light brown eyes.

It twisted something inside of me, something that I did my best to stamp out. A whisper of jealousy that hadn't quite worked its way out of my system after all this time.

Even after she had made her feelings about me painfully clear.

"Laird Davin." The slightly mocking emphasis on my title was so subtle, I might have missed it, had I not known her so well.

But I did.

At least, I thought I had.

Looking at her now, I could almost believe I had entirely fabricated the version of her with stars in her eyes and snow in her hair and a soft smile on her full lips. Then again, hadn't that version of me been a lie as well?

That's all we were to each other, in the end.

Perfect, tempting lies.

THREE
Galina

THE CROWDED BALLROOM was almost a relief after the suffocating greeting in the Great Hall.

At least here, I could escape Davin's scrutinizing cobalt gaze, if not Alexei's bruising grip. Fortunately, the latter seemed just as happy to avoid the Lochlannians, which was...unsurprising.

Prejudices between our people ran deep, and Clan Wolf, in particular, still held grudges from the decades-past war. The duke's son had been killed in battle. His brother had died more recently, courtesy of Rowan's soldiers, leaving my betrothed as the heir.

Davin's presence certainly didn't help matters where Alexei was concerned. He knew we had been acquainted in the past, but he hadn't actually seen Davin until tonight. And while Alexei was certainly attractive enough, Davin's face was very nearly perfect, from the sooty eyelashes that framed his painfully blue eyes to his well-defined jaw.

His obsidian hair was in a constant state of being just disheveled enough to hint at his favorite pastime, and he was muscular without being bulky. No, his looks had never been an issue.

It was his personality that was the problem.

At least my parents weren't showing such obvious bias toward our neighbors to the east. They were engaged in what looked to be a fairly involved discussion with Queen Rowan.

For my part, I was content, or at least resigned, to let Alexei lead me through several dances, during which I definitely did not notice Davin and the array of courtiers surrounding him at any given time.

He was an excellent dancer, though I knew that already. What was it he had said?

There are dances in the villages back home.

Der'mo. I had been such an idiot to believe him.

His familiar chuckle drifted over to me, and I fought to keep my features neutral.

"Is everything all right, Galina?" Each of Alexei's words landed like the edge of a blade, sharply honed, precisely aimed to be a warning rather than an inquiry into my wellbeing.

"Of course. I'm a bit parched is all," I said, letting an embarrassed flush take over my cheeks.

"Sit down and rest. I'll get you a drink." It wasn't a suggestion.

Though it wasn't uncommon for a husband to take the lead here, Alexei had managed to take an arrangement built on trust and protection and turn it into a dictatorship before we were even married.

I squashed the traitorous line of thought before it could show in my features. Besides, it wasn't an unreasonable suggestion, and he was fulfilling his end of the duties by taking care of me.

Still, I stood on the side of the dance floor for longer than was strictly necessary before turning to go back to our table. I was so lost in convincing myself not to hate my fiancé that I nearly plowed right into someone on the way back to my seat.

"Oh, my apol—" I began in my own Socairan dialect.

The word abruptly cut off as I realized it was my least

favorite Lochlannian I had almost run into. He raised a single black arrogant eyebrow.

"Apologies," I repeated in the common tongue, though my tone was markedly frostier.

He opened his mouth to respond but was interrupted by Alexei's return. Agitation rolled off of my fiancé in waves.

"Your drink, my darling." He spoke in Davin's language as well, handing me a silver goblet.

Davin looked from the goblet to me, a humorless smirk gracing his lips.

"Excellent vodka, don't you think?" he asked conversationally.

Aalio.

He knew perfectly well that I didn't like vodka. He might have been the only person who knew, for that matter.

"Delicious," I agreed, taking a deep sip.

It tasted like astringent. Pungent. Bitter. Dry.

Disgusting.

Davin's smirk widened, and I wondered if there was any way for me to accidentally spill this *excellent* vodka all over his perfectly tailored navy waistcoat. Before I had the chance to find out, Alexei's hand came around my waist in a proprietary gesture as he said something pointed about us taking our seats.

I nodded to Davin with all the goodwill I couldn't quite muster, then allowed Alexei to lead me away, pretending I couldn't feel the weight of Davin's gaze and the weight of my fiancé's ire.

Pretending.

That seemed like all I did these days.

ALEXEI WAS ANGRY.

He practically stormed down the hallway as he escorted me back to my rooms, well before the ball had ended.

That shouldn't have been anything new, but tonight, his fury felt different—far more palpable. I ran through a mental checklist of everything I had done over the course of the evening. What I had said. Who I had spoken to. How much I had eaten or smiled or fidgeted.

His grip tightened as we reached the door to my rooms, the pressure carving my charm bracelet into my wrist. I wondered if he had broken the skin, though I tried not to look or wince.

He let go, and I enjoyed the relief of being safely back in my room for all of five seconds before he followed me over the threshold.

"My Lord?" It was as close as I could come to an outright objection without offending him.

He could be rough in his handling, but he had never before breached even the slightest bounds of propriety. Without responding, he closed the door behind us, his shadow following mine along the dimly lit walls. Something dark glimmered behind his eyes, though his features were as cold as ever.

"I had thought, Galina, that you were promised to me. Am I wrong about that?" His tone was low, dangerous.

"No, My Lord," I told him, cursing the tendril of fear that crept into my tone.

It was ridiculous. Alexei was overbearing, even aggressive at times, but he had never actually hurt me.

Not really.

"Then why were you talking to the Lochlannian?" He stepped closer, until the smell of his wintergreen mouth rinse all but suffocated me.

My breath stuttered in my chest.

"I wasn't. I was only apologizing for nearly bumping into him." Emotions warred within me, desperation to explain and indignation that I should have to.

And fury, somewhere too deep down to reach, buried behind the foreboding feeling that was taking dominance over the rest.

"It would be a mistake to treat me like an idiot, Galina." He was close enough now that his breath was hot and sticky on my cheek, his massive form looming over me.

"I know that." That was true enough.

Alexei missed very little. Not a hair out of place, not a glance or a gesture, and I hadn't been nearly subtle enough in hiding whatever complicated feelings I had about seeing Davin again.

I had let my emotions get the better of me, even after my mother had tried to warn me, and this...this was the price.

"Then tell me who he is to you," Alexei demanded.

"He's no one to me." *Not anymore.*

"And who do you belong to?" he pressed.

No one, you possessive bastard.

For a brief, unreasonable moment, I pictured Rowan leading her army and felt a familiar stab of jealousy toward the flame-haired queen who was braver in the face of a war than I could manage to be in my storms-damned bedchamber.

Hating myself just a little more with each word of acquiescence, I still couldn't help but say what he wanted to hear.

"You, My Lord." Gathering the last vestiges of my dignity, I straightened and backed away from him. "Now if that's all, I should be getting ready for b–"

I didn't get to finish my sentence, because Alexei darted forward with a lightning-fast movement, wrenching me toward him by the arm and slamming me bodily into the wall.

Tears pricked at the back of my eyes, a welt already forming where my head cracked against the stone.

"We weren't finished talking." He bit out each word. "You do belong to me, Galina, and I will not share you with anyone, let alone that Lochlannian *svolach.*"

Bastard.

Interesting that Alexei chose the exact word I had used to describe him mere moments ago. He seemed to be waiting for a response from me, and I had no choice but to oblige him. I never did.

"I told you," I said, my voice shakier than it had been before, "he is nothing to me."

Alexei took a deep breath, exhaling through his aquiline nose, his almond-colored eyes boring into mine. "So you say. If I find out you're lying—"

A knock at the door startled us both. His gaze snapped to the door and back to me, narrowing in suspicion. The blood drained from my face. I didn't think Davin would come here when we had nothing left to say to each other, but if he had...

My pulse galloped within my chest, drowning out every other sound for several heartrending seconds.

Alexei stalked over to the door, opening it with a steadiness that belied the rage in his eyes. I stood straighter, holding my breath for a count of three before a familiar voice reached my ears.

"I came to check on my daughter, though I must say I'm surprised to see you in her rooms when the vows have not yet been exchanged."

The air left my lungs in a relieved whoosh, my father's voice as comforting now as it had been when I was a child having nightmares.

Only now I was an adult, living one.

"Apologies, sir." Alexei almost sounded sincere. "She was feeling unwell, so I helped her inside."

"I see. I'll take it from here," my father said in a tone that brooked no argument.

"Of course." Alexei's hands turned to fists at his side, the tan skin on his neck blushing with a furious red. Slowly, he turned to me. "Goodnight, *Radnaya*. May you rest well."

Had anyone ever hated being called *my dear* more than I did right now?

"Goodnight, My Lord," I forced myself to respond.

May you casually die on the way back to your chambers.

My heartbeat slowed to something resembling a normal speed, though my thoughts were still fuzzy and my head still pounding. Alexei was gone, for now, but it wasn't like I was rid of him. I would never be rid of him.

Tucking my trembling fingers into my sleeves and trying to ignore the pain coursing from my head down my spine, I turned to face my father.

"*Malishka*," he said quietly, coming in and shutting the door behind him.

One word, and the tears threatened to spill over again.

"Papa," I responded, barely breathing while I waited for him to ask the inevitable question.

Or worse, to fling an accusation.

When he spoke, though, it wasn't at all what I was expecting.

"I had an interesting discussion with our new queen tonight," he began.

I nodded mutely. I didn't know where he was going with this, but my father was not one for idle chatter, so I listened.

"She was frustrated about the treaty," he commented in the same conversational tone. "It would seem that she had wanted the extradition clause for women removed, but the dukes forestalled her. So all she could do was get a caveat added. Apparently, any lady who is married or betrothed to someone in Lochlann cannot be sent back to Socair."

His words hung in the air between us, suspended along with my very palpable disbelief.

He couldn't be suggesting what I thought he was. It was treason for him to even think about going against the duke's wishes—brother-in-law or not.

I let out a long, slow breath.

"That was an interesting conversation topic for a ball," I breathed.

His crystalline eyes met mine gravely. "I took a scholarly interest, of course."

"Of course," I echoed numbly.

The only thing my father had a scholarly interest in was medicine. He despised politics. Which meant he had asked for me. For *this*.

"Since you're unwell, *Malishka*, I'll send your carriage home in the morning and make your excuses for you."

Tomorrow morning, when the Lochlannians are leaving. And he had said that he would send my carriage home, not me. Deliberate wording from a deliberate man.

I didn't speak. I couldn't.

None of this made sense.

Then he pulled something from his coat and set it down on the vanity next to us with a clink. A small red pouch tied with a black string.

Gold.

"In case you need it on your journey," he said, his warm gaze meeting mine. "Of course, I'll miss you, but I'd rather you do whatever is best for your health."

He turned to go before I could question him any further. Not that I would have.

We spoke in subtleties, and against all odds, I knew what he was trying to say.

He was offering me an escape, one that meant we might never see each other again. Did my mother know? Did she disagree? I couldn't ask him that, either.

So I said the only thing I could to his retreating back.

"I'll miss you too, Papa."

FOUR
Davin

"Why do you have to leave tomorrow?" Rowan grumbled, pouring us both another healthy serving of vodka.

The others had long since gone to bed, leaving me to spend one last night with my best friend before I had to go back to Lochlann without her.

"Because sadly, I have to usher in the southern social season this year with my illustrious presence." And I had to make a damned good showing, wooing the nobles and villagers alike for the next several months.

"Naturally, you *are* the marquess of Lithlinglau—most esteemed and revered of all Lochlannian estates," she said dramatically, raising her crystal goblet in the air.

I chuckled and followed suit.

Unfortunately, she wasn't wrong. My estate was a veritable kingdom unto itself, being both the largest and most influential outside of the two main royal castles.

That was the problem right now.

"And only moderately likely to hold that title," I reminded Rowan, before taking yet another sip.

Though I had been being an arse when I complimented the drink to Galina, I hadn't been lying. It *was* good vodka.

I forcibly pushed away the memory of her standing mere inches from me at the ball, the way her eyes had turned to icicles when she realized I was the one she had very uncharacteristically stumbled into. I wanted to think about *that* even less than I wanted to think about my ownership of my own stars-damned estate being contested in five months.

Admittedly, the man who had left it to me hadn't been my father by blood, but he had been my father by law. He had also been a massive arseling, right along with everyone else in his family who would have inherited in my stead.

More than that, the Andersons had made no secrets of their political leanings—namely, dethroning my entire family so they could split our kingdom in two. The cherry on top was that they didn't give a single damn about the people.

"You can't possibly think the Assembly will vote against you," Rowan said, pulling me from my rather sour thoughts. "The Andersons have no claim. You were the named heir."

I shrugged a shoulder, leaning back against the small, elegant sofa. The Assembly was comprised of representatives from every estate, plus a few for the villagers, and every member had their own interests in mind.

"I think that the Assembly cares more about politics than facts, and the Andersons have done an excellent job convincing everyone that I'm incompetent and lacking in stability." Not that it was hard for them after Rowan and I nearly threw our kingdom into war over a bit of vodka smuggling. "And half the lairds are still upset we didn't retaliate against Socair for that little snafu wherein you were kidnapped. Twice."

She shook her head, her expression going solemn.

"How they lived through one war and want another is beyond me," she said. "I would happily go the rest of my life without seeing another man bleed out from battlefield wounds."

My stomach churned, as it always did when I was

reminded how close she had come to death this past year, fighting in Socair's civil war. And to hear tell of it, that war had only been marginally worse than the one between our two kingdoms over twenty years ago.

It was little wonder the people on either side of the Masach Mountains hated each other.

"Well, that might be where we're headed if the Andersons take Lithlinglau. There's no telling what they would do with that kind of power, but I'm sure a full-blown rebellion wouldn't be out of the question."

Rowan's eyebrows climbed into her crimson hairline. "You think this is about more than just their birthright?"

I pursed my lips.

"I think," I began slowly, running my fingers along the grooves of the crystal goblet, "that Tavish has had the same dubious claim to this estate for twenty years, and yet, it's only now that we're seeing a new group of rebels form, and we're less stable than ever, that he's decided to bring it before the Assembly."

I had no proof, but it was the only explanation that made sense.

Rowan sat up straighter, one of her curls bouncing free of the obsidian crown on her head. "Then I'll come back with you, show a united front."

"You have your own kingdom to worry about now," I reminded her gently.

Something in her features was too discerning for my liking. "That doesn't mean I stopped caring about the kingdom I left behind."

Or the people she left behind, she meant.

"I know that, Row, and I wasn't implying otherwise. But this is your life now." I gestured to the crown on her head and all of the responsibility that came with it. "You stopped our people from going to war with Socair. I'll stop them from going to war with themselves."

Her curls swayed with the small shake of her head. The motion dislodged her crown, and she tugged irritably at it.

"What a team we make," she said, wincing as the black spikes tangled further in her endless mass of hair. "First creating problems, then solving them."

I chuckled, unable to argue. It was a rather unfortunately accurate accounting of more of our lives than I wanted to think about. Though she was half-joking, guilt churned behind her eyes, an echo of my own.

Leaning over, I batted her hands away, helping her disentangle the crown like I had so many times when we were kids.

"What are you going to do?" she asked, placing her hands in her lap.

I turned to set her newly freed crown on the table behind me, taking the opportunity to fortify my expression before facing her once more.

"I'm going to attempt to win them over with my substantial charm, and if it doesn't look like that's working, I'll...show them I'm stable." My parents had strongly hinted at how that might be possible in their letter.

Rowan's bright green eyes darted to my features, reading the truth in them. "You can't be serious. Who?"

I had given this some thought, though I had mostly only been successful in ruling candidates out.

"Not Fiona," I said with a shudder, thinking of one of the more...*motivated* ladies at court. "She'd be likely to murder me and take my estate for herself, and all of that work would have been for nothing."

Rowan smirked knowingly. "You mean like your mother did?"

"She has never confirmed those rumors," I reminded Rowan, leaving out my personal, very strong suspicion on the matter.

"Nor denied them," she said with a shrug. "Who else is on your list?"

"I don't know, Row." I ran a hand through my hair. "It'll probably be Gracie."

She was pretty, one of the nicer girls at court, and we had... enjoyed one another's company on more than one occasion.

Rowan shook her head, staring at the gilded sconces on the wall and downing the rest of her drink.

"I hate this for you," she said quietly. "You, of all people, deserve love. Not some passing compatibility."

"Yes, well, I doubt that was ever really in the cards for me." I deliberately ignored the sinking feeling in my chest.

Maybe that was true, but giving up the possibility of something more still tasted strangely like grief.

Shoving that thought down as deep as it could possibly go, I slapped my hands down on the table, getting up to refill Rowan's vodka.

"Enough of that, cousin. We're not wallowers, and we're not spending our last night talking about all the dreary politics I'm going home to."

A smirk tugged at her lips, though sadness lingered behind her gaze. "I regret to inform you there are no taverns nearby."

I made a face. "This really is the worst place in the world. Well, I would suggest pranking your surly husband, but I suspect he might actually murder us for those efforts."

A light laugh escaped her, just as I had known it would. "Murder *you*, maybe."

"True," I acknowledged, grateful for the shift in mood. "He already doesn't like that I'm prettier than he is."

Rowan laughed harder. "Yes, he was expressing that very thing to me just this morning. The jealousy was palpable."

"As I suspected," I said, shaking my head dramatically. "Well then, best not rub salt in the wounds of his overwhelming insecurity."

It was another few hours of making fun of Socairans and rehashing bittersweet stories before she was yawning more than she was actually speaking. Despite her protests that she wasn't tired, she did eventually leave with one last hug, promising to see me off in the morning.

Only a few minutes after she was gone, a knock sounded at the door.

I huffed out a laugh. She had probably forced herself to get a second wind just to be stubborn.

I pulled the door open, a smile already on my lips.

"You're ridic—" but the word died on my lips, because it wasn't Rowan standing in the hallway.

It was Galina.

The First Misstep

GALINA

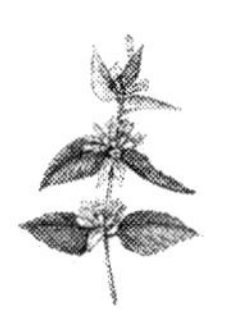

A Year and a Half Ago

I had called Davin an idiot, but I was no better, using my uncle's name to save a man who probably deserved the beating he was getting.

And now, less than an hour later, I was in his bedroom, having already gone to my room to fetch a small satchel of herbs. For all that I had judged the other courtiers for throwing out a lifetime's worth of good behavior for him, I was effectively doing the same.

Then again, I was still fully clothed, so I counted it as a win.

"Dare I ask which of their betrothed you cavorted with?" I inquired as I applied a poultice to the blossoming bruise on the side of his face.

Even with his lip swollen and his cheek well on its way, the sight of him casually sprawled across his bed was...difficult to ignore. Not that I would ever go there.

He shot me a rueful glance, wincing when it tugged at his split lip. "A couple of them, apparently, though in fairness I didn't know they were spoken for. Perils of being in a new court and all."

My eyebrow lifted of its own accord. "Would it have stopped you, if you had?"

"Yes." He put a hand on his chest in a display of offense. "I do have *some* scruples."

Oddly, I believed him. What reason could he have to lie about it now?

"Dare *I* ask how you know about medicine?" There was amusement in his tone, in spite of the circumstances.

"You can ask," I said dryly.

He shot me a demanding look. They must treat their guards very, very well in Lochlann for this one to have gotten so spoiled.

"You must be an only child," I mused aloud.

He arched his brow, wincing slightly as it pulled open the cut on his forehead.

"Technically," he said, letting the word linger in the air alone.

When it was clear he wasn't going to expound until I did, I sighed and answered his question. I wasn't sure why I cared, but I found myself unusually curious.

"My father had no sons and a great deal of knowledge to pass along." It went without saying that it had been in secret.

Davin was many things, but he wasn't the *laskipaa* he let people believe he was. At least, not entirely. I had gleaned that much just by observing him this past week.

A long beat of silence passed between us, his ocean eyes watching as I worked on blending some cedarwood oil, sage, and a bit of honey to help with the concussion he undoubtedly had.

When it was ready, I handed him the small cup, forcing him to drink down every drop.

"So 'technically'?" I pushed.

He nodded slowly. "I had cousins, and a close friend who

was like a brother to me. We all grew up together and spent our summers together at their...house." He abruptly changed the subject. "Why were you on that rooftop?"

Because I'm even more of a prisoner in this kingdom than you are.

I schooled my features, having no intention of answering that one.

"Where else are you injured?" I asked instead, taking the empty cup from his hands.

He raised both of his eyebrows this time, but only responded with, "my abdomen."

I looked to where his tan-and-navy jacket was buttoned securely over his chest. A flush rose to my cheeks before I could stop it.

It was ridiculous. It was just skin. I had seen plenty of men without their clothes on. In Clan Ram, men and women sauna-ed together. This would be no different.

Of course, he noticed. The uninjured corner of his mouth tilted up, causing the smallest dimple to appear in his cheek.

"Don't worry, Lady Galina. I promise not to seduce you," he assured me in a voice that was most certainly designed to do just that.

"How very comforting," I said, my tone brisker than I felt. "In turn, I promise not to let you."

I gestured for him to unbutton his jacket before I could think better of it.

As soon as his fingers went to deftly undo his buttons, I averted my gaze, busying myself with...well, nothing. There was nothing to do except stew in how awkward this was and wonder whether I was a liar for the promise I had made.

Whether we both were.

FIVE
Galina

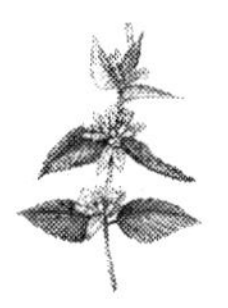

Present Day

Though I had returned my father's farewell, it still seemed impossible that I wound up standing outside of Davin's door, having only narrowly missed the queen's exit.

Davin stopped midway through his sentence, the teasing smile dying from his lips.

I had spent hours pacing my room, planning for this moment, this conversation, but now that I was here, all of the breath abruptly fled from my lungs.

We stared at each other for a long moment while I attempted to gather my wits about me.

"Lady Galina?" he prodded, arching a single eyebrow.

It was strange to hear my full name on his lips, when he had only ever called me Lina. Strange that he had no problem recognizing me by the small bit of my face that was visible.

His voice was low, cultured enough that I berated myself all over again for ever believing he was a commoner. Even if the common tongue was my second language, Davin exuded nobility.

That was the reminder I needed to straighten my spine.

There was nothing here but a history I could go my whole life without revisiting, and I had far bigger problems to face.

The burgeoning bruises that tugged at my spine when I stood taller was evidence enough of that.

"May I come in?" I meant for the words to sound neutral, but each one fell like an icicle, shattering in the weighty tension between us.

If my request shocked him, he didn't show it, though curiosity and wariness churned in his cerulean gaze.

"I told the soldiers you were expecting me," I said quietly.

Of course, I had kept my head down in hopes that they wouldn't know who I was, and it was hardly unusual that Davin would be expecting a random woman to show up at his door.

He blinked. "Did you now?"

For half a heartbeat, I wondered if he would turn me away, if all the bravery I had mustered to come here would be for nothing. Then he shifted back to allow me entry.

"Well, we wouldn't want to make a liar out of you." He might have been teasing, but for the barest edge to his tone.

The hypocrisy of that sentiment coming from him was enough to chase away any residual nerves. I stepped into his rooms on markedly steadier legs than the ones that had carried me here.

Once he shut the door, I took a moment to inspect the space before lowering my hood, just in case he wasn't alone. The last thing I needed was for my presence here to generate gossip that would make its way back to Alexei.

The room was vacant, though a half-empty bottle of vodka and two glasses rested on the table near the fire, one his, and the other, presumably, Rowan's.

He watched me expectantly, his easy stance far more casual than the probing look in his eyes.

"I need to know if you meant what you said," I began carefully.

"About the vodka being good?" he referred back to our conversation at the ball.

Storms. He was still such a *laskipaa*. And, unfortunately, my only real hope for getting out of here.

Taking a deep breath, I centered myself, my eyes landing on my favorite charm. A sprig of rosemary, to remember my family when I was in Wolf.

Or Lochlann, as the case may be now. The thought bolstered me.

"About the life debt," I clarified.

Davin straightened, his brow furrowing.

"What is it that you need?" he asked in a more serious tone.

It didn't escape my notice that he hadn't actually answered my question. I had wanted to wait to reveal what I needed until he gave me some sign of agreement. Weighing my options, though, I realized I had exactly none.

The power rested entirely with the man in front of me.

So, something altogether new and different for me, I thought sardonically.

"I need to go to Lochlann," I admitted, holding back as much of the truth as I could, for now.

He assessed me with a sweeping glance, crossing his arms. "That's hardly worthy of a life debt."

It had been easy, in his absence, to forget how storms-damned perceptive Davin could be when he wasn't flirting and smirking and being generally disarming.

With a sigh, I continued with the most important part. "I need to go as your betrothed."

He blinked several times, his arms dropping to his sides. The last time I had seen him this surprised was...well, the last time I had shown up at his door in the middle of the night, albeit for very, very different reasons than the ones I had tonight.

Looking at his disheveled black locks and his open shirt

laces, I realized that was the absolute last thing I needed to be thinking about right now.

"You want to get married?" he finally said.

My head throbbed from its earlier contact with the wall, from this conversation, from everything about this storms-damned situation. That was the only excuse I had for my uncharacteristic bluntness.

"Of course not." I couldn't quite keep the irritability from my tone. "You've made it quite clear you don't want to marry anyone, and I don't want to marry you."

He almost looked offended.

"Well, then," he said with a shake of his head, stepping further into the room and taking a seat near the fire, gesturing for me to do the same. "What is it that you do want?"

Once I was seated, I took a deep breath and launched into an explanation of the law, the caveat, and my plan to find another arrangement in Lochlann. He listened without interruption, waiting until I was finished to speak.

"You spoke of the treaty laws, but what about your uncle? Isn't disobeying the clan duke punishable by death?" he asked.

It was. Or Unclanning, which was arguably worse, between the forehead brand and the life spent starving, ostracized from your family and your people. Rowan had made strides in that direction, but the reality was still bleak.

But, in the hours since my father had left my room, I had thought this carefully through.

In the incredibly unlikely event that Uncle Mikhail would ever forgive me for this, he couldn't be seen supporting my decision to break my betrothal contract, not without serious consequences to the clan.

"Well," I said with more confidence than I felt, "he can't kill me if I'm not here."

Davin eyed me for several precarious moments before finally asking the question I had been dreading the most.

"Why would you risk that?"

Fortunately, I had spent the last several hours concocting a believable reason. The truth was out of the question. I had no proof and no desire to be even more vulnerable with Davin than I already was.

"I want to study medicine. But the noblewomen here don't do such things, as you know. And Alexei"—I forced myself to say his name casually—"is very old fashioned." *And an aalio.* "He would never allow it. Even if he did, there isn't anyone here who would consent to teach a lady. But I understand that things are different in Lochlann."

I clamped my lips shut before I could oversell the lie. Though, it wasn't entirely untrue. My dream right now was a life free of Alexei. A life with any freedom at all, really. Beyond that, learning more about herbs and working with them did sound nice.

Davin eyed me while I kept a guileless expression pasted to my features.

"And you'd risk your life for that?" His voice was lined with disbelief.

Though it was a fake dream I was defending, I found myself bristling, all the same. It could have been real, and would have been just as far out of my reach.

A bitter huff of air escaped me. "I realize that you have lived in a world that bends and stretches to accommodate your every need, *Laird* Davin, so it must be difficult for you to understand what it is to be denied the opportunity to study or, hell, exist in a world outside of what's expected of you. You can't possibly know what you would or wouldn't do for that chance."

He clenched his jaw. "Perhaps not, but I do know what it is to be trapped a kingdom away from your family and wonder if you'll ever see them again. So I'm asking if you've thought this through."

No. I haven't had the luxury of time to think this through. I tried not to let him see how affected I was by his words, by the fact that I hadn't even gotten to tell my mother goodbye.

Davin and I had never had honesty between us, though. So I took a deep breath, willing the words to ring true as I spoke them.

"I wouldn't be here if I hadn't."

SIX
Davin

THE FIRST TIME Galina came into my life, she was an unexpected savior.

This time, she was determined to be my undoing.

I stood to pour myself a drink, less out of desire than because I needed a moment away from her endlessly icy gaze. There was half a bottle of red wine left, along with the rest of the vodka.

Wine, it was.

I poured us both a glass, taking my time uncorking and recorking the bottle while I sifted through my options.

I could tell Galina no. But even if I hadn't owed her a life debt, she had come to me asking for my help—in her usual highhanded manner, but asking, nonetheless. Could I really leave her trapped in a life she hated, even after everything?

Aside from that, I did owe her a life debt. I had made an oath.

On the other hand, when I returned to Lochlann with a whirlwind betrothal that lasted a couple of weeks, I would ruin any chance I had of winning the vote to keep my estate.

If I was right about my not-quite-cousin's ties to the rebellion, letting him get his hands on the resources of Lithlinglau was not a chance I could take.

Blowing out a sigh, I considered potential solutions.

I couldn't ask Gallagher to take on my life debt, or to betroth himself to a stranger, even for a short period of time.

Rowan had complained endlessly about the limitations to her power on the throne regarding the backward-arse Socairan laws, so I knew that wasn't a possibility.

That left only one real option.

I turned around to face Galina. Her features were carved into careful nonchalance, and she sat with unnatural stillness. For a moment, she looked almost fragile.

Then her eyes snapped up to meet mine, full of the same unyielding strength I had come to expect from her. I returned to my chair, fortifying myself to make my counter proposal as I handed her a glass of wine.

"I can't be betrothed to you for two weeks, then call it off," I began.

She froze, and I held out a hand to stay her response.

"I'm not saying no," I assured her. "But there are more things at play than you realize. I don't know if you're aware of the situation in Lochlann with the rebels. They would target you just for the land you came from, let alone trying to marry one of their own."

"Are they worse than the Unclanned here?" she asked without inflection.

I considered that for a moment. While the Unclanned bore their mark on their foreheads and were completely ostracized from their clans, the rebels back home were more insidious. Otherwise, they were probably about the same.

"Not necessarily," I allowed.

She made a gesture for me to get to my next point, and I went on.

"We'll need to make sure this can't come back on Rowan."

"That won't be a problem," Galina said smoothly. "Since I

left the ball a bit early tonight, my father is sending me home to recuperate. By the time anyone notices I'm gone, it won't have anything to do with the queen or the palace."

I took a long sip of my wine. There was only one more real issue, but I was starting to think it wouldn't sway her.

I could hardly make sense of the fact that we hadn't spoken in over a year, and now we were here, and I was about to make an offer I couldn't take back.

"Then we need to plan on doing this for six months," I told her. "That's time enough to get me past an upcoming issue regarding my estate, and long enough that we won't look unstable when we call it off, which will be better for you as well."

She swallowed, scanning the room for several heartbeats before returning her attention to me. "Won't it make it harder for me to find another match, betrothed to you for that long?"

I scoffed. Already, I could imagine how the vultures would descend. Galina was gorgeous, titled, and accomplished. With my family's support, it would be no problem finding her a marriage, even if she couldn't secure her dowry.

Being betrothed to me would only help that cause.

I ignored the part of me that rebelled against this entire plan, knowing it was the most feasible one.

"Hardly," I answered her. "They'll want you just because they think you belong to me."

Not that she ever had, or ever would. Not that I even wanted that anymore.

I watched the gears turning in her mind as she weighed the situation in her familiar, inscrutable fashion.

"All right," she agreed after only a handful of minutes. "I agree."

Was she really so desperate to leave? Why?

Though her explanation hadn't exactly felt like a lie, I had never known Galina to want any life other than the one she was raised into. And if she had, she sure as hell didn't admit it, let alone act on it.

Yet here she was, barely blinking at a suggestion she would have turned down flat a year ago.

I didn't ask her why she was willing to leave her betrothed. Overbearing arseling that he was, perhaps she didn't feel she owed him an explanation.

Or perhaps it was just as easy for her to walk away from everyone else in her life as it had been for her to walk away from me.

I took another swig from my glass, watching as she did the same.

"All right, then," I eventually echoed. "But I need you to understand that we have to make this look real."

Galina's lips twisted bitterly. "I'm sure that won't be a problem for either of us."

At least one of us was sure about that. It already sounded like a nightmare to me.

SEVEN
Galina

DAVIN and I stayed up the entire night ensuring there were as few holes in our plan as possible. Eventually, we traded our wine glasses for tea.

Somehow, the sight of Davin brewing a pot of tea over the hearth felt almost as surreal as the entire insane idea we had cooked up.

Then again, we both had our reasons for needing this to work.

I clung to that comfort, to the reminder that he wouldn't back out, as I sat outside in the dark, freezing carriage, tensing at every set of footsteps that passed by and hoping with everything I had that they didn't belong to Alexei.

White clouds billowed out in front of me in the frosty morning air, fading in and out with each stilted breath. Silently, I counted down the seconds until we would be on our way.

Davin had escorted me to the carriage as soon as it pulled up to the front door, passing me off as a shy lady friend. Between his rank and his reputation, no one argued with that explanation.

I was fine until he went back to say goodbye to the king and queen. Then I took advantage of my solitude to imagine every possible thing that could go wrong.

My trunks were nondescript enough, easily hiding among the others, but someone who examined their contents might recognize them as mine.

What if Alexei insisted on going after "me" and discovered the carriage my father had sent out this morning was, in fact, empty?

What if someone had seen me under this hood?

My fingers absently traced the cut that the wolf charm had left imprinted in my skin as I considered scenario after scenario where everything could unravel.

The door wrenched open, and my lungs seized in my chest, my heart racing faster than I thought possible. But it was only Davin, followed by the red-headed twins.

He climbed in first, blocking me from view with his broad form long enough for them to sit across from us on the bench. The duke noticed me first. He froze.

"Lady–"

"Nope," Davin cut in smoothly, closing the velvet curtains just as soon as the door locked into place.

Gallagher closed his mouth with a suspicious glance as the carriage jolted into motion.

"Best not to say her name just now," Davin explained casually, settling in entirely too close to me on the narrow bench.

Not that there was anywhere else to go, but his body heat emanated uncomfortably to me, his elbow brushing my arm each time he shifted.

"I both feel compelled to ask and dread the answer," the young duke said with a sigh.

"Both of which are fair," Davin acknowledged. "But that will have to wait until the inn."

"Davin Allesandra Jenine Pendragon," the duchess drawled, rubbing her temples.

"That's not my name," he turned to assure me, as if I didn't know.

Though, to be fair, I supposed it could have been. I had only ever known him as Davin.

"It is entirely too early for me to worry about defending your very precarious honor, so just answer me this; is anyone going to try to kill us for this?" Lady Gwyndolyn asked with far less concern than the question warranted.

Davin looked down at me, but I wasn't sure what he was searching for. Permission to tell them the truth? My opinion on the matter?

There was a time when I could read him—or at least, I had thought I could. Then everything I believed about him turned out to be a lie, and it became impossible to trust my judgment where he was concerned.

I returned his gaze indifferently until he turned back to face his cousins.

"Probably not today," he finally replied.

"All right then. I'm taking a nap," she announced. "Budge over, Gal, and wake me if we get attacked so I can run away and leave Davin here to face it all alone."

Her brother chuckled, making more room for her to lay her head on his shoulder.

"No one likes a liar, Gwynnie," Davin shot back, not at all bothered.

"That's not my name," she echoed his earlier words.

"Apologies, *Gwyndolyn*," he said with false sincerity.

She glared at him, and I surmised she didn't appreciate that name either.

They continued with their bickering, both looking to Laird Gallagher for support. Though my heart pounded with each turn of the wheels, their banal chatter was oddly soothing. Familiar, even.

A memory came to me, unbidden, of a moonlit rooftop.

"Why do you keep coming out here?" I asked with a sigh, as soon as I spotted him standing in my usual corner.

"Because you come out here," he said with a smirk.

I rolled my eyes, something I hadn't dared to do since I was a child. "Yes, to be alone."

"But wouldn't you rather my sparkling wit to keep you company?"

"You aren't half as funny as you think you are."

"And you aren't half as serious as you pretend to be."

I let out a sharp breath that was definitely not a laugh, shaking my head.

"Fine. You can stay if you stop talking."

He had not, in fact, stopped talking.

But he had stayed and then came every night thereafter for reasons that confused me until they didn't. Until I was stupid enough to believe it truly was my company he was seeking out, and not the things that I let slip when my guard was down.

"Galina," a deep voice eventually startled me from my thoughts.

My fingers froze reflexively on my bracelet. For a brief, unreasonable moment, I was in a different carriage with a different man beside me, his fingers digging into my skin like claws poised to tear it from the bone.

A wave of humiliation washed over me when I realized those fingers belonged to me, and the man beside me wasn't the one I was running away from.

I forced my hands to relax, schooling my features into something serene as I shot Davin a questioning look.

"Oh, can we acknowledge her presence now?" Gallagher asked with a trace of sarcasm.

His hazel eyes darted back and forth between Davin and me, and I had the sinking feeling that he saw more than I wanted him to.

If Davin noticed his cousin's assessing gaze, he didn't comment on it.

"In here, at least, but we should still save the rest," he responded before turning his attention back to me. "As I was saying, Galina, we're well past the Obsidian Territory."

His shoulders had eased slightly, belying the tension he had been concealing behind his banter before now.

I wanted to join him in that relief, but this wasn't the hardest part. I still had to get out of Socair, still had to talk my way into the tunnels and trust that Alexei hadn't noticed me missing by then.

I nodded, acknowledging what Davin had said.

"We've got a solid day's ride until we stop at the inn," he went on. "There will be breaks, but I'll keep things vague with the guards until tonight, like we talked about."

"All right," I said, my voice more clipped than I intended.

Things were still tense between us, made even more uncomfortable by the knowledge that we only had a handful of days before we had to start our very fake love story.

Though, that really wasn't new for me.

If I could stand at Alexei's side and pretend to like him, I could damned well do it with Davin. The man might have been a liar, but he wasn't a monster. And at least I wasn't stupid enough to let myself believe it was anything else this time.

"You'll share a room with Gwyn," Davin added, pulling me from my thoughts once again.

"Oh, will she?" Gwyndolyn challenged, not bothering to open her eyes from where she was leaning against the back of the carriage.

"Well, I'm certainly not sharing a room with you," her twin responded. Then he turned to me, offering a tentative smile. "Don't mind her. She's always grouchy before breakfast. Or lunch. Or dinner, really."

The duchess let out a snort that might have been a denial or a confirmation. Either one.

After that dubious exchange, I settled into a cautious

silence for the rest of the ride, wherein I tried not to think about everything I was leaving behind.

Or worse, the uncertainty I was hurtling toward.

EIGHT

Davin

It should have gone unsaid that this whole cloak and dagger routine with Galina meant that we were keeping her identity a secret. Still, I found myself reiterating the importance of that fact to the soldiers.

I mentally noted each man's reaction. The impassive look in Scottie's eyes, the anger in Arran's. Others, like James, looked more apprehensive than upset, and a precious two were unfazed.

"Ye can't be meaning for us to protect one of *them*?" Arran asked, his presumptuous tone grating on my nerves.

"That's precisely what I mean." My voice was even, but I fixed him with a pointed stare.

He shifted uneasily, looking away.

At least telling the twins should be easy after this. I hadn't quite gotten around to mentioning that Galina would be accompanying us all the way to Lochlann while we were in the carriage today.

"More importantly," I went on, "we need this to be kept silent."

"For her safety?" Scottie asked with a note of incredulity.

"And ours," I told him.

He opened his mouth to argue, but James cut in.

"We just want to make sure yer no' in danger, mi'laird," he said, his tone cautious. "But, of course, we trust you. It's just our responsibility to get ye home safely."

"I appreciate that, and I don't anticipate any of us being in any added danger as long as we keep this to ourselves," I explained, my eyes darting from James back to Scottie.

The latter stood tall, rubbing a hand over his cropped blond hair, his expression still guarded. Between the time we had spent together training at the castle, and his on again off again dalliances with Gwyn, he was more familiar than the others.

He also seemed to have influence over the rest. So, I needed his support. Finally, he raised his hands in surrender.

"Listen, James is right. That's all this is," he said by way of explanation. "We just want to make sure we all know what we're getting into when we get back home. We're your men, My Laird. Of course, we'll do as you ask."

He said that last part with a hard look at Arran, who nodded tersely.

Though the situation was stressful enough without the clear lack of support from my men, it was also understandable. They knew the risks of upsetting the Socairans just as well as I did, and it was only fair that they would be worried, too.

After we finished up at the stables and I once again ensured their word to remain silent, we moved inside the inn where I bought them dinner and a pint of ale.

While it was mostly a gesture of goodwill to spend time with them, there was a small, decidedly unreasonable, part of me that might have lingered longer than usual just to avoid the Lochlannian inquisition that was waiting for me upstairs.

Eventually, I ran out of ways to procrastinate, and there was nothing for me to do but face it. After ordering dinners for the rest of us, I finally headed upstairs to our room.

Gal and Gwyn were waiting for me, of course, the former

seated at a square table with his arms crossed and his expression expectant. It was a rather spectacular impersonation of his father, really.

"Galina is in the bath." Gwyn gestured toward the cracked door of our adjoining rooms.

She was lounging on one of the narrow beds, her legs crossed at the ankle as she snacked on some crusty bread and hard cheese that Rowan had sent with us.

"All right, then," I sighed, taking a seat on the other bed. "Let's get on with it."

I explained as succinctly as possible, leaving out only the life debt, which I had less than no desire to get into.

They held each other's gazes for several long seconds, a silent conversation passing between them before Gal finally spoke up first.

"You kept this from Row?" he asked, bringing up a hand to run over the stubble on his jaw.

His question stabbed at the guilt already festering inside me.

"Yes," I said slowly. "Because she couldn't have kept it from her very cantankerous husband, who most certainly would have stopped us."

Gal nodded, conceding my point, and his sister broke in.

"So, wait. You're...bringing her to Lochlann with us?" Her eyes were wide as saucers, her half-eaten cheese wheel forgotten in her shock.

"Why else did you think she was in the carriage for so long?"

She sat up on the bed, then. "I don't know. Some last Socairan hurrah before we reached the border?"

I bit back a snort. Seeing as Galina fled so quickly after our first *hurrah*, I doubted seriously she was desirous of a last one.

"Decidedly not," I answered her.

Gallagher cut in again.

"It's not that I'm not sympathetic, but given...everything,

do you think the benefits of this"—he hesitated, searching for a word—"*arrangement* outweigh the risks to Lithlinglau? That the people will even accept her?"

He sounded equal parts challenging and curious. Gwyn nodded her agreement.

"Stars know I understand wanting more than a dutiful marriage, Dav, but what about the rebels?" she pressed. "They aren't thrilled with our newfangled friendship with Socair as it is. You really think they'll just accept her with open arms?"

I considered that, my mind going back to how well my conversation with the soldiers had gone, and they weren't even privy to the entire story. They were just one small piece of this equation, but their reactions had been a fair gauge of what was to come.

"Not to mention, the scandal when you eventually call off the engagement—" Gal added before I finally interrupted.

"Yes, I've considered those things. I wouldn't have brought her if I hadn't."

"I'm not sure that's strictly true," Gwyn countered, her judgmental auburn brows rising to her hairline. "No offense, but it would hardly be the first time *Little Davin* has led you astray."

"Yes, offense, Gwyn. There's nothing little about—"

A pillow came hurtling toward my face from Gwyn's bed, and I barely blocked it in time. Gal made a circling motion to get back to the point.

"I did think it through." *Mostly.* "This might only be the best of several rather mediocre plans to secure the vote, but it's what we've got."

Gwyn popped another bite of cheese into her mouth, surveying me closely, like I was a carnival monkey. Her brother, on the other hand, was gracious enough to pour two glasses of vodka and a glass of water, handing the latter to his sister, since she hated both the taste of alcohol and the way it made her feel.

He stretched his arm out to hand me the other glass of vodka, but when I went to take it, he pulled back.

"And you're sure it's not more than that? It wouldn't be the worst thing in the world if the betrothal was real."

I snorted, thinking of Galina's vehement denial last night.

"Maybe not to you," I told him.

And of course, that's when the door to the adjoining room pushed the rest of the way open.

Galina stood in the doorway, her wet hair braided back from her face. Anyone else would have looked like a drowned rat. But even fresh out of the bath and bundled in a bulky dressing gown, Galina was alluring enough that I had to forcibly avert my gaze before I made an arse of myself staring at her.

She was like an ice sculpture, though, pristine and perfect and endlessly cold.

As if to prove that thought, her tone was even more frigid than usual when she broke the uneasy silence that had fallen.

"Your bath is ready, Lady Gwyn," she told my cousin.

Gwyn nodded her thanks, following Galina back into their room and shutting the door with a brief goodbye. A hush rang out in their wake, Gal and I both sipping thoughtfully at our drinks.

I cleared my throat uncomfortably. "As I said, it's a short-term affair."

He shook his head, his eyes churning with an emotion I couldn't quite read.

"They always are with you."

They Loyalty Conundrum

DAVIN

A Year and a Half Ago

It was harder being back at Elk than it had been at Ram. Though Rowan had only spent a few days here, this place reminded me more of her.

Of failure—mine, specifically—to keep her safe from this mess we had landed ourselves in. Though through the spies I had discovered and the network I was amassing, I was trying like hell to find a way to get her home.

Galina's presence was a small reprieve from those thoughts. She had come with us to "discuss marriage options" with the heir to Clan Elk, something she had been resolutely stoic about.

Of course, she was that way about everything.

Tonight, like every night, she found her way to the glacial rooftop. And like every night, she sat down just far enough away to pretend we were both here by happenstance.

I held out my flask to her and she took a long swig—longer than usual—pulling a face when she was done. I raised my eyebrows.

"Was your night with our favorite dishwater lord so horrible?"

"You're horrible," she muttered, though there was a smile in her voice. "And so is this," she added, shooting an accusatory glance at the contents of the flask.

Three weeks. That was how long it had taken her to admit she didn't like vodka, and still, that small glimpse of the person behind her perfect façade felt like a victory.

I tilted my head. "Why do you drink it if you don't like it?"

"It's what's expected of me," she said with a delicate shrug.

"And you always do everything that's expected of you?" I pressed.

"Not always," she said, her eyes darting pointedly from the balcony to the flask to me.

Touché.

"Then why this? Would your uncle really punish you for having the nerve to request chilled white wine instead?"

She raised an eyebrow at my knowledge of her preferred drink.

"It's not about fear," she explained. "It's about loyalty. You must have seen by now that Socairans take appearances seriously. If I disobey my uncle or insult someone by snubbing their family's noble distillery, that reflects badly on the entire clan."

I could hardly argue that. Wasn't that what Rowan and I had done? Disobeyed the king by smuggling vodka, and gotten caught by the enemy doing it? And it had, in fact, reflected badly on all of us.

Still, I thought of everything else Galina did because it was expected of her. I pictured her sitting demurely next to Lord Theodore—or *Theodope*, as I fondly thought of him. Would she smile graciously at every boring, noble thing he said, like she didn't notice or care that he was besotted with my cousin?

"So your taste doesn't come into account, then?" I

wondered if she realized that I was talking about more than her choice in drink.

When her searching eyes met mine, I suspected that she did.

"Is loyalty really loyalty if it's only on your terms?" Her quiet words were more of a declaration than a question. "At that point, you're simply making a choice to go in line with something so long as it fits with what you already wanted to do. That's not loyalty, it's convenience."

I thought about my family back home, about the lengths to which Rowan went to keep me safe, the lengths to which I would go to do the same for her. How many times had Avani covered for us even after she warned us not to do something, even though she took the most blame from our people as the heir to the throne?

I nodded, conceding Galina's point.

"Besides, he's hardly the worst I could do," she added with another long drink.

My lips tugged up into a smirk. "What an overwhelming endorsement. Perhaps one day, I shall be lucky enough to receive similar praise from my future wife."

"Will the future Mrs. Davin be a love match, then? Or just someone who falls all over themselves at your powers of seduction?"

My smile widened. "Both would be preferred, obviously, though the latter is certainly the priority."

She let out a delicate snort as she held the flask back to me, and I wondered if the vodka was going to her head tonight.

"What? You've never even considered wanting more than Lord *Hardly the worst I could do*?" I demanded, taking a swig.

Galina shook her head. "Believe it or not, most of the marriages here are happy ones. People build their lives on principles, not some fleeting feeling that's intangible and indefinable at best."

“And at worst?” For some reason, my voice came out a rasp.

She met my eyes, something clouding her expression I couldn’t quite read.

“And at worst…” She paused, her hand closing around the flask once more. Her slim fingers entwined with mine for a single heartbeat before she pulled the drink back toward herself, never breaking eye contact. “At worst, dangerous.”

My heart pounded harder in my chest with every second she held my gaze. I wondered what she would think if she knew the truth about me, wondered it often enough that I could almost forget about the danger to Rowan and myself, and hell, even what position Galina’s uncle might put her in if he knew how important I was to Lochlann.

Dangerous.

I couldn’t find it in me to argue that point at all.

NINE
Galina

Present Day

THE NEXT DAY on the road was nearly as tense as the first had been.

Not only was I still plagued with anxiety about whether I would safely reach Lochlann, but a night's rest had allowed me to consider everything I had no real capacity to think about the day before.

Thousands of questions ran through my mind about our plan, my future in Lochlann, my prospects for marriage, and everything Davin had hinted he was going home to.

The cousins weren't quite as chatty today, either, though Gallagher did make an effort to engage me in a couple of conversations about Socairan medicine.

All in all, it was a relief when we reached the inn, knowing I could finally get some answers out of Davin. This time, it was Gwyn and Gallagher who stayed behind, either to help the soldiers, or to talk to them.

The greetings Davin received as we walked through the doors of the inn were familiar, and almost downright warm. He couldn't possibly have been here more than twice, but leave it to Davin to win over the enemy in that amount of time.

Of course, some were warmer than others. The dark-haired young maid who showed us to our rooms was particularly happy to see him, her honey-colored eyes not so subtly raking up and down his body.

"Thank you, Marjatta," he told her in obnoxiously flawless Socairan.

Color me utterly unsurprised that he knew her name.

"Of course, Laird Davin," she simpered. "Let me know if there's anything else I can do for you."

I'm sure he will.

He dismissed her politely, again in perfectly accented Socairan. While most of the nobles in Socair learned the common tongue growing up, the Lochlannians—according to Rowan—knew less than nothing about Socair, let alone the language.

Davin must have picked up more than he let on when he was stuck here, probably using pillow talk to practice. My fists clenched before I could stop them.

When *Marjatta* finally left, Davin turned to me with something like amusement dancing in his gaze.

"I didn't," he said, answering a question I hadn't asked.

I hurriedly cleared my features, which must have been giving away more of my thoughts than I intended.

"It's hardly my business," I said airily.

He arched a sardonic eyebrow, and I staunchly ignored him, though I did wonder at the truth of my response.

Socairan men had their faults, but adultery was a taboo. Not that it didn't happen, just as Alexei's manhandling did, but there were few quicker ways to bring dishonor upon your name than disrespecting your spouse.

Unless, of course, you disobey your duke, as I have done.

Somehow, I doubted things were the same in Lochlann, on either count. Everything had happened so fast that I hadn't had the time to give much thought to what Davin would be doing during our arrangement, but it was probably a mistake to assume he would bother being chaste.

As long as it didn't come back on my prospects, I supposed I had been right the first time.

It wasn't my concern.

Instead of being relieved at my indifference, Davin took a deep, irritable breath through his nose. "Indeed. Well then, dinner and a bath should be sent up shortly."

Though I was desperate for both, especially the latter, I knew we weren't done here yet. He started to walk away before I stopped him.

"We probably should talk first."

He turned back, raising an eyebrow when I stepped aside and gestured for him to join me.

Wordlessly, he followed me into my room, shutting the door behind him.

The room was luxurious but small to the point of being claustrophobic when Davin was standing this close to me. Taking several steps back, I put as much distance between us as I could, until I could no longer smell the faint scent of his shaving balm.

Sitting down at the small breakfast table near the window, I sifted through the list of questions I'd thought of in the carriage, narrowing them down and selecting the most important ones to ask.

"Tell me what we're walking into in Lochlann. I don't want to go in blind." *Again*, I wanted to add, but we both knew the word was implied. "What is this vote you have coming up, and why is it so important that you look stable for it?"

I nearly leapt out of my skin when the heavy oak door pushed open before he could answer. My heart galloped and raced in my chest even after the twins walked in, looking very distinctly unlike Alexei.

"No need to worry about knocking, Gwyn," Davin sighed.

"I wasn't going to, since it's my room," she responded with a saccharine smile, plopping down on the bed.

"To answer your question…" Davin turned back to me. "My right to own Lithlinglau is being contested, and there's a vote in a few months that will wind up being more political than factual."

Something niggled at my memory, a conversation where he had mentioned that his mother was married to someone who was not his father at the time of his birth.

"An entire council is getting together to decide whether or not you're a bastard?" I delivered the words evenly, but Gallagher snorted out a laugh anyway.

A muscle twitched in Davin's jaw.

"More or less," he intoned.

I mulled that over. "What happens if they vote against you?"

He pursed his lips. "I lose Lithlinglau."

"So you'd have no holdings?"

"Well, no. Just…*different* holdings," he corrected.

I fought down a rare surge in my temper, already frayed by the very real danger I was in each day we weren't safely out of Socair while Davin apparently had all the stress of losing his favorite holdings to other, slightly less desirable holdings.

"That sounds like a real catastrophe," I deadpanned. "Truly, it's a difficult life you lead."

Davin massaged the bridge of his nose with his thumb and forefinger, but it was Gallagher who responded.

"The problem isn't Davin keeping the title or the estate," he began gently. "It's that—"

"The Andersons are arseholes," Gwyndolyn supplied.

Gallagher shrugged. "Pretty much, that."

I couldn't help but glance at Davin who was already preemptively glaring.

"Yes, Galina," he said. "Before you ask, I am quite certain I'm not related to them by blood."

"More importantly," Gallagher interrupted, "the Assembly is quite certain of that."

"Then why is there a vote?"

"Because I'm trying to get them to agree that since my mother was married to Laird Anderson at the time of my birth and he claimed me as his heir, the law applies...even though my real father eventually adopted me."

I blinked several times, trying to wrap my head around the complex politics and familial drama.

"Understandably," he went on, "there isn't much precedence. So it will hinge largely on a popularity vote and whether they think I'm the best person to run the estate, which is where our very important and believable betrothal comes in."

"Yes, very believable, the way you two barely look at each other," the duchess chimed in.

Gallagher frowned. "She's not wrong. And the soldiers talk."

Davin cleared his throat. "Well, it needs to be kept under wraps until we reach the tunnels anyway, but I'll be sure to gaze longingly into Galina's eyes at every opportunity thereafter."

To think, there had been a time when I believed he *was* staring longingly into my eyes. At least I knew better now.

"This is all a lot of trouble to go to just because you don't like someone," I commented.

Davin ran a hand through his hair, tousling the short obsidian strands. "It's not that I don't like them—though I don't, for that matter. It's that Lithlinglau has both substantial resources and influence, and I don't trust what they would do with those things."

"No one does," Gwyn added. "When I said arseholes, I

meant arseholes who want our family off the throne by any means necessary."

"We suspect," Gallagher cut in.

"We know," Gwyn corrected. "We just don't have proof."

"Let alone the fact that they care little and less about any of the people who would be under their purview," Davin added. "My aunt and uncle can't be everywhere, and it's my job to care for Lithlinglau."

His aunt and uncle, King and Queen of Lochlann. That was still difficult for me to wrap my head around when the Davin I knew had been a commoner.

This one was a marquess, in charge of trade agreements for the whole kingdom and more territory than my uncle's entire clan. It was hard enough, leaving everything I knew behind. Worse still to realize my partner in this ruse was a stranger.

But it was still, eternally, better than the alternative.

I wondered if I would ever get the opportunity to stop living my life by that dubious standard.

THE NEXT FEW days passed more quickly than I expected them to.

My years of extensive etiquette lessons had included Lochlannian customs, but it had been some time since I reviewed them. So I took advantage of the endless hours in the carriage to be sure there were no gaps in my knowledge, and to learn as much as I could about the Lochlannian court.

It was a convenient distraction from the blinding panic that overtook me every time the carriage slowed, when I was sure Alexei or my uncle had discovered my subterfuge.

In fact, we were so immersed in discussing the nuances of

court politics, I was almost surprised when the gaping maw of the tunnel came into sight.

Soldiers stood sentry on either side of the narrow entrance, darkness pouring from the pathway that would lead me further from home than I had ever been.

And I abruptly realized that even though I had prepared for this, I was in no way ready. Because this was it. If I turned around right now, I could find a way back to my estate before anyone knew I was missing. My father would help cover for me, that much I knew by now. I could still go home, and...

And what?

Marry Alexei?

Davin's deep voice intruded on my thoughts. "Having second thoughts about our whirlwind romance?"

Was I that obvious?

"No." The word left my lips before the thought had finished forming, but it resonated down to my soul.

No, I would not go back. *Could not.*

Pushing down the last lingering bits of apprehension, I squared my shoulders before leaving the carriage. The Lochlannian soldiers split to let me pass, alone, to the Socairans stationed at the tunnels.

This was one of the tenets of our plan, to make sure it couldn't come back on Lochlann or Rowan that Davin had absconded with Socair's highest ranking eligible lady, and that it couldn't come back on my family or clan that I had fled from my betrothal.

Davin insisted on remaining close enough to intercede if necessary, though.

There were men stationed evenly all along the border leading to the tunnels, but only two directly at the mouth. They shuffled as I neared, their eyes widening.

"My Lady," the closest officer said, stepping forth. "How can we help you?"

"I'm here to enter the tunnels," I said as flatly as I could muster.

The soldier looked uncertainly at the carriage behind me. "Are those your escorts?"

"The queen has mandated that a lady does not need an escort to travel," I responded, my tone far steadier than my insides. "But the Lochlannian party has graciously agreed to share resources and protection in the tunnels."

He exchanged a look with his partner.

"Do you have consent from your father or your husband?"

Though I was allowed to travel alone, the law had not yet extended to my being able to do so without authorization.

"I have the permission of my betrothed. His insistence, actually." I was absolutely not letting my father take the fall for this, and it was true.

Technically, Davin was now my betrothed.

The man turned to his logbook, a quill already poised over the open page. "What's your name?"

"Galina Zhakarov."

His blond eyebrows climbed into his hairline. "Sir Mikhail is sending his niece to Lochlann?"

I gave him an unassuming smile. "As I said, it's at the behest of my betrothed."

Out of the corner of my eye, I saw Davin pause in the middle of moving from the carriage to one of the narrow wagons suited for travel in the tunnels. I gave him a subtle gesture to show that everything was fine, and he continued after only a moment's hesitation.

The soldier looked from the Lochlannians to me, his brow furrowed. I registered the exact moment he decided this was not his problem. After all, if I was lying, they would fetch me back and it could hardly come back on them when I claimed to have permission.

If I was telling the truth, and he stopped a duke's niece

and insulted the queen's family in one go, that was another story.

"You'll need to sign," he said, gesturing toward the logbook.

"Of course."

I stared at the words he had written just above a small black x.

Galina Zhakarov, traveling to Lochlann at the behest of her betrothed.

Dipping the quill in an ink pot, I fought to keep my hands from shaking as I sealed my fate with a single signature.

Then I stepped into the tunnels to wait for Davin, letting the darkness swallow me whole.

TEN

Davin

THIS WAS my third trek through the tunnels since Rowan and I were trapped in them for days on end with no light or water, and each subsequent journey was only marginally more fun than that one had been.

The northern pass—the only other route between our kingdoms—wasn't accessible this time of year. Even if it had been, we couldn't afford the weeks it took to traverse. So we were left with the suffocating tunnel that had been roughly carved through the mountain itself for the sole purpose of bringing war to our people.

My shoulders tensed as soon as we left the last lingering ray of sunlight behind. In contrast, Gwyn breathed a sigh of relief.

"Thank the stars we're finally out of that kingdom."

"Because the tunnels are so pleasant in the early autumn chill." Sarcasm coated each of my words.

"At least here, no one is trying to muzzle me," she bit back.

"Don't speak too soon, Twinsy," Gallagher said. "It depends on how loud you get in this very cramped space."

She punched him in the arm, and he might have made a face at her. It was impossible to tell in the low lantern light.

As the hours crept by, I was grateful for the steady stream

of chatter that Gwyn and Gal kept up. The longer we spent in the endless, suffocating darkness that had nearly claimed my life, the harder it was for me to be entertaining.

Galina, too, was even quieter than usual. She sat stoically at my side in the narrow, open wagon, once again unnaturally still. She didn't complain about the damp air or the rapidly dropping temperatures or the pervasive smell of dirt.

She didn't say anything, really, except for the occasional *Yes, My Laird*, and *Thank you, My Laird* when I offered her food or water.

When we finally stopped for the night, though, she let out a small sigh of relief—the only indication that her experience thus far had been less than tolerable.

I held out a hand to help her down from the wagon, and she gave me another appreciative nod, leaning in closer when the soldiers' eyes were on us. The familiar scent of rosemary and lavender wafted from her, bringing with it a visceral slew of memories I could have done without.

Galina, looking sardonically down at me, her tone chiding and unimpressed as she called me a laskipaa.

Her gentle hands contrasting her sharp expression when she treated my bruises.

Her soft, unexpected laugh on an empty rooftop.

Her hair falling in silky waves around us while—

"Thank you, My Laird." The echo of the empty, perfunctory phrase she had been using all day was enough to pull me from those thoughts.

None of it mattered now, anyway. I had been wrong to think the few scattered moments where I saw a truer version of her meant anything, in the end.

Though something about the way she locked eyes with me made me wonder if I wasn't the only one caught up in memories of the things we never were.

GIVEN our rather limited options for accommodations, we were forced to make camp in cramped caverns just off the main tunnel. The soldiers slept in the tunnel itself, alternating with guard shifts. Not that we expected any trouble, but it would be foolish to rule it out, especially in light of all the...circumstances.

Then again, some of the guards themselves were a bit of a problem. I didn't like the lingering glances they shot Galina's way. Some were for obvious reasons, but others...I wasn't as sure.

I wanted to trust my men, but her safety wasn't something I was prepared to gamble with.

In that vein, I laid out Galina's fur-lined bed roll closest to the cavern wall, and furthest from the opening, since she was the only one who couldn't physically defend herself. Gwyn would insist on being closest to the opening, for the opposite reason.

My roll went next to Galina's, while Gallagher's was sandwiched between mine and his twin's.

Galina returned from where she had been filling up the soldiers' canteens, a job she had taken upon herself apropos of nothing. The men accepted her help with varied reactions.

While some of their anger had faded as they spent more time around her, some of them remained just as resolutely stubborn and biased as ever, barely even thanking her when she handed them their canteens.

"That one's yours." I pointed to her bedroll.

"And yours?" she asked, her gaze already settling on the one next to it.

I nodded, bracing myself for an argument, but she only

returned the gesture with resignation, settling wordlessly into her blankets.

Gwyn and Gal joined us shortly after. As cold as it had been during the day, the temperature fell even more with each passing hour. The twins passed out quickly, huddled together for warmth. I pulled the furs more tightly around my shoulders, leaning closer to Gal to share some of that heat, and thought back irritably to a time when it had been that easy for me to sleep.

Though, I wasn't sure that would ever have been true when it was this cold.

Galina had to be freezing.

The stilted, uneven breaths coming from my right attested to that. At the very least, she wasn't sleeping, either.

With a sigh, I forced myself to reach out.

"You can move your bedroll closer, you know," I said, my whisper echoing off the cavern walls.

"I'm fine right here," she insisted.

"It's freezing," I pointed out superfluously.

"For you, perhaps. I'm Socairan. We're used to the cold." Her teeth clacked together on that last word, but she held steady in her resolve.

I let out an irritable breath. She was so stars-damned stubborn when she wanted to be, which only seemed to be where I was concerned.

It wasn't like I wanted her any closer than she wanted me. I had drowned in plenty of memories today as it was.

"Right," I muttered. "I must have forgotten all those nights you spent sleeping on the ground outside."

She sucked in a breath to respond, but another voice cut her off.

"For the love of all that is sacred, Dav, she said she's fine," Gwyn hissed. "So either shiver yourself to sleep or budge over closer to Gal, but if you don't stop talking, I will smother you with your own pillow."

Galina let out a huff of air that sounded suspiciously like a laugh. Reluctantly, I shuffled nearer to Gallagher, leaving Galina to her obstinance.

Only a handful of minutes went by before Gwyn's snores echoed off the cavern walls.

It was going to be a long night.

ELEVEN

Galina

THIS RUSE WAS ALREADY WORSE than I could have imagined.

Not worse than pretending to like Alexei, but unexpectedly jarring, playing out pieces of the life I had let myself want when I was still naïve enough to believe Davin wanted it, too.

It was safe to say he never had, especially after he essentially told his cousins that a life with me was the worst thing he could imagine.

It shouldn't have stung. It wasn't new information, by any means.

Regardless, there was no fear here—at least, not toward Davin. No slow degradation of pride. So I could manage.

I reminded myself of that every time he brushed against my arm in a display of intimacy or placed his arm protectively around me when the men stared. Though most of the soldiers had sated their curiosity about me in the first day or so on the road, a few still eyed me far too often for comfort.

We ate in the wagons to preserve time, then stopped to use the ever-dignified makeshift latrines. It was the first time I was jealous of Gwyn's lighter skirts, as mine were much more difficult to maneuver in such a precarious position.

After that, we finally stopped for another frigid, sleepless night.

Davin stayed next to me while I took over the job of refilling the men's canteens. They didn't all appreciate the gesture, but it was important to me to contribute in some small way.

"Come on, Love, I'll show you to our cavern." Davin stressed the nickname just enough that I noticed, gently guiding me with the pressure of his fingertips on my lower back.

His comment and accompanying gesture served their purpose, and the two men who were staring quickly glanced away.

I wasn't sure what to make of all their attention. It felt like more than mild curiosity or attraction. Then again, this entire tunnel had a foreboding energy to it, so maybe I was unfairly projecting that onto them.

Either way, I didn't argue when Davin led me to a tiny cavern again, even when I realized it was too small for four. Whatever else could be said of Davin and me, he had a vested interest in my safety now.

I settled wordlessly into the furs that were entirely too close to his, trying not to inhale his irritatingly familiar scent of cloves and spiced bergamot.

Hours went by as I watched the flames flicker out in our lantern.

It was somehow both too loud and too quiet at the same time, with the echoing sound of a steady *drip, drip, drip* of water falling from somewhere above us, and the faint scurrying of mice or rustle of wings belonging to creatures that I didn't want to think about for too long.

Another shiver rattled my frozen bones. It was even colder tonight than yesterday.

My heavy limbs trembled as I attempted to bury myself

further in my blankets. I gritted my teeth to keep them from chattering, trying in vain to warm myself.

"You're being ridiculous." Davin's low voice came from far too short a distance.

I didn't bother to pretend not to know what he meant. Instead, I contemplated whether he was right.

Last night, waking up any closer to him had felt like the worst thing in the world. But there was less body heat in this cavern without the twins, and waves of cold were emanating from the frosty cave walls directly to us.

We were never going to sleep this way.

I tried to imagine myself in front of a roaring campfire, sipping my favorite ginger and cinnamon tea. Burrowing further into heavy furs on a soft bed. Anything to make myself forget about the cold, damp, hard ground of these storms-damned tunnels.

But it was no use. Besides, I could hear Davin's ragged breathing, belying his own shivers.

With a resigned sigh, I rolled over until my back was pressed entirely against him. He inhaled sharply in surprise.

"Satisfied?" I asked.

"Hardly," he rasped out.

His breath was warm against my neck, eliciting a shiver I desperately hoped he would blame on the cold. He hesitated for only a moment longer before resting his arm over mine, cocooning me in unexpected warmth.

I squeezed my eyes shut, forcing away memories of the last time we were close enough for me to feel his breath on my skin.

At least this was our last night in the tunnels. Then it was just...another six months of this charade.

Davin was already up by the time I awoke the following morning.

Sadly, that didn't seem to make our ensuing day any less uncomfortable. Then again, everything about this trip was uncomfortable.

Even the twins were less talkative than usual as the hours wore on.

I wondered if they all missed the sunlight the way I did, or the feeling in their fingers and toes, or any smell other than the dirt and sulfur of the mountains.

When we finally emerged from the tunnels later that evening, our party let out a collective sigh of relief.

The gentle shafts of sunlight stabbed at my eyes as we transitioned from the wagons to the waiting carriages. Somewhere through my blurry vision, I vaguely discerned a new contingent of men who were eyeing me with varying degrees of curiosity and disdain.

Ladies in Socair were treated with something close to reverence, certain bastard fiancés notwithstanding. We might have been regarded as somewhat ornamental, but there was respect, all the same.

So, this casual contempt was new for me.

I was supposed to be helping Davin win them over, but it took everything I had not to glare back with my own icy scorn.

Instead, I smiled demurely, reminding myself that the only thing I cared about now was a hot bath and a real bed that I could sleep in far, far away from Davin. Not stupid prejudiced soldiers who looked at me like I was a circus attraction.

When they inquired about my presence outright, Davin hedged, but I waited until we were safely ensconced in the carriage to question him about it.

"Second-guessing yourself?" I injected the words with as much nonchalance as I could, though my gut twisted at the very real possibility.

Davin rubbed a hand over his face, smearing the slightest bit of dirt across his brow. I shuddered to think what my own face looked like. Or my hair. Not that the Lochlannians had much room to judge on that front.

"No, Galina. There's just no need to advertise our betrothal before we're safely behind the walls of Lithlinglau," he explained.

I froze, overcome with visions of Alexei's eyes, narrowed and furious as he dragged me right back beneath the mountain.

"So, it won't be official for another two weeks?" I asked with far more serenity than I felt.

That was how long Davin had said it would take to get to his estate from here, by carriage. I doubted my ruse about going back home would hold up quite that long, and that wasn't a gamble I cared to take.

"No." Davin shook his head, much to my relief. "I'll send a letter to my aunt and uncle from the inn, declaring it. Anyone who comes through the tunnels needs permission first, and that goes directly through Castle Chridhe, so that will kill two birds with one stone."

Gallagher whistled under his breath, pulling my attention toward him. He looked about as tired as I felt. Faint bruises hung beneath his eyes like crescent moons, and, like Davin and the rest of the men, he had several days' worth of stubble.

"You'd better tell him not to write Lithlinglau until you can get there," he said to Davin. Then, to me, he explained further. "Auntie Jocelyn might actually murder Dav if she has to hear about his betrothal from Uncle Logan."

Gwyn winced, and Davin made a face. "Good looking out, Cousin."

I didn't ask the obvious question, whether she would be upset hearing about it in person as well. Whether both of his parents would. Davin had been resolutely silent on the matter, and I supposed it didn't make much of a difference.

Though, everything I heard about Princess Jocelyn made me wonder if she was even more terrifying than their notorious king.

IT WAS a short ride to the inn after that.

The building was a solid, artless rectangle, smaller and simpler than anything I would have expected Davin to choose. Several of the other buildings on either side of the inn appeared newer and even nicer, but with a hand on my back, he led me into this one.

As soon as we stepped inside, I could see it was nothing at all like the inns we had stayed at in Socair. For one thing, there were so many people, and they were all so different from one another. Where my people were mostly tall and muscular with olive-toned skin and sharp, defined features, Lochlannians were apparently an array of color and size and shape.

Just in this tavern, they ranged from a freckled man so pale he was nearly translucent to a tiny woman with deep umber skin and piercing blue eyes, and several in between—closer to the twins' shade of light brown.

And while the inns in Socair had been filled with the typical hum of conversation, perhaps a booming laugh on occasion—this was something else entirely.

It was a cacophony of people talking over each other in boisterous conversation, cheering when they were victorious at a game involving mugs of ale and a small ball. One notable gentleman was drunkenly singing a song that brought a flush to my cheeks.

I felt Davin's gaze on me, and I forced myself to look a bit less scandalized.

He chuckled anyway, the smarmy bastard.

"Are they always this...outspoken?" I asked, choosing the word carefully in case I offended anyone close by.

"This is nothing," he said with a disarmingly casual grin. "It's barely sundown."

A round woman with graying hair made her way over to us, and Davin angled himself in front of me. Intentionally?

"Did you miss me, Ms. Agatha?" he asked in a teasing tone, barely audible over the din.

"Don't try to charm me, mi'laird, when we both ken well yer cousin is the nice one," she said with affection.

"I'm wounded," Davin said, just as Gallagher chimed in, "I always tell him the same thing."

My lips parted in surprise. My uncle would have died before allowing a villager to be so familiar. Or rather, he would have killed.

The woman's gaze landed on me, then, her countenance going flat.

Davin went on like she hadn't paused, telling her how many rooms and meals we needed in a deceptively casual tone. His congenial smile was intact, but there was a glint of authority in his eyes, a set to his jaw that said he wouldn't tolerate commentary on the matter.

"Yes, mi'laird," she said, her tone more subdued.

In the time Davin had been talking, the other patrons had gradually started to notice my presence. What my olive-toned skin didn't give away, my embroidered, high-necked gown certainly did.

The looks I garnered ranged from suspicious to outright hostile. I squared my shoulders, pretending not to notice.

"Thank you, Ms. Agatha," he told her, a hand on his chest. "This is why we love to stay in your fine establishment."

My lips parted in surprise. Though I knew, logically, that women here were allowed to work, owning an entire inn was another story. Did she have men who worked for her?

Gallagher's teasing voice broke into my thoughts. "That and your apple turnovers, of course."

Ms. Agatha shook her head but was smiling as she left to take care of ordering the baths.

Davin glanced around the room, then to me like he was weighing something.

"We'll head up, and you can bring dinner," Gwyn told Davin and her brother with a smile that didn't quite reach her eyes.

It wasn't hard to figure out why it would be better for me to go upstairs. Davin had told me already that there would be rebels who wanted to kill me just for the sin of being born on the wrong side of the mountain.

I had no desire to argue with going up to our rooms. The people could get used to me gradually, but there was no sense in turning this room into a powder keg—not for any of our sakes.

Gwyn grabbed an apple from the counter, calling over her shoulder to have it added to her tab before gesturing for me to follow her up the stairs. I did, trying to ignore the weight of the glares that accompanied us until we were out of sight.

When we got to the room, Gwyn sprawled out on the bed. It was small for two people, but I couldn't bring myself to be concerned about Gwyn's blanket thievery or her snoring when it meant I didn't have to snuggle up next to Davin.

My mind returned to the woman downstairs, the one who apparently owned the inn. Was that common? How had she come by it to begin with?

"Did Ms. Agatha's husband leave this inn to her?" I asked, trying to parse out the circumstances that led her here.

Gwyn eyed me, likely because engaging in idle conversation was not something we did. In all our nights on the road, we had never actually spoken one-on-one.

"Not that I know of," she finally said, rubbing her apple

against her dress before taking a large bite. “But I’m sure Davin has her life story memorized.”

Of course he did.

Because that’s what he did, got people to talk to him, to give him information he needed. I had no doubt that was what he was doing now, working the room downstairs to figure out what had transpired here in his absence.

It was a skill I might have admired, had I not been on the receiving end of it before.

The duchess's voice startled me out of my thoughts. “For whatever it’s worth, not everyone here is a prejudiced arsehat. There are tensions, obviously, but you won’t have to deal with as much of that closer to Lithlinglau. It’s harder up here, where they lost people to the war.”

I blinked at her once, trying not to bristle at the comment.

The war had taken place over twenty years ago, back when Lochlann was still two kingdoms and Socair was ruled by a tyrant. My clan had been forced to fight in it.

“I could argue that your family was far more responsible for that war than mine, but they’re treating you just fine,” I said smoothly, meeting her assessing hazel gaze.

She surveyed me, leaning back against the wall. For a moment, she looked markedly older than her twenty-two years, all traces of her usual flippancy gone.

“Don’t worry,” she sighed. “There are plenty of people who haven’t gotten over our family’s role in the war. I’m sure you’ll meet them soon enough.”

I contemplated the fairness of that.

Gwyn’s mother had wanted to get out of a betrothal agreement, so she had married someone else, breaking the contract. It had always seemed impossibly selfish when I heard the story, but I was starting to understand it now.

I wondered if I could make myself go back to Alexei, if the alternative was starting a war.

If I had been wrong about the culpability falling solely on myself, if my clan was going to face the repercussions for what I had done alone, then that was a question I might be forced to answer sooner rather than later.

TWELVE
Davin

When Galina left, I swept a glance around the tavern, trying to gauge everyone's reaction to her presence as dispassionately as possible.

My usual smirk felt like it was pasted to my face, but I kept it up anyway, trying to hide the irritation I felt at the innkeeper's clear disdain for my…well, my nothing. But she was still a person.

With a sigh, I made my way to the barman while Gallagher took a seat at one of the long tables.

Alastair was usually the talkative sort, but he was close-lipped tonight.

I was forced to abandon my more congenial approach for some decidedly less friendly conversation, wherein I made a thinly veiled threat to tell the man's wife about his questionable liaisons at the local brothel.

His eyes widened, and he shot a fearful glance around the tavern.

"All I can tell ye is, there were a couple o' men in here last night, talking about the Socairan wen—the Lady Galina," he corrected himself quickly. "They weren't happy to hear she was coming with you."

It took every tool in my substantial arsenal to keep the shock from my features. No one should have known she was coming, and certainly not her name.

"What else did our rebel friends share?" I asked, outwardly nonchalant.

He shook his head, and I sighed. I hated to lose him as a future source, but I needed to know what he knew.

"Come on now, Alastair." My voice was quiet and cajoling. "I'd hate to let on how forthcoming you've always been..."

The blood drained from his face.

"So, if you just tell me what you know, I'll laugh like we're sharing a joke, and I'll head back upstairs," I assured him with a shrug.

He swallowed, nodding.

"They didna say anything else, but they weren't just the regular sort. They were from the Uprising."

I bit back a curse. This upstart group of rebels had been cropping up everywhere, though so far, as little more than a whisper in the wind.

It had crossed my mind that the entire outfit was more of a scapegoat than a real threat, a convenient boogeyman in the night to blame for every bit of death and dissension that had come our way since Rowan's wedding.

Alastair's fear was real enough, though, and he hadn't hesitated this way in the past.

True to my word, I let out a light chuckle, sliding several coins across the bar before strolling casually from the room. There was a prickling feeling between my shoulder blades, like someone was watching me all the way out.

It was Galina who answered my sharp rap at the door, and I couldn't suppress a scowl. Did she even realize how vulnerable she was by doing that? She hadn't so much as called to see who was on the other side.

"Guess you just open the door for every assailant who comes along," I told her, the barman's words still echoing in my ears.

She shot me an irritable look. She was already freshly bathed and dressed in a thick dressing gown, her hair in a damp braid pulled over one shoulder.

"I recognized your knock," she informed me curtly. "And I assumed if you were knocking, it was with the expectation to have the door opened."

It was easy to forget, sometimes, how familiar we had once been. How I had come to her rooms with regularity, often enough for her to know my knock...even now, apparently.

I swallowed back the uncomfortable emotion I didn't have time to dissect. "Just...let Gwyn open next time."

"Yes, My Laird." The phrase she had uttered demurely in front of the men was dripping with sarcasm now.

My cousin emerged from behind the screen that hid the bath, her hair wet and her expression mock-offended. "Glad to know you're willing to sacrifice me for the cause, Dav."

I shrugged. "I'm sure you'd take several down with you, Gwynnie."

Galina glanced between us, but I waited until Gallagher had joined us to explain to everyone at once.

"The rebels knew Galina was coming," I said evenly. "And they're, apparently, not thrilled about it."

Several beats of silence passed before Gwyn broke it.

"The Socairans told them?"

I shot her a dark look, but it was Gallagher who responded.

"Most of the rebels hate Socairans," he said with an apologetic glance at Galina. "And why would they endanger one of their own?"

"Because they're mad about her marrying Dav?" his sister suggested weakly.

"They shouldn't have known that yet," I reminded her.

Gwyn cast around for another reason, looking at the ceiling like it held the answers she was so desperate for. And I didn't blame her.

I wanted there to be another reason, too. I wanted anything other than the sick realization curdling in my gut right now.

Galina's eyes met mine, and I knew she, too, had put the pieces together.

"Maybe they just want to sow dissension," Gwyn finally said, sounding about as convinced as I felt.

"Gwyn," I said quietly.

"Davin." She said my name like a denial, a warning.

"We have to consider the possibility that it was one of our own," I told her as gently as I could.

It was the only real possibility, but she wasn't ready to hear that yet.

Gwyn shook her head. "That's a dangerous road to go down."

"It will be dangerous for Galina—hell, for us all—if we *don't* go down that road and we're wrong," Gallagher countered gently.

Galina's low tone cut into the ensuing silence.

"Couldn't you set up something to..." She cast about for a moment, a rare reminder that the common tongue was not her first language. "Lure them?"

I considered that for a moment, looking between Gwyn and Galina while an idea formed in the back of my mind.

They looked nothing alike. Gwyn's eyes were hazel to Galina's blue, her braid wavy and crimson where Galina's was sleek and honey colored. They were both tall and slim, though. Gwyn's shoulders were more muscular, but in a cloak, that would be difficult to see.

I thought back to when I had admonished Galina not to open the door, because she couldn't defend herself.

But Gwyn could.

I exchanged a look with my cousin, and her gaze slid over to Galina before she dipped her chin in assent. Taking a deep breath, I faced the other two occupants of the room.

"I have what is either a very good or a very stupid plan," I announced.

Galina narrowed her eyes, but Gallagher only sighed.

"Oh good," he deadpanned. "I was just thinking how we had a shortage of those."

THIRTEEN

Galina

I WAS BEGINNING to think that being in constant danger was my new normal, no matter where I was.

It was a toss-up, really, between rebels who wanted to kill me on one side of the mountain and a monster who wanted to own me on the other. *Der'mo.* The latter wasn't even a real option anymore, not now that my uncle would know I had disobeyed him.

Rebels, it is.

I waited for the fear to sink in, the panic, but the past two weeks seemed to have drained me of those emotions. Frustration, however, I felt in spades.

I was so tired of being the weakest link to this party. Though I could work my way around a ballroom or a court dinner, the journey here had made it clear how perilously few life skills I had.

So, Davin wasn't wrong. I couldn't defend myself, not against Alexei and not against these rebels, but that didn't mean I was willing to sit back while someone else died in my stead. Even if that person was Gwyn.

"I appreciate the political implications of me dying on

Lochlannian soil, but surely you aren't willing to risk your own cousin in my stead?" I pointed out.

Of course, Gwyn snorted, but Davin looked at me consideringly. Then, in a lightning-quick movement, he pulled a dagger from his boot and hurled it directly at the duchess.

The blade hurtled through the air directly toward her face in a whisper of wind and steel. There had been no warning, no noise, no sign at all that he was about to attack her, and yet...

She snatched the blade out of the air with a bored expression. My mouth fell open in shock. I had barely seen her hand move.

Smirking, she twirled the dagger around in her fingers before handing it back to Davin with a flourish, like it was a playing card.

Gallagher rolled his eyes.

"If you two are quite finished with your theatrics..." He turned to me. "As much as it pains me to feed her ego, my sister isn't in much danger from an assassin. The only one who can really best her is our father, and I doubt he'll be showing up trying to murder her—"

"Unless he finds out about her liaisons with his soldiers," Davin added with a shrug.

"I like to think he'd kill them first," Gwyn said. "Give me some warning."

I cut in before the conversation could get completely derailed, as it had a tendency to do with the cousins.

"I won't deny that was..." I searched for words to adequately describe what I had just seen. "Impressive."

Gwyn's expression was smug, and she gestured for me to continue.

"But what happens if there is more than one?" Though her reflexes were amazing, anyone could be outnumbered.

Gwyn opened her mouth to respond, but Davin stopped her with a gesture. Rather, he gestured to Gallagher, who grabbed his sister's arm and tugged her toward the door.

“Come on, Twinsy. Ms. Agatha was making shortbread when I left.”

She started to argue before catching whatever look he was giving her.

“Fine,” she said, following her brother out into the hall. “But you’d better not be lying about the shortbread—”

Her words cut off when Davin shut the door. He crossed the room to me, his expression more serious than before.

“We won’t do this if you really aren’t comfortable with it,” he began.

“I’m not,” I assured him.

He held up a hand. “But at least hear me out first.”

Reluctantly, I nodded.

He met my eyes directly. “This really is the best plan.”

I arched a skeptical eyebrow. “Have you even considered other options?”

He almost looked offended. “I have, actually. I would never put my cousin in unnecessary danger, but Gwyn isn’t just a duchess. She’s a soldier, and a damned good one at that. She wants to root the rebels out as much as I do, and this is a way for us to do that.”

That explained why she had agreed to do it at all, given that she had made no secret of her indifference toward me.

“We will have measures in place to keep her safe,” he went on, “which is more than I can guarantee for you. I know you don’t trust me in general, but could you at least consider trusting me with this?”

His cobalt gaze seared into mine, willing me to believe him. I considered his words. If nothing else, he had taken his life debt seriously, had done his best to keep me safe so far, up to and including trying to convince me now.

“And if the rebels don’t fall for it?” I pressed, half to buy myself time and half because I truly wanted to know.

“That’s why we’re sending soldiers with you and Gallagher as well, a few trusted men who weren’t in the tunnels,” he said.

"Don't let his laid-back personality fool you. Gallagher spars with Gwyn every day of his life. He's plenty skilled as well."

"And you?" I couldn't help but ask.

When I met Davin, I had believed he was a soldier. Even after I knew the truth, it hadn't hit home to me until now that I had no idea how capable he was of defending himself. All men in Socair trained for the military. Was that true in Lochlann as well?

I didn't want to care, didn't want to feel this churning in my gut, knowing he would be standing between the rebels and their perceived target, but I couldn't quite seem to breathe when I pictured his azure eyes blank and unmoving.

His brow furrowed, the hint of a cocky smirk tugging at his mouth.

"I can hold my own."

With most people, I would have had some idea of whether they were posturing, but I had long since lost confidence in my ability to determine whether Davin was lying.

I had no choice but to believe him. To try to trust him on this, as he had asked me to.

Instead of admitting that outright, I asked a different question.

"What do I tell your parents?"

His shoulders eased with the implication that I was willing to accept his plan.

"I won't leave it to you to explain everything. I'll send a letter, and they likely won't question you too much until I'm there." He made a dubious face before amending that statement. "Probably. If all else fails, just use your resting Socairan face to deter their inquisition."

I glared at him, and he raised his eyebrows.

"That's the one."

Shaking my head, I relented. "All right. I'll go."

I'll trust you on this one thing.

It was another sleepless night.

I had never ridden a horse for longer than a few leisurely hours, and my muscles were screaming with the effort of staying upright in the saddle through the endlessly dark forest.

The sun was peeking over the horizon when we finally stopped to sleep. I had just enough time to eat and bathe before Gallagher crept somewhat apologetically into my room.

"I'll sleep on the couch, of course, but it's not safe for you to be in here alone," he explained.

I had already surmised as much. It made me feel further from home than crossing the mountains had, the ease with which we both breached this propriety.

"Of course," I said, with a dip of my head. "Did you talk to the soldiers?"

Gallagher sighed, falling onto the small sofa against the opposite wall.

"More like they talked to me," he said. "Though, I suppose it's to their credit that they waited until we were all the way here to ask where the real Gwyn was."

At my apprehensive expression, he turned his head toward me, giving me a gentle smile.

"We knew we couldn't keep this from them," he reminded me. "It's why we chose the men we did. We've also let them know we have an eye out for traitors and sworn them to silence. It's everyone else we're worried about finding out. So, if we pass anyone on the road, be sure to proclaim loudly that you could beat them in a duel, and they'll have no problem believing you're my sister."

I couldn't help the small smile that crept onto my lips.

Gallagher returned it, running a tired hand over his face while guilt pricked at my insides.

"I'm sorry you had to go to all this trouble," I told him sincerely.

He waved a dismissive hand. "This is hardly the first time we've had to change our plans because of the rebels."

I nodded tiredly, settling into bed. It should have been awkward, preparing to sleep in a room with a man I barely knew, but Gallagher had a calming presence about him.

Only once I was under the blankets and propped against my pillow did I force myself to ask the question that had been relentlessly churning in my mind.

"Are you worried?" My voice was barely a whisper.

Gallagher heaved a sigh, shifting to face me. "I have hopes that Davin will keep my sister from being too reckless. They'll keep each other safe."

I nodded, shoving the apprehension back in the box where it belonged. Davin wasn't mine to worry about, and Gwyn certainly seemed to be able to take care of herself.

Another few minutes of silence ticked by, but I didn't seem to be the only one struggling to sleep. Gallagher was the first to speak this time.

"What will you do when you're finished helping Davin?"

I raised an eyebrow, surprised Davin hadn't shared this part of our arrangement. "If I go without a betrothal contract, my uncle could demand my return. So when we're nearing the end of the six months, Davin will help me secure things with the most likely...candidate..."

I trailed off as the awkwardness of me being thrown together in a room with the second most eligible lord in all of Lochlann dawned on me.

"So you're going to be quietly searching for a husband while you're betrothed to Davin?" There was no judgment in his tone, only curiosity.

Which was just as concerning.

I searched for a polite way to tell him I would rather die

than marry into Davin's family, but he preempted me, speaking quickly before I could respond.

"I wasn't offering. Not that you aren't lovely." He winced. "But I'm afraid there's a lass in the village who might be inclined toward murdering one or both of us, which is something I feel we've had our share of already."

He gave me another of his easy smiles, adding, "That's not common knowledge, by the way, so...now you know one of my secrets as well. I hope you didn't..."

"I'm not offended," I said, letting out a relieved breath. "Quite the opposite."

He scrutinized my expression.

"So I see. Now I'm wondering if perhaps I should be offended," he said drily.

It was my turn to scrutinize him.

He had the same light-brown skin, crimson hair, and hazel eyes as his sister, but Gallagher was decidedly masculine. There was a light stubble on his square jaw, and the muscles in his broad shoulders were evident, even with his shirt on.

Add to that his understated humor and thoughtful mannerisms and general lack of being an *aalio*, and I suspected he knew he had nothing to be concerned about.

"Not unless you'd like to be offended on Davin's behalf," I admitted. "I can think of few things worse than having to see him at every family engagement for the rest of my life. The next six months will be more than enough."

He choked on a laugh. "I suppose that answers the question of why you aren't just sticking with this arrangement. It's probably for the best, then. Stars know our family has enough gossip surrounding us without *the royal family stealing one another's fiancés* added to the mix."

The word *gossip* made me wince a bit.

"Do I even want to know how much gossip this arrangement will generate?" I gestured vaguely to myself.

"No." He softened the blunt word with a lopsided smile.

"Well. Thank you for your honesty."

Gallagher leaned his head against the arm of the couch, pressing in further against the cushions. "And thank you for yours."

It was too bad that he was taken *and* Davin's family, really. I didn't feel anything close to attraction for him, but he was kind. Safe.

And safe was something I would never take for granted again.

FOURTEEN
Davin

Gwyn fussed with the high-necked Socairan gown for the thousandth time in the handful of minutes since she put it on, and I subtly nudged her with my elbow.

Straightening, she made her way into the carriage. Thank the stars it was still dark outside, because her confident stride was nothing at all like Galina's delicate footsteps.

I followed her in to find her yanking at the neckline once more, huffing irritably.

"Problems?" I asked cautiously.

She forcibly placed her hands in her lap, shooting me a sideways glance.

"This entire situation is a problem."

"One you volunteered for—insisted on, actually," I reminded her, trying to keep the bite from my tone.

"I'm not talking about this." Gwyn gestured to herself. "I'm talking about all of it. I'm talking about the fact that you're so keen on villainizing our own but won't even consider that Galina might have let the truth slip to someone before she left."

I took a deep breath, calming myself before I bit something back at her. She had a legendary temper under the best of circumstances, which these most certainly were not. The carriage took off with a jolt, rocking me back in the seat.

"I'm not *keen* on blaming our own, but we both know Galina being the source doesn't make any sense," I told her quietly, leaning forward. "The far more likely scenario—the only real scenario—is that it was one of our men."

At least one, I thought to myself but didn't see the need to add insult to injury. Not that I was enjoying this any more than she was.

She scoffed, shaking her head. "James and Scottie were practically in the nursery with us, and the others have trained alongside us for years. They aren't just our men, Davin. Some of them are our friends."

With a sigh, I tilted my head back against the carriage wall. She wasn't wrong, and I couldn't pretend it didn't sting. But it didn't change anything.

"And some of them are our enemies," I said softly.

Gwyn let out a sharp breath, turning her gaze to look out the window.

"Are they?" she asked, her voice even lower than mine had been. "Or are they *her* enemies?"

Again, she wasn't entirely wrong, though I wondered how quick she would have been to split that hair if she had felt more warmly toward Galina.

There was more than one sect of rebels. Our only real saving grace at this point was that they wanted conflicting things. There were those who desired nothing more than to go to war with Socair, by any means necessary. Some wanted a new monarchy, others a democracy, and still others believed the kingdom should be split.

Even then, they couldn't decide who they wanted on the thrones or councils, so they never worked together. Whatever they worked for, though, their commonality was in working against us.

We still didn't know what, exactly, the Uprising wanted.

"If they're willing to betray their monarchy for their cause, doesn't it amount to the same thing?" I pointed out.

A pained expression passed over my cousin's features.

"I suppose so," she allowed. "But why *do* you trust her?"

Did I trust her? There was a loaded question, let alone why.

"It's complicated," I said truthfully.

Gwyn's cheeks flushed with indignation as she sat forward on her side of the carriage.

"I'm here, Davin." She flung a hand between us. "I'm going along with your plan, willing to play bait, willing to consider that men I train alongside every day are the traitors rather than a woman I met a week ago, all on your word. So, you don't get to tell me it's *complicated*. Uncomplicate it. What is there between you?"

I opened my mouth to say *nothing*, but Gwyn cut me off with a scathing glare.

"And don't you dare say *nothing*, because as much as I absolutely despise feeding into your ego, even the Socairan ladies weren't immune to your charm. Yet this one is willing to play house with you for half a year, and I know you aren't cruel, so you clearly aren't concerned about her getting attached."

I scoffed. "I seriously doubt Galina has ever gotten too attached to anything in her entire life."

She had walked away once already. Stars, she had practically sprinted. The life she wanted might have been in Lochlann, but it sure as hell wasn't with me.

"See, that right there, Cousin," Gwyn growled. "I might not be Gal, but I'm not an idiot. Why are you so sure she won't care, and why is she the only woman in two kingdoms who is unattached but appears to want nothing to do with marrying you?"

Suddenly this carriage was a little too cramped, and I was far too sober.

I ran a hand through my hair, wanting nothing less than to have this conversation right now.

But one look at my cousin's sincerely frustrated expression as she fidgeted with the Socairan gown she hated reminded me that she was right. She was putting her life on the line for my half-arsed scheme. I owed her this much.

Besides which, Gwyn was family. I didn't want to lie to her.

"We were...friends," I began slowly. "Close friends."

Gwyn already looked dubious.

"You don't have female friends outside of your cousins. Hell, you don't really have any close friends outside of..." she trailed off before she could mention Mac, and I forged ahead.

"Nonetheless, we were. And then, for a brief time, we were...more than friends."

She relaxed back against the bench again, apparently satisfied now that I was talking. Pulling one of her ever-present snacks from her satchel, she shot me a small smirk.

"A *very* brief time?" she teased. "Is that why she hates you?"

I narrowed my eyes at her implication.

"Don't be ridiculous. I'm quite certain she enjoyed herself immensely." It took everything I had not to lose myself in memories of just how immensely, the flush on her cheeks, the frantic whispering of Socairan words I didn't have the capacity to define until much later.

"So she, what?" Gwyn pulled me from my thoughts, which was probably a good thing. "Felt taken advantage of?"

I forced myself to think about the rest of that night, her showing up at my door. *I don't want to take it back. I want to take it for myself.*

Then the next morning. *I came for a bit of fun before I had to get back to real life.*

The last part was like a bucket of ice water, sufficiently dousing any of my feelings about the former memory in a wave of bitterness once again.

"No." The word came out in a single sharp breath. "She didn't feel taken advantage of."

"Then what in the storms-damned hell happened?" Gwyn demanded, a trace of impatience in her tone.

"I...don't know," I said, wishing the words were a lie. "She was fine one minute, leaving to make sure no one noticed she was gone. I assumed she would come back, but then...she didn't," I shrugged.

Gwyn furrowed her brow but didn't interrupt.

"Then," I went on, the words coming out of me in a rush. "I caught wind of the fact that she was leaving without so much as saying goodbye. So I sought her out in time to hear a frigid sentiment about how she had used me for a good time, and we always knew it was going to end this way."

That was more information than I had strictly planned on giving.

Now that the words were out in the universe, I couldn't help but examine them. Galina wasn't much of a live-in-the-moment type of person, but she wouldn't have been the only Socairan lady who approached me out of an unwillingness to lose their maidenhead in front of six dukes, as was still the custom for witnessed consummation there.

To her everlasting credit, Gwyn did not remark on the irony of me getting used. She only asked, "Well, did you?"

"Did I what?"

"Always know it was going to end that way?" she clarified.

Had I? I should have, certainly. Even if I had been trying to find a way to tell her the truth. To see if it changed anything.

Then that morning happened, and everything went to hell. In hindsight, her behavior made even less sense, but I couldn't afford to dwell on that right now.

"Yes," I finally said. "I suppose I did."

Even after all this time, the words tasted like a lie.

The First Dance

DAVIN

A Year and a Half Ago

Music floated up through the open rooftop door and the windows of the floor below, remnants of the ball Galina had left behind.

She was quieter than usual tonight, examining the stars like every single one was keeping a secret she was determined to discover.

Or perhaps I was projecting, knowing the secrets I was keeping. It was getting harder to lie by the day, but I couldn't tell her who I was.

It would risk Rowan's life if the information got in the wrong hands. And even if it didn't, I wasn't ready to consider all the implications of what that truth could mean.

Though, all of this was coming to an end soon, one way or another.

Galina would be distracted by finding a new husband, and I… I might finally be going home. Or I would be just as soon as my family could dig their way through the rest of the rubble from the cave-in.

After months of carefully obtaining information and

rooting out spies had finally come to fruition, I'd been able to secretly get word back-and-forth to my uncle, and I knew they were doing everything they could to bring Row and me home.

Which was what I wanted, obviously.

"What is it?" Lina's low voice startled me from my thoughts.

I hadn't realized she had switched from deciphering the stars to deciphering me.

"It's nothing," I lied automatically.

She gave a small delicate sound of disbelief, arching a dark-blonde eyebrow in question.

I sighed, twisting to lean against the balcony, meeting her crystalline gaze.

"I'm worried about Row," I said, wanting to at least give her something true.

"Row?" she echoed, and I cursed myself for being distracted.

Bollocks.

"Princess Rowan," I corrected, keeping my tone light.

Galina looked away, then, focusing back on the stars above us.

"Are things really so casual in Lochlann?" Her tone was light, but it felt forced.

"Not always," I admitted, trying to stick closely to the truth. "But I know the princess well."

"I'm sure you do," she muttered. "Probably nearly as well as you know half the ladies in the estate by now."

I laughed out loud, prompting an irritable blink from her.

"No, Lina. Not like that," I clarified. "I would never..." I trailed off because I couldn't very well tell her Rowan was my cousin, and more like my sister, at that.

"Complicate our relationship when it's my job to keep her safe," I finished.

I could practically hear Rowan suppressing a laugh at the

idea that I would keep her any safer than she would keep me. I was decent with a sword, but she was probably better.

"Ah, so she isn't one of those ladies who comes to your rooms at night so you can teach them important things like how much ice to put in Lochlannian drinks?"

The corners of my mouth twisted up, and I bit back another laugh.

"Hold on now, that's not plural. Only *one* lady did that." I nudged her with my shoulder. "And who am I to fault her for wanting to learn about her neighbors?"

She arched a judgmental eyebrow, and I shook my head.

"She really is only a friend," I answered. "Rowan, I mean."

There was a charged pause before Lina spoke again.

"So more like me, then," she offered, still looking decidedly elsewhere.

No. Not at all like you. Because I definitely never resist the urge to run my hands through Rowan's hair or wonder what her favorite white wine tastes like on her lips.

"Exactly," I said with a smirk.

Something indiscernible flitted behind her eyes. Then she blinked, and it was gone before I could read it.

Behind us, the music swelled to a crescendo, pulling me from thoughts that would send the nearest stuffy lord into a panic and make the ladies clutch their pearls.

"What made you leave earlier than usual?" I finally asked. "Not a fan of dancing?"

She let out an uncharacteristically wistful sigh. "Actually, I love dancing. That might have been my only incentive to stay."

For the first time since I met her, she looked almost...sad. Which was my only excuse for what I did next.

"As it happens, so do I." I pushed away from the stone railing, stretching out a hand for hers.

Galina's countenance turned skeptical. "You dance?"

"Obviously." I drawled the word. "There are dances in the villages."

That wasn't a lie. There were, and I had even been to them. As their laird.

She hesitated only a moment before placing her hand in mine.

It was warm despite the late-night chill, and for a little while I let myself pretend that everything was different.

FIFTEEN
Galina

Present Day

GALLAGHER and I traveled at the same relentless pace for nearly a week, sticking as much as we could to back roads until it was time to stop at an inn for the night.

There wasn't much opportunity for conversation, but Gallagher was as congenial as ever, helpfully telling me about the royal family and the court and anything else he thought I needed to know whenever we stopped for breaks.

He didn't say much about Davin's parents, which made me slightly nervous.

Would they be upset about the arrangement? Lithlinglau was Davin's, so in theory, it was his decision whether I stayed there, but his father was a prince. At home, I knew what to expect, but here... Here, everything was different.

Even the landscape.

The Lochlannian countryside was nothing like the snowy mountain town I hailed from or the storm-swept plains near the Obsidian Palace.

Here, there was an abundance of life.

There were sprawling purple-and-gold hills, punctuated

with lakes and rivers and streams. Fat, wild birds and antlered creatures ambled through the tall grass, and more than once, we had to stop while the soldiers shooed enormous fluffy cows from the path.

It was all too open and vaguely chaotic, much like its inhabitants.

The buildings were different, too. In the mountains, we built up, but here, the estates were sprawling. And ugly. Made from blocks of solid gray stone, they seemed to be built for defense rather than beauty.

I stuffed down a wave of homesickness, trying not to think about the gilded, colorful domes that always welcomed me back to my family estate.

And then, Lithlinglau came into view.

Somehow, I knew this was Davin's home before Gallagher even announced it. Despite my best efforts, I must have made a face, because the duke chuckled under his breath.

"Welcome to the most coveted estate in all of Lochlann."

I didn't have to wonder why.

It was the largest castle I had ever seen, and unlike the other Lochlannian estates that we'd passed, it was far from ugly. It was all pristine white turrets and elegant wrought-iron balconies nestled in the rolling hills and silhouetted by a sparkling blue lake.

The castle wasn't without its defenses, either. An outer wall made of the same white stone and topped with wicked-looking iron spikes edged the property, leaving an enormous amount of space for stables and grazing animals.

For all that Davin had talked about politics and rebellions, I wondered if part of him just couldn't bear to part with this place.

We entered the gate, making our way to the back of the property on a path of black-and-white gravel, lined by artfully trimmed hedges.

I almost laughed out loud, remembering the sheer number

of times I had pictured Davin's quaint family home in a village somewhere. There was, in fairness, a village in the distance. One that he owned.

After we dismounted, Gallagher led me in through the main doors, past several curious maids, and straight up a gleaming white staircase.

I was no stranger to opulence. The clan estates in Socair were filled to the brim with antique furniture and jeweled chandeliers. In Ram, nearly all of the windows were stained glass, and my uncle had a collection of jeweled eggs worth more than my father's much-more-modest castle.

This was a different kind of wealth, everything large and open and modern and bright. It felt almost empty, by comparison.

We came to a halt at the end of a well-guarded hallway, stopping just outside of a sage-colored door.

Gallagher rapped his knuckles against the frame.

"It's Gal," he called through the wood.

A deep voice told us to enter.

Gallagher opened the door, gesturing for me to follow. No sooner had I crossed the threshold than I halted in my tracks.

Because Davin was standing in the center of the room.

Or, rather, a slightly older version of Davin. The man had the same cobalt eyes and onyx hair, though his was graying at the temples. His build was identical, too. Tall and broad-shouldered, but not quite bulky. And when he smirked, it tugged at his lips in exactly the same way.

He stood next to a diminutive blond woman, her elegant features drawing in confusion as she scanned first the two of us, and then the empty hallway.

"Where's Davin?" Prince Oliver asked.

His voice was different from his son's, less clipped and more drawling, and currently edged with a trace of panic. It was a reminder that only two years had passed since their son disappeared beneath the mountains.

"Safe," Gallagher responded quickly. "On his way. He sent you this."

While Prince Oliver took the letter, Davin's mother turned to me. There was a clear question in her navy eyes.

"This is Lady Galina Zhakarov," Gallagher said, gesturing to me.

"Lady Galina of Clan Ram?" Princess Jocelyn clarified, her perfect blond eyebrows climbing into her hairline.

It would be easy to think Davin had gotten nothing from her, but the similarities were in the nuances. The cadence of her speech, her clipped, cultured tone, and the subtle way she assessed me with a single, sweeping glance.

Gallagher nodded, exchanging a look with the princess that I couldn't quite read while I swept into a curtsy.

Had she memorized the entire Socairan court? Knowing her son, it wasn't unlikely.

"And our son's betrothed, apparently," Prince Oliver added. "For the time being."

I held my breath for her reaction.

Princess Jocelyn blinked several times, the expression almost eerily reminiscent of her son.

"It's a pleasure to meet you, Lady Galina," she said after a beat.

Her husband echoed the sentiment.

"And you as well," I responded.

"Dare I ask how one might be betrothed 'for the time being'?" A bare hint of exasperation lined her voice.

She was already holding her hand out for the letter, which Prince Oliver swiftly relinquished to her. She scanned the contents, her lips quirking in displeasure before she smoothed them back out again.

"Very well, then," she finally said, her hands falling to her sides, fingers tightly gripping the parchment. "I'm sure you'd like to get some rest after the journey you've had. We can get to know each other better in the morning, but in the meantime, Gallagher can show you to your rooms. The blue ones," she added.

Oliver shot her a sideways glance, and the corner of Gallagher's mouth tilted up. I got the feeling there was a joke I wasn't quite in on.

"Yes, Auntie Jocelyn." He dipped his head in assent.

"And Gal, come right back," Prince Oliver added pointedly.

"Yes, Uncle Oli." This time, Gallagher's tone was more resigned than polite.

I didn't envy him that conversation.

Once we were safely in the hallway, he let out a slow breath.

"Well. That could have gone much worse."

He wasn't wrong, though I still wasn't entirely certain how it had gone. They hadn't actively tried to make me leave, which was something. If anything, they had almost seemed to...accept it.

I wasn't ready to let my guard down, though.

I knew all too well the dark secrets that could hide in beautiful places.

SIXTEEN
Davin

The days since we left Hagail had been more than enough to remind me why I never shared a room with my cousin.

Her mood continued to decline, and I found myself missing Gallagher's laid-back nature, or hell, even Galina's icy stoicism next to Gwyn's increasingly short temper.

That wasn't helped by the fact that each night we pretended to go to our separate spaces before one of us would sneak to the other's room. We had no way of knowing what form in which an attack would come.

In an effort to smooth things over, I had taken the liberty of purchasing her favorite snacks each time we stopped at a village or town.

Unfortunately, even those had limited effects.

Tonight, we again went through the routine of sneaking Gwyn out of the carriage and into the inn—her hood pulled low over her face. I wrapped an arm around her shoulders for show, as well as to force her to walk with a shorter stride.

Honestly, it was a miracle that none of the soldiers suspected us yet. Or if they did, they didn't let on.

Once we had the keys to our rooms, I ushered *Gwyn-Lin*a

up the stairs, but didn't make it five steps before I was followed by the dulcet tones of the innkeeper's daughter.

"Davin?" She said my name like a question, and my cousin let out a low laugh.

I groaned internally, kicking myself for not choosing a different village to stop at for the night.

"Have fun with that," Gwyn whispered, the first bit of amusement in days lining her features.

When I turned to face Bess, I *accidentally* stepped on my cousin's toe. She hissed a curse under her breath, but I covered over the sound with a loud apology.

"I am so sorry, Darling. Did I hurt you? Why don't you go rest your feet in your room? Yes, the door is just there," I said, pointing to the second door on the left.

It would be a hell of a lot easier to let Bess down gently without Gwyn's snickering giving us away.

When I turned back to face the girl, her eyes were still trained on Gwyn's retreating form. Any hopes I had that *Galina*'s presence would deter Bess were dashed when she put a questioning hand on my arm.

"Good evening, Bess," I began, and she took a confident step forward just as I took one backward. "Could we get a bath sent up for my lady?"

Might as well start laying the groundwork for that announcement.

It didn't hurt that it would serve as a polite deterrent for the incredibly young girl who had tried to approach me on every single visit I made to her father's inn.

Bess's large brown eyes flitted to the door as it closed behind Gwyn, then back to me.

"So it's true, then? That you brought back a Socairan?" There was a hard edge to her tone, and I internally bristled.

She had practically spat the word *Socairan*, using it like a slur. Interesting, though, that the rebels had managed to spread word this far.

"It is indeed," I assured her. "And I should go make sure she's settling in."

"Of course, mi'laird," she said in a tone that implied the opposite. "I should get back to work."

I blew out a slow, relieved breath when she walked away, grateful Galina hadn't actually been here to witness that exchange, lest she hate me even more. Stars knew she would never believe I hadn't touched the girl.

Then again, Galina *couldn't* actually hate me much more than she already did.

That was a small comfort, at least.

I WOKE up to a hand over my mouth.

Gwyn's intense gaze bored into mine, evident by the low light of the lanterns. Blood rushed to my ears as the scrape of metal sounded at our door.

Someone was breaking into our room.

Half a heartbeat later, the familiar click of a lock sounded. I kept perfectly still, watching as the moonlight bounced off of the door handle. It dipped downward before the door itself was gingerly pushed open.

Gwyn curled up into my side, feigning sleep, but I knew she was silently reaching for one of the many blades she kept on her person at all times.

Whoever it was, they were skilled. The gentle clinking of keys muffled as our visitor tucked them into a pocket. The intruder shut the door noiselessly before creeping across the aged floorboards without a single scuff of their boots or groan of the wood.

No one tried to stop them, so either the two guards outside her door were complicit...or they had been silenced.

A flash of silver glinted above us. In a single fluid motion, Gwyn slipped from the covers and spun behind the man, covering his mouth with one hand while she restrained him with the other.

"Surprise, arsehole," she taunted in a low tone.

His eyes did, in fact, widen in shock, probably as much because a woman had bested him with such ease as because that woman was clearly not Socairan.

I kicked his dagger out of his hand and it went flying across the floor, skittering to a halt just beneath the window. Gwyn pressed her knee to his lower spine, and he groaned behind her hand as he sank to the floor.

While she kept a hold on him, I drew my own dagger, cutting a couple strips from the blankets and using them to tie him up and gag him. Gwyn released him from her grip, pushing him none too gently until he was kneeling with his back against the wall.

"What's the matter?" she asked, mock pouting down at him. "You were expecting someone else?"

As soon as she moved the gag to let him speak, the would-be assassin spit in her face. Before I could react, Gwyn's fist connected with his jaw, snapping his head back with a resounding crack.

I held out a handkerchief. She reached out for it without taking her eyes off the man, wiping off her cheek and looking like she very much wanted to punch him again.

"Look at that." I tutted. "You've already made her angry. I might be tempted to help rein in that legendary temper of hers if you tell me what the Uprising wants, or is it just death to Socairans?"

I was sure to speak in a tone that conveyed how very unimpressed I was by that idea.

He bared his teeth in a macabre smile, stained red with his blood.

"We want you gone. All of you," he said meaningfully, looking from me to Gwyn.

This wasn't just about Galina. It was about our family.

"Well, good luck with that," my cousin shot back. "You would hardly be the first to try."

I wanted to share in her confidence, but something in the man's gaze gave me pause. *Arrogance.* This was not the look of a man cowed. It was the look of a man who knew something we didn't.

He raised his eyebrows in a clear challenge, chewing viciously at the inside of his cheek. At least, that's what I thought he was doing, until I heard a crack.

Had he broken his own tooth? Had Gwyn broken it when she punched him?

But when he smiled again, there was something more than blood running over his lips. Dread pooled into my stomach, an alarm sounding in my head.

"Cut his ties," I told Gwyn.

She shot me a questioning look but did as I asked.

For all the good it would do.

"Too late," he confirmed. "We're closer than you think."

He bit out each word in a rasp, a sharp contrast to his harsh, mocking tone from before.

Gwyn severed the binds on his hands just in time for him to slump forward. His body was racked with a violent tremor, then another until he was seizing.

"Hold him down," I all but yelled.

She anchored her hands at his shoulders, and I started on chest compressions, already knowing they wouldn't save him. This was what I got for splitting away from Gallagher.

Then again, if I hadn't, Galina would be dead.

And now I was put in the infuriating position of trying to save the man who would have killed her.

"Damn it," I cursed, just as foam bubbled forth from his lips.

It was pink at first, fading into a deep crimson until it turned black. Veins burst in his eyes, a deep purple that spider-webbed down his face into his chest.

Then he was still.

I sat back, checking automatically for the pulse I knew I wouldn't find.

Gwyn let loose a string of curses that made mine look mild by comparison, then silence fell. We stared at each other, trying to comprehend what the hell had just happened.

I wasn't sad to witness the demise of the man who had tried to kill a defenseless woman in her bed, but any hope we had of finding answers had followed him in death.

Which, I suspected, had been the point.

I ran my hands through my hair, repeating every moment of our interaction in my head, playing it all out again and again, wondering what I might have missed.

He had poisoned himself—unless someone else had poisoned him, but that seemed unlikely. There had been a crack. Was he carrying poison in his mouth somehow? A glass vial?

I couldn't very well go poking around where he might have a deadly poison, but perhaps the village healer could tell us something.

Faintly, I registered Gwyn saying my name.

"Davin," she said again, more firmly.

I followed her gaze to the assassin's chest. His shirt had come loose at the laces, falling to the side and revealing more inky veins that stood out in contrast against his pale skin.

But that's not what she was staring at.

There, branded into the skin above his heart, was the image of a snake coiled around a broken crown.

It surely wasn't a coincidence.

The rebels until now had been disorganized, disgruntled, and as susceptible to bribes or corruption as anyone else. But this one was willing to have their cause branded into his skin.

Not only willing to kill for what he believed in, but willing to die for it.

If they were all like this, we had a problem, because what they apparently believed in was the end of my family's reign.

By any means necessary.

SEVENTEEN
Galina

A KNOCK on the door startled me from my deep sleep, and I sat up with a gasp.

Was I in the guest rooms at Castle Wolf? Was the maid here to fetch me for breakfast with Alexei? Blinding panic overtook me when I realized I might be late, might be less presentable, might be anything that would give him cause to be upset with me.

I shot out of the overly plush bed before my eyes were even fully open, stopping short at the feel of the polished wood floor beneath my feet where there should have been a bear skin rug.

Belatedly, I registered the light that stabbed at the back of my eyelids, more than the heavy drapes at Wolf would have allowed.

I finally forced my bleary eyes open to the sight of sunlight filtering in through sheer ivory curtains, painting the room in a hazy morning glow. A delicate golden chandelier hung from the center of a high, painted ceiling, simple and elegant and decidedly un-Socairan.

I was at Lithlinglau Castle. Safe. *For now.*

The vast, open rooms were an artwork of creams and pale

blues and gold accents. They were delicate and feminine, undeniably pretty, like the rest of the estate.

Perhaps this was where Davin's women always stayed.

That thought was irritating enough to pull me back to myself. I inhaled two deep lungfuls of air to calm my racing heart before I called for the person—presumably the maid—to enter.

Sure enough, it was Anna, the woman who had assisted me the night before, followed by two younger maids.

"I apologize for oversleeping," I said, smoothing down my nightgown.

"Ach, no, milady. Ye needed the rest." Her gaze lingered on the dark circles under my eyes, and she looked like she only narrowly refrained from adding a comment about how I still did.

Of course, I hadn't slept much.

Instead, I had spent my midnight hours exploring my suites and the balcony, stopping just short of taking the stairs to what I presumed was a rooftop. I wasn't sure if there were sentries posted, and there was no doubt plenty of suspicion on the random Socairan who had shown up claiming to be betrothed to their laird as it was.

Sleep had only claimed me a few short hours ago, and it had been fitful at that.

"Nonetheless, I can be ready quickly," I said.

"There's no hurry," Anna responded in a softer tone, one that belied her no-nonsense features and equally severe graying bun. "I daresay their highnesses willna starve if ye take an extra minute or two to dress for breakfast."

I nodded, unsure exactly how to respond to that.

Anna didn't seem bothered by my lack of response. She just turned to give orders to the maids about where to place my borrowed gown and cosmetics.

I had wondered last night if she was chosen because Princess Jocelyn had scoured the estate for a maid who hadn't been on the receiving end of Davin's affections, but now I wondered if it was because Anna was a more senior member of the staff. A more trusted member.

For my sake? Or for her discretion?

I wasn't sure.

Either way, I was grateful for the latter when she helped me disrobe after sending the younger maids away. My bruises were pale remnants of what they had been, but even if she had missed them in the low candlelight the night before, there was no way she didn't notice them in the sunlight.

She didn't comment or even pause, though her hands were exceedingly gentle as she pulled my corset over them. She kept up a steady stream of chatter, doling out information in her blunt manner.

"Lady Gwyn willna miss the pink gown since it clashes something awful with her hair, so I took the liberty of taking in the shoulders for ye. I'm told yer things are arriving shortly, but we'll have some gowns made for ye in no time as well."

After she helped me into it, I wasn't certain I wanted any new gowns—at least, not in the Lochlannian style. The bodice was low and wide, leaving my shoulders and my collarbones entirely exposed. Instead of the heavy brocaded material I was used to, or even the wool of Gwyn's traveling dresses, the pale silk hugged my skin, clinging to my modest curves.

Anna asked me how I preferred my hair, following my guidance until she had it braided in an approximation of my usual style. She topped it off with a silver circlet, then fastened matching understated jewelry around my wrist and neck.

"Are these Lady Gwyn's as well?" I asked.

"No, milady. Princess Jocelyn sent these up."

It was an unexpectedly thoughtful gesture, one that left me even more curious about Davin's mother.

Before I could comment on it, another knock sounded at the door. I tensed reflexively.

“He must have come to escort you to breakfast,” Anna said easily.

“Of course,” I said, forcing my shoulders to relax.

In Socair, I had always been escorted when visiting the other Clan estates. I wasn’t sure why I expected things to be different here. Perhaps because it was hard to picture Gwyn waiting patiently in her rooms for someone to come collect her, no matter where she was.

Anna started to tidy the room while I went to open the door. I was expecting Gallagher’s crimson hair and easy smile, or perhaps the unfamiliar features of a guard.

Instead, it was Prince Oliver.

EIGHTEEN
Davin

The last few hours of the night were a whirlwind of calling the magistrate and the healer while we kept Gwyn's presence a secret and tried not to let on to our men that two of their own were dead.

We had found the guards stashed in a linen closet, their throats slashed, with no defensive wounds. The assassin couldn't have gotten them both that quickly. He could have had help from one of the villagers, but the men on guard were well-trained enough that they should have been on alert for anyone who wasn't one of their own.

So at least one of the men left standing was a traitor.

I brought a carafe of coffee and a tray of food to my room, where Gwyn was still hiding out. The healer had just left the room next door, having no insights on the poison except that it had come from a false tooth implanted in place of the assassin's molar.

"You knew this would happen," Gwyn said when I shut the door.

She didn't move as I set the tray on the table in front of her, just stared at the wall like she could see straight through it to the other side, to where the magistrate stood a silent vigil over the three bodies that were cooling on the bare wood floor. The assassin and our men.

Men who had died because we hadn't warned them when we set this plan in motion. I had hoped that they had been the traitors, that they had run. It would have been better than finding their corpses and knowing we may as well have wielded the knives ourselves.

I sank into the chair across from Gwyn, pouring us both a cup of coffee.

"You knew, too," I said, sliding hers across the table.

There was no more heat to my tone than there had been to hers.

We were both too tired for that. Tired from a lack of sleep, tired of having to make decisions that meant good men died for the sake of rooting out the bad.

"Yeah," she said softly, taking a sip. "I suppose I did. I just wanted you to be wrong."

"I wanted that, too, Gwynnie." Running a hand through my hair, I got to my feet. "You should stay here and eat. I need to go tell the men."

She didn't bother offering to come with me. We both knew she couldn't lie well enough for what I was about to do.

I went downstairs to where the men were all eating breakfast. Bess shifted guiltily as soon as she saw me, the first test to my resolve.

I would deal with her after.

First, I needed to make sure whoever was responsible for last night didn't get spooked and alert anyone who might be back at Lithlinglau. It had already taken everything I had not to take off straight away without handling any of this, just to make sure Galina and Gallagher were safe.

I had responsibilities, though, so I gathered the men outside to talk to them.

I started with the truth, that we had gotten a tip about a traitor.

The words hung in the air, long enough for me to catalog reactions. The blood drained from more than one face, but it made sense for them to be afraid. It wasn't incriminating, yet.

Next, I spun a tale of an assassin who attacked, only in my story, he was very chatty after we caught him, calling out the traitors by name. This was the worst part, impugning the honor of the men who died for their loyalty.

We would make it right, when this was over, but it still churned my gut to say the words aloud. Even more so to watch the oh-so-subtle signs of relief overtake more than one of my men.

Because they were guilty? Or because they believed we caught the men who were?

Finally, I lit the final match to the powder keg, telling them that I had switched out Gwyn for Galina and apologizing for the necessary subterfuge. There died any hope that I was wrong about the traitors.

There were a few mouths drawn in disappointment, others twisted in anger.

But only two men exchanged a look filled with the barest hints of panic. Whether they were concerned they had almost gotten Gwyn killed or that they had passed along faulty information to their precious Uprising, either was all but an admission of guilt.

Pasting a smile on my face, I told them to ready the horses, as we would be on the road in no time.

Then, while they were distracted, I told the innkeeper and his daughter to accompany me upstairs. There was still a chance that I was wrong, or worse, that I had missed someone.

Gwyn wasn't surprised to see Bess. We both knew there were only so many ways the rebel could have gotten the key.

Bess, on the other hand, let out a squeak when she beheld my cousin. Horror settled into her expression, her mouth dropping open as she shook her head back and forth.

I shut the door, and the innkeeper Jon turned to me, his wide eyes confused.

"What's this about, mi'laird?"

"Yes, Bessie, what *is* this about?" Gwyn asked, her jaw rigid, her eyes blazing with accusation.

Bess took a step back.

"We need to ask your daughter some questions," I answered when she said nothing.

"Bessie?" Jon's voice trembled, and I hated the necessity of what we were about to do, hated that the rebels pulled in a young, stupid, jealous girl for their ends.

Mostly, I hated that there were people in the world who could be swayed toward facilitating murder for petty, ridiculous reasons like prejudice and spite.

"No," she said, her voice coming out as a strangled cry. "I thought she was... I thought you were... I didn't know, I swear! I would never have wanted her to get hurt."

Gwyn's hand twitched toward her sword, and I shook my head subtly. She glared but nodded. Jon's face had gone ashen, and he appeared to be mute with shock.

"Of course you didn't," I agreed with Bess, my tone conversational. "I think we both know you would never let the duchess get hurt."

Her shoulders sagged in relief, and I went on. "Just an innocent, defenseless woman whose very existence offended you."

The blood drained from Bess's face. Her father ran his hands over his bald head, his face stricken.

"Are you going to execute me?" she asked weakly.

"Not if you tell us what we need to know," Gwyn said plainly.

Jon took a sharp inhale. "Tell them, Bessie."

Several tears tracked down her cheeks when she met my eyes. "It was Scottie."

Was I relieved to have it confirmed? Disappointed? I wasn't even sure.

And if he was guilty, Arran most certainly was as well.

Gwyn met my eyes with her own tumultuous ones. I could practically see the thoughts playing out in her head.

Scottie, who had grown up at Castle Chridhe as one of the orphans from the first war, who had trained with us from the time we were kids. Who had kept her bed warm more than once.

"Was there anyone else?" Gwyn demanded.

"Not that he told me. We were...*alone* when he asked for the keys," Bess admitted, avoiding looking in her father's direction.

It was an effort not to laugh at the ridiculousness of it all. She had no problem admitting that she had happily been an accessory to murder, but admitting that she was in a compromising situation with a man was still somehow embarrassing for her.

She hadn't named Arran, but I doubted she was lying for him. More likely, she had only known of Scottie's involvement.

"What's going to happen to me?" she asked through her tears.

"Nothing, for now," I said, already turning to go. "Stay in here until we're out of sight."

Gwyn followed half a second later, staring at me in disbelief.

"You're just going to let her go?" she hissed when we were out of earshot.

"Of course not," I assured her. "I said *for now*. I'll write to the magistrate from the next village, strongly encouraging him to take a hard line with this."

She nodded with a savage sort of satisfaction, but all I felt was the overwhelming anxiety that we were missing something. There were more of them. The assassin had made that clear.

Were they with Gallagher and Galina, even now?

Trying for a lighter tone, I elbowed my cousin. “Why don’t you use your woo woo twinsy senses to check in on Gal?”

“You laugh, but—”

I let the mask drop long enough for her to see the very real panic building up in my mind. She surveyed my features, her eyes softening.

“I would know if something had happened to him,” she told me. “I would feel it.”

I nodded my thanks. All my teasing aside, I believed her. I knew they had a connection that was only made stronger by their fae heritage. In the past, she had always known when Gallagher was in trouble.

And if he was safe, then Galina was, too.

That would have to be good enough for now.

NINETEEN

Galina

Davin's father stood back from the door, granting me space to enter the hallway.

"Your Highness," I greeted, dipping into a curtsy.

The movement was still strange, and I found myself wondering why the Lochlannians thought it was a sign of respect rather than an awkward dance move.

"Good morning, Lady Galina. I suspect if I told you not to worry about formalities, it would fall on deaf ears," he said with a raised eyebrow.

The expression was so reminiscent of his son that I was grateful for the chance to look at the polished beams of the floor as I gave him a demure smile.

"I'll certainly try, Prince Oliver," I said smoothly.

"That's better. We'll be on to just Oliver in no time." His tone was gently teasing. "I hope you don't mind, but Gallagher went to assist the healer's apprentice with treating an injury in the village, so I took it upon myself to escort you to breakfast. If you need more time, though, I'm happy to wait."

Was this truly a world in which a lady would tell the king's brother that she minded his personally escorting her somewhere, or better yet, that he could wait in the hallway until she had perfected her cosmetics?

Or were those merely formalities?

"I'm glad for your company," I told him, stepping out into the hallway and closing the door behind me. "I hope everything is all right in the village."

His smile was casual, but his gaze was scrutinizing as he offered his arm. "I'm sure Gallagher and Mistress Maisey will get them fixed up in no time. Breakfast isn't far today, since it's just down there on the other floor of the family wing."

He gestured toward the smaller staircase down the hall, which meant that I was staying in the family wing as well, rather than the one reserved for guests. Was that normal for a betrothed here?

In Socair, betrothed couples were generally housed on opposite ends of the castle, for at least the appearance of propriety.

Prince Oliver led me down a set of stairs into another hallway.

"My and Jocelyn's suites are just down here," he told me.

Unlike the main part of the castle, this hallway was lined with portraits. Nearly all of them appeared to be by the same artist.

Oliver walked at a steady pace, giving me time to peruse the walls.

"My cousin painted them," he said. "Gal and Gwyn's mother. She truly has a gift."

"They're stunning," I said truthfully. "Is she...like Lady Gwyn?"

Skepticism bled into my tone. It was impossible to imagine the vivacious woman sitting still long enough to paint these vivid renderings.

He barked out a laugh. "No. Though in fairness, no one is quite like Gwyn. It's Gal who takes after Isla, though Gwyn did get her temper."

I couldn't help but smile as I surveyed the series of portraits.

Instead of the stiff poses I was used to, she had captured the subjects in moments. In one, there was a beautiful dark-haired boy with fair skin and bright blue eyes smirking up at a nearly identical man who stared back down at him with adoration.

A glance at the prince showed he was looking at the same picture fondly.

"He was probably trying to get out of trouble with his mother that day," he said with a wistful smile.

There were several more paintings of Davin and his parents, some with other adults I didn't recognize, then one of six teenagers lounging by a lake. Four of the six sported crimson curls, all but Davin and a boy with shaggy chestnut-colored hair. Davin and his cousins, and...a friend? Another cousin?

A red fox curled next to the girl who I assumed was Princess Avani, something the artist must have added for whimsy.

"That's the lake you passed on your way in," the prince offered.

I nodded, though it was truncated when I caught sight of the next painting.

Davin and the only other non-redhead from the picture before, each with an arm slung around the other's shoulder and holding a mug of ale in their free hands. They wore identical smiles, genuine and unrestrained and just the slightest bit mischievous.

"That's Mac," Oliver said quietly.

The name brought forth a memory of Davin on the rooftop at Elk Estate.

"There was some gossip regarding the circumstances of my birth," he had said. "But Mac never cared what anyone thought of him, and it made it easier for me not to, either."

"You were close?" I surmised.

"Like brothers," he confirmed.

There was something wistful in his tone.

I peered over at him. "You aren't anymore?"

He turned his head toward the balcony, far enough that I couldn't make out his expression when he spoke.

"He's gone now." The words were somber, final, leaving no doubt of their meaning.

I had no experience with comforting anyone. My relationships at court were shallow at best, and I had no younger siblings or cousins to speak of. Hesitantly, I placed my hand on his.

"I'm sorry," I said sincerely, feeling how ineffectual the words were.

He flipped his hand to entwine his fingers with mine, squeezing them gently.

"So am I."

I had wondered about that night more than once, sure no one could fabricate that kind of grief, and just as certain that he wouldn't have bothered to show me something real when nothing else was.

But it had been true, after all.

Is that better? Worse?

Infinitely more confusing, to be sure.

Belatedly, I realized Prince Oliver was studying me, perhaps waiting on some sort of response.

"His best friend growing up," I supplied, not wanting to comment on how carefree Davin looked or how different it was from the man I had left only a few days ago.

Oliver's eyebrows shot up in surprise. "Dav told you about Mac?"

I paused, unsure whether it was information I was supposed to be privy to.

His features softened. "It's all right, of course. I was only surprised because Davin doesn't usually talk about him."

"His options for company were fairly limited," I said

wryly. "And I'm sure you know how he feels about Theodore."

The prince let out a low chuckle. "I do, indeed, though his dislike certainly makes more sense now."

Fortunately, we arrived at the breakfast room before I had to respond to that.

I doubted seriously Davin's feelings about Theodore had anything to do with me or my former pseudo-betrothal, but I couldn't very well argue with the prince.

ONCE BREAKFAST WAS SERVED, Princess Jocelyn kindly dismissed the servants, so we had privacy in the room.

I braced myself, pulling my armor in more closely and donning my...*resting Socairan face.*

But, once again, the inquisition I was expecting didn't come.

"How are you finding your rooms?" Jocelyn asked innocuously, adding a sugar cube to her cup of coffee.

Was she trying to put me off my guard? This kind of conversation was as natural to me as breathing, though, so I responded easily. A compliment, something specific and as genuine as possible.

"They're lovely. The bed was so comfortable, I nearly didn't want to leave." That was true.

Though I mostly didn't want to leave because I didn't want to have this conversation.

"You must be tired from your travels," Oliver added. "I must apologize, on behalf of Lochlann, for the welcome you received. Would that our people were more tolerant."

"I'm certain that's a problem faced on both sides of the mountain," I allowed.

They took turns asking questions and commenting until I finally realized this wasn't their way of putting me off my guard. Instead, they were testing me.

Jocelyn confirmed my suspicion when she finally gave an approving nod.

"It appears whatever plan you and my son have concocted between you just might work."

I didn't feign surprise. We weren't hiding it from them, after all, and I wasn't remotely shocked that Davin's plan had merit.

I had witnessed his skills in action, after all. Still, their acceptance was a relief, so I gave a gracious nod.

Though part of me couldn't help but wait for the other shoe to drop, wondering if they were only biding their time until Davin got home.

"We'll introduce you as a visitor to the arriving courtiers." Jocelyn's tone was all efficiency now, though there was still an undertone of warmth. "Let them assume what they will, then save the official announcement for when Davin returns."

"The courtiers are coming here?" I asked.

She gave an affirmative dip of her chin. "Lithlinglau is launching the autumn-winter social season, so some have arrived already, and others will be here shortly. I expect an even larger turnout than usual as it's Davin's first year hosting the opening ball since he became acting laird."

"Yes, the ladies can be quite...exuberant," the prince added with a smirk.

I took a long sip from my coffee cup, less because I needed to and more to conceal my features while I processed what he had just said.

Wonderful.

It wasn't that I hadn't known on some level how many women would be after my fake fiancé. Even with the vote, it was a win-win for them. If he won, they would be the next

Lady of Lithlinglau, and if he lost, well, they would still be marrying one of the royal family members.

I had been so focused on so many other things, I hadn't given much thought to how exhausting it would all be, ingratiating myself into a new court that was already full of enemies.

I had no choice, though. At least I had been raised for this. On the road, I had been less than useless, especially next to Gwyn.

But this... This, I could do.

THE NEXT FEW days were a flurry of arriving courtiers who met me with various levels of disdain.

In fairness, not as many of them appeared to be concerned about me being Socairan as they were about me taking their precious marquess off the market. It would have been easier, if I could have told them he was all theirs.

There were two women who stood out more than the others. Lady Fiona Shaw and Lady Gracie MacBay. They had arrived in a carriage together, apparently having been staying at Fiona's southern estate, something which Gracie looked decidedly displeased about.

Gracie was pretty, with light-brown hair and a sprinkling of freckles across her rosy cheeks.

But Fiona was flawless.

Midnight tresses hung in loose waves over her bare shoulders, pinned back at the sides with ornate combs. Her gown was low cut, expertly hugging each of her curves in a way that had nearly every man in the room helpless to keep their eyes off of her. I was pleased to note the prince was an obvious exception.

Gallagher, slightly less so, but he did an admirable job of at least trying to avert his gaze.

Fiona was well aware of the effect she had, angling her body just so as she expertly wound her way through the crowd. In fact, I suspected that nothing the woman did was unintentional.

She assessed me with deep-blue, kohl-lined eyes, like a predator searches its prey for weaknesses.

Though her questions were outwardly innocuous, I got the sense she was cataloging my every answer to twist toward her purposes. Gracie was her polar opposite, warmer and kinder and clearly not a fan of Fiona's.

But there was something too knowing in the familiar way they both said his name, endearing in Gracie's case and possessive in Fiona's.

I guarded my words even more carefully than usual before politely excusing myself to sit at a table far, far away, hoping I could limit my interactions with them.

We were at another of our daily teas where I smiled and complimented and worked on charming the court, which was markedly easier with Jocelyn's help.

She had managed to weave a story of star-crossed lovers without actually admitting I was here for Davin. As I sank into the seat next to her, she was again, working toward that end.

"Of course," the princess said in a conspiratorial tone. "She had to come visit after Davin had told us so much about her."

It was no mystery where her son got his lying skills from.

"Indeed," Lady Fenella said. "How did they meet?"

It was a good thing I was used to being talked about as though I wasn't in the room, because Lady Fenella did a fabulous job of it. Though, it was better than when she directed her words at me, speaking loudly and overenunciating like she thought I struggled to grasp the common tongue.

Jocelyn shot me a subtle look that told me she knew exactly how irritating it was before smiling at the odious woman.

"I gather they met at court during my son's...extended stay in Socair, but it seems their friendship blossomed on a rooftop, of all places."

Despite years of training, I nearly choked on my tea. That had not been in the letter, and I certainly hadn't mentioned it. Jocelyn's sideways glance took on a whole new meaning now.

I had no idea what to make of any of it.

Lady Fenella nodded, looking intrigued, if not exactly charmed. The feathers in her headdress seemed to quiver with the force of her curiosity as she took in my seated form.

"Well, I can see the appeal, I suppose." With that dubious compliment, she moved on to loudly complaining about the lack of decent prospects for her son when Gwyndolyn refused to entertain suitors.

The sad part was, she was probably some of the more desirable company at this table. Most of my other options were staring daggers at me.

Worse still was knowing that in the end, I really was no different from any of them. I, too, had wanted to believe that Davin belonged to me on some level.

And I, too, had been wrong.

The Broken Promise

GALINA

A Year and a Half Ago

The snowstorm had hit with little warning, blanketing the grounds in white and leaving the rooftop inaccessible. It was unfortunate, as I could have used the blast of cold air to cool down after an evening of having the most advantageous back-up nuptials I could hope for discussed by Sir Iiro and Uncle Mikhail.

I knew better than to call for a maid when I returned later than usual to my rooms. Davin, I had learned, hated to be alone. When the weather was too bad to make it to the rooftop, he inevitably sought me out here.

So, when the telltale pattern of his knock sounded on my passageway door, I didn't even bother to turn around before calling for him to enter. Instead, I stayed at my vanity where I was yanking pins out of my hair.

The door opened and shut quietly, then there was the sound of liquid being poured before a glass of white wine appeared in my periphery.

I raised my eyebrows, wincing as a pin got stuck.

"I *borrowed* a bottle from Theodope's stash," he said with

a shrug.

"He hates when you do that," I said sardonically, referring both to the thievery and the nickname.

"I know," Davin's mischievous grin reflected in my mirror, and it was impossible not to return, despite my sour mood. "But I figured you could use it after tonight."

I stopped fighting with my hair long enough to take a hearty sip before returning to the damned pins that were intent to nest in my braids for the rest of my life.

"I could, indeed. It's one thing when my uncle arranges my marriage, but Iiro—" I stopped just short of insulting the duke of the clan we were visiting.

Davin really was a terrible influence.

"I'm just glad he's leaving tomorrow," I finished up, finding that it was true.

In the years that I had known him and had known his brother, we had gotten along well enough, which had always been a relief since I was supposed to marry Theodore. But now... Now everything was uncertain and Iiro was putting his nose in places it didn't belong. He had no say in the affairs of another clan if his people weren't involved.

"I hadn't heard that," Davin said. "But I think I'll have a drink to celebrate."

A string of curses escaped me as another pin got stuck in my braid. The maid who had done my hair had clearly made it her personal responsibility to ensure that this particular set of braids lasted for the rest of my life.

"I don't think he's telling anyone, but Inessa mentioned it," I said distractedly. "He has some business with Eagle."

Davin stopped in the motion of pouring his drink, coming to cover my hand with his. "Here, let me."

"Does your skill repertoire extend to hair now?" I asked, though I promptly quieted when he did, in fact, start expertly undoing my hair.

"I'm sorry, Lina, you were saying?" he intoned, his fingers

rubbing a soothing pattern in each spot he removed a pin.

Lina. He had taken to calling me that after just three days of meeting on the rooftop at Ram.

I wasn't sure if he even knew what a breach of Socairan etiquette it was, how intimate it was to call someone by a shortened version of their name.

Though, if he had known, he probably would have just done it sooner.

I told myself that was why I hadn't bothered telling him.

"I shouldn't be surprised, given your favorite pastime," I murmured.

The words came out breathier than I intended them to, warmth spreading down from each place his hands touched.

"I'll have you know," he said, gently sliding another pin from my hair and setting it down on the vanity, "that I learned this from my incredibly demanding cousins, thank you very much."

His voice was lower and closer than I expected it to be, robbing me of my own.

When he finished with the hair in the back, his hands came to my shoulders, gently turning me on my stool until I was facing him. He moved more slowly then, carefully working out the few remaining pins in my hair.

The light scrape of Davin setting the last pin on the vanity was louder than it should have been in the silence that had fallen over us. His lips parted, but no sound came out. I raised my eyebrows in a question I wasn't entirely sure I wanted the answer to.

He cleared his throat. "I've just never seen you with your hair down."

"Oh," I said lamely, my hand coming up automatically to sort it into place.

"No, it's... I like it."

Had I ever seen Davin flustered before?

His gaze flitted to my lips, still parted in surprise, then

back to my eyes. I saw the question in his features, and I knew with every fiber of my being that the answer should be no.

A solid, resounding no.

Several heartbeats passed, my chest rising and falling as flames ignited low in my belly.

I was so tired of denying everything I felt for him. Of denying everything I felt, period.

Whatever he saw in my face had his hand moving to gently tuck a strand of hair behind my ear, had him leaning forward, dipping his head down so, so slowly. He gave me every opportunity to pull away.

And I didn't take a single one.

"Lina." He said my name softly, his warm breath a caress against my lips.

"You promised not to seduce me," I reminded him, though I made no effort to move.

I wasn't sure if I was teasing him or stopping him. I wasn't sure which I wanted to be doing.

"And you promised not to let me," he responded in an even lower tone, his mouth hovering impossibly close to mine.

There was doubt buried in the playful words, so I put it to rest.

"I suppose we're both liars."

His eyes widened in surprise. One heartbeat passed, and then another, an eternity before his perfect lips finally pressed against mine. They were warm and soft, already sending a wave of delicious heat through every part of my body.

A breath escaped me, something that almost felt like relief to finally be touching him the way I had wanted to for longer than I cared to admit to myself.

I pushed to my feet, wanting – *needing* to be closer to him. His hands traced a gentle path from my shoulders down to my waist, leaving a trail of fire in their wake.

I couldn't resist darting out my tongue to taste him. He groaned softly, the sound reverberating through me. Then he was tasting me in turn, his tongue twining with mine, his hands clenching around my ribcage while his thumbs rubbed tantalizing circles.

Awareness coursed through me, catching me off guard with its intensity.

I wanted *more.*

Fisting my hands in his shirt, I tugged gently until he was walking me backward. Then we were in my bed, Davin's lips skating down my jaw and my neck. Heat pooled like lava through every part of me, igniting me straight down to my toes.

I let out a noise I didn't realize I was even capable of making, and Davin cursed softly, pulling me even tighter against him while his mouth returned to mine.

When we talked, Davin would alternate between teasing me and scrutinizing my responses, everything he did far more intentional than he openly admitted. It was no different here.

He explored my body with his lips and hands, carefully, deliberately, gauging my reaction each step of the way.

I didn't know what I was doing, but I did know that we still weren't close enough. The way my blood raced through my veins made me feel like we would *never* be close enough.

My hands moved to the top button of his shirt, as if of their own accord, and he halted in his ministrations.

His dark eyes latched on mine, my name escaping his lips on an exhale. He said it like a warning.

I sat up, forcing him to ease into a more upright position. "You don't want–"

He pressed a finger against my lips, cutting off my words.

"Of course, I want," he assured me. "Stars, Lina, sometimes it's *all* I want. But this isn't something you can just take back."

I hardly heard him over the racing of my heart, but I knew he was right.

Other girls at court had been less concerned about that,

but...my uncle was already arranging another marriage. There were expectations from him, and from my future husband.

Then there was Davin, with his bee-stung lips and his disheveled hair and his hooded eyes looking at me like I was the most perfect thing he had ever seen.

Indecision warred within me. My silence was apparently answer enough because Davin backed away, kissing me on the forehead.

"Do you want me to go?" he murmured against my skin.

No.

"It would probably be for the best," I said instead, hating myself for every proper word.

He nodded, opening his mouth like he was going to say something before closing it again. Then he was gone, leaving an empty silence in his wake.

Empty but for the furious beat of my heart, each thud an accusation, a fresh wave of regret.

I stood to pace the room, trying to make sense of my racing thoughts.

I thought of Iiro looking me over like a prized mare before deciding who might deign to accept me as their bride.

Then Davin, his voice echoing in my head.

Haven't you ever wanted more for yourself?

Sometimes it's all I want.

I was so sick of thinking, sick of constantly doing the right thing instead of being allowed to *feel*, to think about what I wanted for a change.

And what I wanted was Davin.

My feet moved before I could second-guess myself, carrying me down the passageways to where I knew I would find Davin's room.

He answered at the first knock.

"Lina–"

"I don't want to take it back," I told him. "I want to take it for myself."

TWENTY
Davin

Present Day

The next few days saw Gwyn and I sleeping in shifts with one eye open.

We may have known that Scottie and Arran were traitors, but we had no idea how many of our other men were tainted by it.

It was a relief when the white stone turrets of my home came into view. Though I had no desire to face what was coming next, at least the pretense would finally be over. At least I would finally know that Galina and my family were safe.

The black iron door gleamed in the late afternoon sun, opening as my parents and Gallagher came to greet us. Their concerned expressions raked over my cousin and me as we rode up to greet them.

My gaze flicked behind them, searching reflexively for Galina.

"She's upstairs, dressing for dinner," my mother said quietly, leaning in to embrace me as I dismounted my horse.

My shoulders eased, some of the tension ebbing away.

"Do you want us to send someone for her?" Da' asked, clasping my fist with his and pulling me in for a hug.

When I pulled back, I rubbed a hand over my face. "No. I have something to take care of first."

My mother's assessing gaze narrowed slightly. "Well, I do hope we can handle it quickly. Remember that we have guests."

It was a careful reminder that there were more than the usual eyes on us. So, it was undoubtedly a good thing that we hadn't made the arrests as soon as we rode into the courtyard.

"Is there anything I can help you with?" Gallagher asked, crossing his arms in a move that mirrored his sister's current position.

I let out a slow breath. "Unfortunately, yes. We need to call a formation."

After a brief explanation, my parents went back inside to distract the courtiers while my cousins and I headed to the barracks.

Three sharp whistles signaled the soldiers to line up. It was an uncomfortable harkening back to the morning at the inn. We had told the men on the way here that we would be doing this—lying, of course, about the reasons why.

As far as they were concerned, it was to let them all know what had happened on the road. What they didn't know was that we would be searching them for signs of their allegiances.

One by one, we led them to a side room off the barracks, beginning with Scottie.

As soon as the door shut behind him, Gwyn held his arms behind his back while Gallagher forced his mouth open with a wooden bit to remove the poison.

His face reddened, his fury palpable as Gallagher held the fake tooth in his hand, examining it closely. While he did that, I stepped forward and sliced the laces of his shirt open. As the fabric fell away, it revealed a bit of angry-looking skin in the shape of a serpent and crown.

"You. Bastard," I gritted out the words, not even giving him a chance to respond before ordering him to be taken to the dungeons.

From there, things continued to go downhill. Of the ten men that had traveled with us, three were with the rebellion.

By the end, we had discovered thirty-two rebels among the several hundred of our soldiers. Four of them got to their poison before we could stop them, leaving our dungeons filled to the brim with twenty-eight traitors.

Granted, it could have been more. But it was still thirty-two too many. Thirty-two would-be assassins who had been living under my roof, who had sworn allegiance to me.

"Well, at least we have them now," Gallagher offered, though his expression was just as somber as mine and Gwyn's.

"You weren't there, Gal," his sister said bitterly, her boot scuffing the stone floor. "This isn't the end of it."

He sighed and ran a hand over his face. With a nod, he acknowledged that he knew that much as well. We all did. It wouldn't be this easy.

With that auspicious thought, we headed back inside the castle to entertain the courtiers and pretend that the enemy hadn't just made arses of us all.

LIKE EVERY TIME I walked these halls, I looked straight ahead as I made my way through the family wing, avoiding the portraits that haunted me from either wall.

It wasn't just Mac I missed, or even Rowan. I missed the days when the rebels didn't feel like a threat. When I didn't have to make decisions wondering which of my men would die for the necessary gamble to expose a traitor.

When there was no blood on my hands.

Pushing those thoughts away, I made my way to my parents' study.

It was a mark of my mother's concern that she said nothing when I sank onto one of their pristine chairs in my dusty traveling clothes. For several long breaths, I focused on anything but the memory of dead eyes, lips covered in black foam.

The white fur rugs in front of the fireplace. The sound of ice clinking in my mother's glass of whiskey. The rustle of the curtains swaying in the breeze. The gentle, dusky light of the setting sun that made everything glow.

The chime of the grandfather clock reminded me of the time and how little of it we had before needing to head to dinner.

"Looks like you'll have to cut short your speeches of disappointment," I teased half-heartedly.

Da's lips pulled into a wan smirk. "After all this time, surely you know we could manage to make a single, cohesive speech of disappointment."

I scoffed, gesturing for him to continue. "Well, then, by all means."

My mother surprised me by responding first.

"What made you think we would be upset?" she asked sincerely. "The traitors weren't your fault, and the betrothal... The only thing I'm upset about is that you have no intention of following through with it."

I should have seen it coming that Mamá would like Galina.

"Well, between you and Galina, that makes one of you," I muttered, rubbing my temples.

"And you?" Da' pressed, eyeing me with his indifferent spymaster face.

I made sure my own features were carved into neutrality when I answered in a bored tone.

"Still just one." I sighed. Changing the subject before they could push any more on that, I went on. "You really aren't bothered by our plan?"

They exchanged a glance I couldn't read.

"Honestly, no," Mamá said, shaking her head. "It could be good for our relationship with Socair to give people a chance to see them as human. We already know most of the lairds don't have a problem with alliances to the west, so long as they're...advantageous."

That was true, and something I had taken into account. Several of them had propositioned the Socairan lords with marriage contracts on behalf of their daughters when the two men visited to vie for Rowan's hand.

"So as far as the vote goes, you'll look both stable and responsible," Da' chimed in.

I tried very hard to ignore the implication that I was neither.

"That will go a long way toward regaining the favor of the lairds and the people both. Especially Laird MacBay," he continued. "He's here tonight. His son and daughter, as well."

I bit back a wince.

MacBay's estate was to the north what Lithlinglau was to the south. He was a longtime supporter of our family, but that support had been waning since Rowan married into Socair rather than punishing them for their role in our captivity.

Then there was the small matter of my liaison with his daughter, which had, rather unfortunately, made its way to him.

"However," Mamá began, her tone a clear warning, "your show had better be flawless. There was a good chance you could have won the vote before, and I'm willing to admit introducing a Socairan fiancé was a gamble that, while unnecessary, could still sway that further in your favor if it's handled correctly. But if the people—*stars*, if MacBay—gets wind that you're lying, you may as well hand Lithlinglau over to the Andersons yourself."

There was the speech I had been waiting for.

I nodded gravely, not wanting to think about what could happen to the royal family, to the kingdom, with Lithlinglau in the hands of likely rebels, and the oldest family at odds with us.

"That's why we decided on six months, to get us well past the vote so the timing isn't suspicious."

"I'm not terribly worried about that, all things considered," my father said, reaching into a desk drawer. "This, however..."

He handed me a tiny scroll, the nondescript seal already broken.

"Did it come this way?" I asked, gesturing to the jagged bit of wax.

"Oh, no. That was all us." Da' smirked.

Of course it was. They were, in fairness, the unofficial collective spymaster of Lochlann, so I should have expected nothing less.

I unfurled the parchment to find very familiar handwriting.

Dear Favorite Cousin (until now, that is),

Did you, perchance, get back to Lochlann with something of ours? We've been in rather a tizzy looking for it everywhere, and the guards mentioned you might have seen it when you were here the first time.

Of course, I assured them that wasn't the case, because I was quite certain you would have mentioned that to me, your cousin, best friend, former co-captive, and the queen of the kingdom from whence said item hails.

In the unlikely event that you accidentally got away with it, kindly let me know. There are those who would wish for me to tell you to return it at your earliest convenience, but I don't want it to get broken coming back through the tunnels so soon.

A significantly smaller portion of my love than usual,

Row

I FELT a sharp stab of guilt. Though Rowan was joking, she was clearly hurt, which was fair. And yet, I didn't miss her warning. Even now, even without knowing the circumstances, she was solidly on my side.

I pinched the bridge of my nose and sighed. When I looked up at my parents, ready to defend the way we left things, my father shook his head.

"You're both here safe now. That's all a discussion for later. For now, you need to clean up in time to escort your betrothed to dinner."

I bit back a sigh.

I still wasn't sure what to say to her, how to feel about any of this now that the consequences had been made so glaringly apparent.

"Where are her rooms?" I asked.

"Oh, you shouldn't have any trouble finding them. They're the ones across from yours," Mamá said in a tone a shade too neutral.

I narrowed my eyes at her. "Was there something wrong with the other twelve rooms in the family wing?"

She met my gaze with all the innocence she had never possessed. "It was for appearances, obviously."

"Obviously," I deadpanned, turning on my heel to leave.

"Don't forget to stop by the vault on your way up," Da' called after me.

Stars.

Because ring shopping was exactly what I wanted to add to my ever-growing list.

Still, I nodded and headed to the vault. We had to make this *flawless*, and the ring was the next step in that direction.

I was beginning to miss the days on the road when all I had to worry about was someone popping up to murder me.

TWENTY-ONE
Galina

My lack of sleep was catching up to me.

As usual, I had spent half the night plagued by relentless thoughts of what was happening back home, but now, I was struggling to keep the thoughts out during the day as well.

Had anyone discovered that I was missing yet? Had I been wrong about the dangers to my clan, my family? Would they pay for my decision to leave?

And the one thought that resounded above them all… Was it worth it? Had I overreacted to a little manhandling? Or would I have gotten better at keeping Alexei happy in time?

In the rare moments that I could quiet the maelstrom of questions about my home, different worries crept in.

Was Davin in danger because of me? Were we going to make the tensions here worse?

When a knock on the door startled me from my thoughts, I would have been grateful, except that I was still barefoot and hadn't yet put on my jewelry.

"I'll get it, milady." Anna was already moving toward the door while I tugged my slippers on.

I was sure it was only Gallagher. He always escorted me to

dinner. Still, I couldn't quite quell the part of me that panicked whenever I was running behind.

I was already talking when Anna opened the door.

"Apologies, I'm not quite—"

"Take your time," a deep, cultured voice cut in.

I froze, my foot halfway into my shoe. Though the accent was the same, I would recognize that voice anywhere, and it most certainly did not belong to Gallagher. Belatedly, I realized I should have recognized the knock, but I was tired, distracted.

"Welcome home, mi'laird," Anna said, her tone warm and familiar.

I didn't turn around. I wasn't ready to see him yet, to burst the bubble of whatever semblance of peace I had found at this estate.

His estate, I reminded myself.

"Thank you, Anna," he said kindly. "It's good to be back. Would you mind giving me a moment with my betrothed?"

That last word was said with just a bit of emphasis, enough that I abruptly remembered we were supposed to be putting on a show. Pulling on my shoe the rest of the way, I rose to my feet.

Instead of leaving right away, Anna hesitated. "Do you need anything else, milady?"

Was she seeking my permission to leave? Or making sure I felt safe with her going?

I didn't have to feign the blush on my cheeks as I finally looked up, though I faced her rather than Davin.

"No. Thank you, Anna." My voice was steadier than I felt. "I can handle the rest."

Only then did she leave.

"I thought we should talk before we go down to dinner," he said once we were alone.

"Of course," I responded, finally forcing myself to look at him.

I promptly wished I hadn't. That somehow, I could avoid ever looking at him again.

Though he had been dressed formally at the Obsidian Ball, most of my memories of him were as a guard or in travel clothes. The sight of him now, outfitted unmistakably as the laird of this estate, was almost shocking.

His navy jacket was tailored to perfection, a pristine white shirt peeking out from underneath it. His hair was perfectly coiffed, his face freshly shaven. He looked...

Like the man who had seduced half the court in Socair, and here as well, a small obtrusive voice in the back of my head reminded me.

It was enough to pull me from my thoughts, to notice that there were shadows behind the gaze that was just this side of too intent.

"Did something happen on the road?" I asked, realizing I didn't know if everyone had made it safely. "To Gwyn?"

He blew out a slow breath. "Gwyn is safe, though I'm sure she'll be touched that you were so concerned, given how close you two grew on the road. Were you desolate in her absence?"

The corner of his mouth tugged ever so slightly upward, though the expression was more subdued than usual. I got the feeling what he wanted to tease me about was whether I was desolate in *his* absence.

So, I gave him my most saccharine smile. "I hardly had time to notice, what with your entire harem here to keep me company."

A barely perceptible wince crossed his features. He opened his mouth, but I realized I didn't actually want to hear whatever he had to say on the subject, so I cut in.

"Don't think I didn't notice you avoided the question."

He ran a hand through his hair, managing to only make it look more styled rather than less.

"It was more or less what we expected. I can give you the details after dinner." His eyes darkened with an emotion I couldn't read, and he seemed to scrutinize me even more intensely than before.

"Is something else wrong?" I glanced down to check that everything was in place.

My gown was one of the new ones, but it had been made in the Lochlannian style. It was navy with paler blue stitching, and I couldn't help but wonder if the coordination with his own clothing was intentional.

He cleared his throat, blinking to clear his expression. "I'm just surprised that you like the Lochlannian style dresses."

"I don't," I admitted.

At least with Davin, I didn't have to bother with the pretense of politeness. It would almost have been a relief, if everything else about his presence hadn't been so storms-blasted frustrating.

"Then why did you have it made that way?" he asked with a raised eyebrow.

"You said that appearances were important," I reminded him, a trace of impatience in my tone. "That I needed to be...relatable."

His lips pursed, and without another word, he disappeared into my closet.

"Davin!" I chastised him. "You know, when I thought you were a commoner, you had an excuse for your general lack of propriety, but now I know you very much don't."

"Blame it on my upbringing," he called, amusement in his tone.

I shook my head, though he couldn't see me. "I'll be sure and share that with Princess Jocelyn."

He emerged carrying a pale blue scarf, the exact shade of the stitching in my gown.

"I see you've already sussed out which of my parents is more terrifying," he said drily.

Without waiting for a response, he crossed the distance to

me, looping the scarf around once, then twice, before draping it artfully over my shoulders.

He didn't directly touch my skin, but I felt the ghost of his fingertips trailing along my collarbone.

"I'm fairly certain this isn't what anyone down there is wearing," I told him quietly.

His answering smirk was all arrogance. "It will be after tonight."

The worst part was, he wasn't wrong. If I had learned anything after spending several days with the arriving courtiers, it was that Davin was an extremely important figure to the social scene here, upcoming votes notwithstanding.

If his betrothed showed up wearing a scarf with her dress, probably half the court would be wearing one tomorrow.

"What was it you wanted to discuss?" I turned away to put my earrings on and take a welcome reprieve from his presence.

"The rebels," he said, his tone darker than it had been a moment ago.

"What about them?" I asked, catching his haunted expression in the mirror.

"We did, in fact, catch traitors as part of the fun we experienced on the road. Until we know for sure that we have them all, someone will need to accompany you when you leave your rooms. I'll be assigning someone I trust to guard you when you're not with me or Gwyn."

I fastened the silver-and-pearl drops into my ears before turning back to him.

"Or Gallagher?" I asked.

Something flashed in his expression, but it was gone before I could read it.

"Yes, or him, obviously."

I nodded, and his shoulders eased.

"If that's all, I'm ready when you are," I told him.

He hesitated for a solid second before he reached into his pocket, taking a step closer. "Not quite."

A wave of clove and spiced bergamot washed over me, more familiar than I wanted to think about when we were alone in a room with a very large bed.

Davin gestured for my left hand, and I hesitantly held it out. Though it should have been obvious, I was unprepared to feel the cool metal of a ring sliding onto my third finger. When I pulled my hand back, it was adorned with an oval-shaped ruby framed by delicate gold wiring and studded with small, sparkling diamonds.

Red, for Clan Ram.

I let loose a breath, forcing my eyes away from the stunning piece of jewelry.

I tried not to read too much into it. His parents had reminded me more than once that our subterfuge had to be faultless. That's all any of this was.

A perfect façade.

TWENTY-TWO

Davin

IF I THOUGHT I was prepared for the sight of Galina here, in my home, dressed like she belongs here, I certainly had not been.

She had one slim hand wrapped around my bicep, offering the perfect vantage point of the elegant piece of jewelry that was sure to send the entire dinner into a barely contained frenzy.

But I couldn't focus on that when warmth was pooling from each place her fingertips grazed my sleeve.

Sure enough, when we walked into the dining hall, there wasn't a single set of eyes that didn't linger on Galina's hand where it rested on my arm. She valiantly pretended not to notice, dropping gracefully into the seat next to mine.

Gwyn took the seat next to me, while Gal sat next to Galina. I didn't miss the way her shoulders sagged in relief when he smiled down at her.

"Gallagher." Galina said his name with more genuine warmth than she had shown all evening, enough to make me remember that she and I were not actually friends.

But apparently, she and Gallagher were.

"Gwyn," she added in a more stilted tone, nodding to them both.

Gal said something under his breath that made Galina laugh, and Gwyn raised her eyebrow.

"It's nice they've had time to get to know each other in our absence," she said drily, leaning forward so that only I could hear her.

"I couldn't agree more," I replied.

They continued to talk over the first course, their conversation easy. There was something about Lady Fenella's outfit. *Stars*, they had inside jokes already, which was...not irritating. I had known Galina would be looking for a real fiancé, eventually, but it hadn't actually occurred to me that her next best match would be my cousin.

Though, she would have plenty of options, if the way the lairds and their sons were eyeing her was any indication.

After my ridiculously long day, week, and hell, month, it grated on me more than it should have.

Galina fiddled with the delicate stem of her wine glass, candlelight refracting off the ruby in her ring in an array of reds and pinks. Reaching out, I took her hand in mine, running my finger over the stone before entwining our fingers together.

After all, we were a newly engaged couple, so we needed to act a certain way.

It would look suspicious otherwise.

Gallagher met my eyes over Galina's head, his lips pursed in suppressed amusement. She briefly glanced at our hands, her brow just barely furrowing before she leaned into me, peeking up at me through demure eyelashes.

"Davin?"

"Yes, Love?" I asked innocuously.

She blinked, and her expression shuttered. "Is everything all right?"

I dipped my head toward hers, feigning intimacy. "I just didn't want anyone getting the wrong idea."

She let out the smallest sound of disbelief.

"Of course not. That would be a shame." She picked up her drink, talking behind the cup. "Do you think they got the wrong idea when they were *accidentally* falling all over you earlier?"

I cleared my throat. Fiona had, indeed, all but fallen into my lap in a flimsy pretense of greeting Galina.

"Technically," I countered, "only one of them did that, and I made it clear how unwelcome it was."

Galina made a humming sound, her features still perfectly pleasant. "In her defense, I'm sure she feels she has some claim on you, along with...how many others?"

Now, there was a question I didn't want to touch. It wasn't as many as she thought, but more than enough to irritate her.

And though I wouldn't apologize for things that happened when we were no part of each other's lives, I did feel guilty realizing what she had likely put up with in my absence. What she was still going to put up with, now that I was back.

I picked up my own glass, taking a hearty sip. "You've made your point."

"There was no point," Galina lied with a perfectly straight face, her countenance going markedly icier. "Merely an observation. It will be easier if we both remember who the other is."

Would it?

I wasn't even sure we knew who the other was.

We were serendipitously interrupted when my father raised his glass and called for an announcement.

If my hand hadn't still been wrapped around hers, I would have missed the way Galina tensed slightly, an unnecessary reminder that she wasn't any happier about this charade than I was.

My parents, however, gave every appearance of being

thrilled when they spoke of how excited they were to welcome Galina to the family, even going so far as to crack jokes at my expense about how I was finally settling down.

Toasts went up all around, my cousins helpfully chiming in.

Gallagher, "To the genuine love they share between them."

And Gwyn, "To the many, painfully attractive heirs in their future."

I kicked her under the table while keeping an expression of gratitude plastered to my features.

For her part, Galina gave little to no indication of what she really thought about the toasts. Her resting Socairan face was schooled to a neutral perfection.

By the time soup was served, I had never been more grateful to see a bowl of *partan bree* in my life. Galina took one sip of the crab bisque and hesitated before swallowing.

"What is this?" Her voice could have merely been curious, but for the barest hint of tightening around her eyes.

"It's a creamy soup made with pureed crab meat," I explained, watching her expression carefully.

When she dipped her spoon in again, I sighed. "You don't have to eat it if you don't like it. That's not a thing here."

In Socair, there was no greater faux pas than to leave food on your plate, but Lochlannians didn't get off on making people suffer the way our neighbors to the west did.

"Don't be ridiculous," she murmured under her breath. "I'm not going to waste it."

I rested my spoon back in my bowl, giving her a slight shake of my head.

"It won't go to waste," I told her. "It will go to the animals. The only waste will be if it makes a reappearance on the table and the rest of us can't enjoy our soup either."

Galina's eyes met mine as she brought the spoon to her lips once more, something almost challenging in the graceful arc of her hand.

She rarely chose a battle, but when she did, it always seemed to be with me. Even though I had given her a clear out, she was damned and determined to pretend she liked this stupid soup. I wasn't sure why it bothered me so much except that I missed being the person who was allowed to know her.

"Would you like some vodka to pair with it?" I asked, all false congeniality. "Or will the wine be sufficient?"

She pointedly ignored me, turning to my mother instead. "The soup is truly delicious, Princess Jocelyn."

My mother's gracious smile widened into something more genuine when she looked at Galina. "I'm pleased you like it."

All right, then. I pinned Galina with my stare, a smirk forming at my lips.

"She's so shy, Mamá," I said without turning my head. "She doesn't want to ask for more, but I assured her that the servants can whip another up for her."

"Absolutely," my mother said, though her gaze narrowed just a bit at my tone. "If that's what she wants."

Galina's eyes widened with what I was fairly certain was murder, but she passed off admirably as gratitude. "If it's not too much trouble."

The servants did, indeed, bring her another serving. And to her everlasting stubbornness, Galina lifted her spoon with all of the grace of a Socairan swan, ready to tackle the second bowl when Gallagher's hand appeared instead.

"Would you mind terribly if I snagged this from you?" His tone was light and affable, though he threw a reproachful glance in my direction. "Partan bree is my favorite, and we can't get it up in Alech. Too far from the sea to transport."

My mother's scrutinizing gaze darted between them, then to me, understanding dawning in her features. At her side, my father also seemed to take note of the exchange, though he looked more amused than annoyed.

"I could never deny you that, My Laird," Galina

responded to Gallagher, some of the guardedness leaving her countenance.

I spoke up again. “I’m sure we could ask for–”

“Don’t be gauche, Davin,” Mamá cut in smoothly. “It’s far too close to the next course for that.”

Though her court face was intact, I sensed she wished we were at one of our family dinners so she could reach over and swat me on the back of my head. I clamped my lips shut, reluctantly acknowledging that I had been outnumbered and outmaneuvered by my own family.

“Well,” Gwyn muttered from her spot to my left. “This has backfired on you quite spectacularly.”

Somehow, I thought she was talking about more than the soup.

And I couldn’t disagree.

TWENTY-THREE

Galina

AFTER DINNER, we met with Davin's parents in their study.

Though I had spent many mornings breaking fast with the two of them, the dynamic was different now that Davin had returned.

He broke through the uneasy tension that had crept into the room alongside us, holding out a letter as soon as the door was shut.

"Rowan wrote." He took a seat next to me on the small sofa, his leg resting against mine.

The others gave me space to read, Oliver pouring us drinks while Jocelyn seated herself in a chair across from us. I unfurled the tiny scroll and briefly scanned the contents before reading them a second time, more carefully.

Well, then. That answered the question of whether anyone had noticed I was gone.

Was it my uncle trying to get me back? Or Alexei?

It was a small relief, at least, that Rowan appeared to be in our corner, if only for Davin's sake, though I did feel a small stab of guilt at the subterfuge I had unwittingly forced on him.

After scanning the contents a third time, I handed the

letter back with fingers that were surprisingly steady. The flickering light from the wall sconces caught on my bracelet, glinting off the fangs of my least favorite charm.

The wolf's head seemed to be taunting me, and I all but flung my hands back to my lap.

"Well, we can't say we didn't see that coming," I said more calmly than I felt.

It was, technically speaking, true.

But I had hoped, with some unreasonable part of myself, that it might go differently. That Alexei would let this go. That my uncle would find a way to smooth things over.

Something.

Davin pocketed the letter, examining me too closely for my liking.

Prince Oliver cleared his throat. "On that note, I think it would be prudent for me to reach out to Sir Mikhail. As I understand it, marriages in Socair are typically arranged by the patriarch, so we thought he may be more amenable to hearing from me. I would offer to go through Logan, but..."

Jocelyn let out a light laugh before she covered it with her hand.

"My uncle doesn't do subtlety," Davin explained.

Having met Rowan, that was not hard to believe.

"No," Jocelyn confirmed. "But we thought Oli might have some luck. I know you left under...somewhat questionable circumstances. But given the advantages of a marriage to Davin, we wondered if we could perhaps persuade your uncle, delicately, to see reason."

Davin snorted at the unlikelihood of my uncle letting this stand. I said nothing, because I privately agreed with Davin's assessment but still couldn't bring myself to outwardly criticize my duke.

"Though I appreciate your efforts, it wouldn't make a difference," I began. "Regardless of his personal feelings, my uncle can't be seen supporting my decision. My betrothal was to seal an alliance during the war, one which ultimately cost Wolf countless lives."

A familiar wave of shame heated my cheeks. My clan had made an agreement, and I had singlehandedly broken it. Even if I had tried to keep everyone else out of it, the safest course would have been for me to stay.

And still, I had left.

I stamped those feelings down. There was no sense in dwelling on choices I couldn't unmake.

"If it's only me," I went on, "acting out, against his wishes, then the clan can't be held responsible because my uncle—the only one who signed the agreement—won't have gone back on his word."

Jocelyn raised an eyebrow. "Perhaps they'll learn a valuable lesson about excluding women from contracts regarding their own lives. I know Lochlann did."

Oliver looked thoughtful. "So, your plan was to take the consequences entirely on yourself?"

I nodded with all the serenity I didn't feel. "In theory, there won't be any consequences to bear, so long as everything goes according to plan."

"Except the trifling matter of you never being able to return home," Davin added, a muscle ticking in his jaw.

"We already knew that," I reminded him. "It was a calculated decision."

It was the most difficult choice of my life.

He shook his head but didn't respond. I couldn't tell if he was judging me for leaving my family behind when he had almost been forced to live without his, or upset on my behalf.

I wasn't sure what to make of either.

"What if we offered recompense to Wolf?" he suggested a moment later, an indecipherable expression churning in his ocean eyes.

"I couldn't ask you to do that." I was torn between hardly

daring to hope and despising the idea of the scales tipping toward me being in *his* debt.

"No, you didn't ask." He sounded almost accusatory now.

Jocelyn waved a dismissive hand, the motion pulling my attention back to her and away from her son. "You're helping Davin keep Lithlinglau, which helps the whole of the kingdom. It's the least we could do."

Was she really that confident in this whole betrothal arrangement?

"Besides," Davin interjected, "it's not like we want Wolf coming after us."

Was that where the accusation came in? That he thought I hadn't warned him sufficiently about the repercussions?

"Would that make a difference?" his father asked.

"I'm...not certain," I admitted, not having considered it before. "We would need to go through my uncle first, allow the offer to be made through him. So he would still need to accept this betrothal, and it's a risk to leverage any benefits of my particular arrangement with Davin, because if my uncle's approval hinges on that, we'll be right where we began."

Jocelyn and Oliver exchanged a look.

"Well, we'll cross that bridge when we come to it," the prince said, though I got the feeling I was missing something. "At the very least, it can't hurt to try."

With that settled, it was still another hour before we finished crafting the letter to my uncle.

In the end, we settled on language we thought had the best chance of swaying him, ensuring that it absolved Davin and Rowan both of any responsibility. I had insisted on clarifying that I left of my own volition, and that my and Davin's betrothal was not secured until after I left Socair.

It was a last-ditch effort, offering a technicality of the law for my uncle to fall back on, should he decide against punishing me.

"And your parents?" Oliver asked gently when we were

done. "Should we reach out to them as well, or would you like to?"

I considered it, longing gnawing at my insides.

I wasn't sure my mother would want to hear from me, though. Was she disappointed? If I told her the truth, would she be still?

A lifetime of raising me day by day, teaching me everything I needed to know to be a perfect Socairan lady... Did it feel like betrayal when I walked away from it all?

I didn't know.

"...Galina?" Jocelyn was looking at me with concern.

A flush rose to my cheeks.

"Apologies, Your Highness."

"Jocelyn," she corrected gently, not for the first time. "And think nothing of it. It's been an exhausting few days."

"Weeks," Davin corrected.

The truth of that reverberated down into my soul. It had, indeed, been an exhausting few weeks.

"I shouldn't write them until I hear from Uncle Mikhail. Depending on his reaction, I wouldn't want them involved," I decided.

"Very well," Jocelyn said over the chiming of the clock. It was just now nine, but the signs of exhaustion were present in all of us. "Then, I believe the last matter is your former betrothed."

Davin didn't look up from where he was bent over the letter to my uncle, but he did get markedly more still.

Jocelyn went on. "Do you think he would take the news better coming from you or..."

The blood drained from my face.

How had I not considered that I would need to tell him? Had I really thought I could walk away and never have to speak to him again?

Jocelyn's shrewd gaze assessed me, and I was grateful

Davin wasn't looking in my direction. I fixed my features as quickly as I could.

Just when I worried she would draw attention to it, Jocelyn continued in a casual voice.

"Actually, I think it might be better if Oliver writes to him as well. We'll send an official announcement, explain the situation and request that he resolve the matter with your uncle. I'm sure we could make it clear that it's in his best interest to do so." The way she worded that, I wasn't sure if they would be subtly incentivizing him or not-so-subtly threatening him.

I forced myself to breathe, in, then out, forced my tone to be as nonchalant as hers was. "Yes, I think that would be better."

I wasn't sure if that was true or not. Perhaps he would accept it, or Nils would force him to. But Wolf's pride was stronger than their practicality, and there was every chance this would only incense them more.

One way or another, he was going to find out what I had done, if he hadn't already.

And one way or another, he was going to be furious about it.

IT FELT like hours before Davin led me back to my rooms, though in reality, it was only another few minutes. After we dealt with the issues in Socair, he told me about the traitors.

Dread settled into my gut.

It was one thing, knowing an assassin might be after me. Another to know that if we had done things differently, if Davin hadn't talked me into switching with Gwyn, I very well may be dead by now.

Between that and the letters we had just sent out, I was so

on edge that I came to a dead halt when I spotted two hulking men outside my door. My heartbeat thundered in my ears.

Belatedly, I remembered what Davin had said about the guards.

"Ewan and Hamish," he said quietly, his hand on my lower back prodding me into motion once again. "Since there are men stationed around Lithlinglau, they'll switch off guard, but one of them will be here and available to accompany you at all times."

He made introductions when we were closer.

"Thank you, sirs," I told them both.

"Did ye hear that, Ewan? She called us sirs." The shorter guard's accent was thick and rolling, the same I had heard from the villagers on our way in.

"That's only because she doesn't know you well enough to call you *that eejit over there*," the other man, presumably Ewan, responded.

His accent was closer to Davin's, though not quite as posh.

Though I appreciated the gesture of guards, I couldn't help but wonder how these were any more trustworthy than the ones he had caught today. Like he had read my mind, Davin elaborated on his introduction.

"Ewan was once part of Rowan's personal guard, much to his eternal dismay," he smiled as he reflected on some inside joke there. "And Hamish fought alongside my father during the war. I trust them both with my life."

The men stood a little taller at the praise.

"I have business to attend to tonight," he said, gesturing to the guard on the right. "Ewan will be accompanying me, but Hamish will be here if you need anything."

"All right," I said with a small dip of my head.

What kind of business did he have at this hour? Before I could decide whether it was my place to ask, he expounded.

"I need to question the traitors we found today." His

features were guarded, like perhaps he was expecting censure, but I had none to offer him.

His job was to protect his people, and I wasn't naïve enough to believe that didn't get messy sometimes.

If there was one thing I knew about Davin, it was that he did what he needed to do.

For better or worse.

The Dilemma

DAVIN

A Year and a Half Ago

If any lingering part of me had thought that Lina was someone I could get out of my system, last night had effectively robbed me of that notion.

Destroyed it, really, with the feeling of her skin against my lips and her hair running through my fingers, and her lithe, warm body moving in perfect synchrony with mine.

Even now, my pillow smelled like her, like lavender and rosemary and something heady and intoxicating.

All of which was a problem.

I ran a hand through my hair in frustration, staring into the fireplace and wondering what in the hell I was going to do now.

On one hand, my life was in Lochlann, and hers was here. Even if I told her the truth, I couldn't be sure she would want to leave her entire family behind to come with me, especially when things were so uncertain between our kingdoms.

On the other, I wasn't even sure any of that mattered. I wasn't sure she wanted anything at all.

The alarming part was how badly I realized *I* did.

How often I had considered bringing her home to meet my family, had wondered which festival would be her favorite, and whether she would make the same face at whiskey that she did at vodka. How often I imagined a life with her, and how difficult it was becoming to imagine one *without* her.

A light rap at the passageway door startled me from my thoughts. Unreasonable hope surged through me, even though she made it clear she was expected at breakfast with Inessa this morning.

But it wasn't her, of course. It was Aino, one of the maids of Clan Elk, and more importantly, the first of the Lochlannian spies I had found.

She shut the door behind her before crossing to the middle of the room, the better not to be overheard.

"You have news?"

She nodded, speaking in low tones.

"The runner finally got back from the tunnels. The king and Prince Oliver are on their way through, along with their friend, the lady thief. He's passed your message along to them and said they should be well into Socair by now."

It shouldn't have surprised me. Since he had missed out on the first six months of my life, my father had spent every day making up for it. Of course, he would come through the mountains himself.

Hell, I was half surprised my mother wasn't with him.

Still, my stomach sank. All this time I had spent trying to get out of Socair, but now...

It hardly mattered. I wasn't the only one at risk, and it wasn't like I could stay here as a not-quite-captive indefinitely.

"Do you have a message to send back?" Aino prompted when the silence had stretched on too long. "Should I tell them to come here?"

"No. They need to get Rowan to safety first, but..." I hedged, trying to think through a solution, a way to help them without getting them caught.

Somewhere in my hazy memory, through the scent of lavender and the taste of white wine and skin, I remembered Galina's lips moving and something about Iiro leaving with the guard.

I swallowed hard. I had forgotten all about it in the hours since she first mentioned it, just an aside, a small note that neither of us expected to be important.

"Tell them—" I hesitated then, realizing that for all the lies I had told Galina, this would be yet another breach of her trust. And after last night...

But could I really *not* use the information she gave me? Could I really withhold it if it meant my family's safety?

Rowan's life was at stake. She had already been hurt. Scarred. I shoved away the guilt, stuffing it down to a place that existed in a world where I had the luxury of making easier decisions.

"Lady Galina mentioned that Iiro is leaving today. Heading west. The guard will move to accommodate him, so my uncle and father should be freer to cut through the north to Bear," I said, letting out a huff of air as I considered my next move. But the bastard owed me, and I knew he would help Rowan. "We can also arrange things with Theodore in his absence, which will make everything easier."

She nodded again, her features turning coy.

"Is there anything else I can do for you?" Her intent was blazing from her dark brown eyes.

When I'd first arrived at Elk, it had been easy to lose myself in Aino. She was something familiar, a small bit of home in a world that was entirely foreign. We had taken advantage of our meetings together to find a connection that allowed us both to forget that we were strangers here.

She had seemed to understand the nature of our relationship before I left for Ram a couple of months ago. Had seemed to welcome it, even. But ever since I had returned, she had been more persistent, even though I turned her down each time.

"Not today, Aino."

Her eyes flitted to my rumpled bed. A dark emotion flashed across her features, but she dipped into a curtsy before I could decipher it.

After she left, I sank down onto my mattress, massaging my temples. Maybe Galina wouldn't understand. Maybe she didn't want what I wanted.

But I would never forgive myself if I didn't find out. I had to talk to her.

Before it was too late.

TWENTY-FOUR
Davin

Present Day

I HAD NEVER SEEN the dungeons this full.

In Alech, sure. That was where Lochlann housed most of our prisoners.

But not here. Not in my home.

Sure as stars not full of men I had trained beside, men I had called friends and counted on to protect my family.

Gwyn's fist connected with Scottie's jaw. Her knuckles dripped with crimson when she pulled her hand back. Whether it was her own or that of the man chained to the chair, I couldn't be sure.

"Come on, sweetheart," Scottie said, spitting a mouthful of blood onto the ground. "This isn't the kind of fun we usually have."

Gallagher barely pulled her away before she lunged at the arseling. Was he trying to goad her into killing him now that his false tooth was gone?

"We can't kill him yet, Gwyn," her brother said calmly, stepping between the two of them.

Then he pulled his fist back and brought it down on Scottie's cheek with surprising force before bending down to growl in his ear.

"I'm a healer, Scottie." He managed to make the words sound menacing. "So, I know how to keep you clinging to life long, long after you wish you weren't. Remember that next time you open your mouth about my sister."

And everyone thought Gwyn was the more terrifying of the two.

Scottie's face paled several shades before he, belatedly, lifted his head defiantly.

I took my chance to resume my questioning.

"Is this a game to you? Do you actually have any loyalties, or do you get off on the betrayal? Otherwise, why?" I left the question dangling in the air.

I had found myself repeating that single word more and more lately.

Why would you betray us? Why did you choose these rebels? Why their cause? Why now?

He scoffed, though he wasn't nearly as confident as he had been before Gal's threat. "Now you care. How fitting."

Once again, I wondered where we had gone wrong with our people to make them think we didn't.

"We always cared. We were your friends, Scottie," I said, trying a different approach.

"Friends?" Scottie forced out a laugh. "We were never *friends*. You lot had no time or concern for anyone but yourselves. This is on you."

It always was these days.

I took a step back, blowing out a slow breath before switching tactics again. He had only been minimally responsive to threats, and clearly wasn't suffering from any crises of conscience.

Time to have a go at his pride.

"So, what happened at the inn?" I demanded. "Were you just too afraid to attack one unarmed woman? I mean, you certainly didn't mind sleeping with a veritable child to bring her into your schemes. Where is it that you draw the line?"

He tilted his head, his anger breaking through.

"Bess is of age," he spat out. "And for the last time, I couldn't care less about the Socairan."

"That's not true, though, is it?" I pressed. "I saw the way you watched her. You wanted her. Is that what held you back? You didn't really want to kill her? Maybe you don't really believe in your little rebellion after all, if you're not even willing to—"

"I couldn't risk my position!" he cut me off, his eyes wide and furious.

Before he could say anything else, a voice called out from a cell down the hall. It was Graeme, another soldier. Prisoner. Traitor. Whatever we were calling them these days.

"That's enough, Scottie," he yelled. "Remember."

I bit back a curse as Scottie's resolve visibly strengthened. Lithlinglau didn't have a torture chamber, as it were, since men were typically sent to Alech if they needed to be questioned. So, we had made due with spacing the men out, and now we were paying for it.

We didn't get a single word out of him after that. The other men, too, were as silent as the grave they were headed toward.

Loyalty might have stayed their tongues, but something in the looks they exchanged pointed to something more sinister. Someone was threatening them.

But who had gotten to them? And when? Who was more powerful to them than the royal family?

What were we missing?

My father and cousins stared back at me, the same questions churning in their eyes, the same tumultuous expressions belying their frustration.

I couldn't take it anymore. I ran a hand through my hair,

pushing away from the wall as defeat settled in right alongside the fury burning through my veins.

"You know what happens now," I said, raising my voice enough to be heard throughout the dungeon. "You will hang. All of you."

I dropped my hands to my side as I paced the bleak hallway, taking in each of their faces and trying not to think of the years I had spent with them. Of the families that would be left without husbands, fathers, brothers, sons.

And for what?

A bitter laugh escaped me. "Though, maybe that doesn't matter much to you, since you walk around with poison at the ready. Ready to just end your lives and destroy your families with the snap of a tooth."

I scanned the room, taking note of each of their expressions. Most of them stood with a confidence bordering on fanaticism. There were a few, though, who faltered ever so slightly.

I pointed them out, ordering the guards to remove them to a different cell, one clear across the dungeon from here.

"Dougal, too," my father added before we left the room.

I nodded. He was right. I hadn't seen it before, but there was something in the set of the man's shoulders, the look in his eyes that spoke more of regret than pride.

Gal stayed with Hamish and the other men while Gwyn came with us. We had barely even closed the door when Dougal's voice sounded.

"We can't," he said, cutting off my questions before I could even ask them.

I rounded on him, my frustration growing.

"Can't, or won't?" I challenged.

"You don't understand," he said flatly, his graying brows pulled together.

"Then help us understand," my father entreated him.

Dougal only clamped his lips shut, just as Scottie had, just as they all had.

I was at a loss.

Underprepared. Underqualified. Unable to do anything to root out this rebellion that had spread through my men, my home, and my life, right in front of our eyes.

My father stilled at my side, studying the men for several long moments before he gestured for us to leave.

"Why are we stopping?" Gwyn hissed at him.

She had never been angry with my father before, but desperation and the sting of betrayal were doing strange things to us all.

"We haven't even really tried questioning—" she began.

My father held up a hand, cutting her off.

"He's afraid," he said, quietly enough for only us to hear.

"They all are," I added. "And not for themselves."

If they had been afraid only for their own lives, they would be talking now to avoid the noose. Hell, even if they were afraid of torture, it stood to reason that they would break before the situation could escalate.

It wasn't just fear in their eyes, though, especially not for these four. It was desperation. A silent plea.

"You think their families have been threatened?" Gwyn asked.

My father and I nodded at the same time. Gwyn spun on her feet, marching back toward the cell, her auburn braid streaming behind her.

"We can help you." She gripped the bars as if she would rip them from where they were welded into the floor. "We can protect your families."

Dougal stepped forward, giving the barest shake of his head.

He had served Gwyn and her parents for over a decade before being transferred here from Alech. Something softened in his gaze as he looked at my cousin. Was he remembering, as I was, a time when he had sparred against the fiery twelve-year-old duchess, laughing when she demanded round after round?

"No, lass," he whispered.

Her shoulders rose and fell with each furious breath that poured from her lungs. Finally, she hit the bars with a loud clang, storming down the hallway and back to her brother.

If I hadn't known her better, I could have sworn I saw a single tear track down her cheek as she passed me. But that was impossible. Gwyn didn't cry, not where people could see her.

He shook his head at her retreating form, his soft voice echoing off the dungeon walls. "You won't even be able to protect yourselves from what's coming."

DEFEAT HUNG heavy in the air between us when we finally climbed the stairs from the dungeons. We had gotten nothing further from the prisoners, nothing we could use.

No one said a word as we made our way to the family wing, all of us still parsing through the events of tonight.

"We'll try again tomorrow," my father finally said when we made it to the first bisecting hallway. "And in the meantime, I'll send a bird to Chridhe and Alech."

He offered us a wan smile before turning to head to his and Mamá's rooms while the three of us descended the stairs to the family hall.

"I wouldn't want to be the one sending that bird," Gallagher said after a tense few steps.

He gently grabbed his sister's injured hand in the privacy of the stairwell. When he pulled away, the wounds on her knuckles were already noticeably improved.

He usually refused to heal small wounds, saying it raised too many questions without cause. It was a mark of his concern for her that he was trying to ease whatever bit of her pain he could, trying to lighten the mood for us both.

I forced myself to banter along. "Yes, I wonder what it will say. Dearest Brother and Sister-in-Law, No one is safe, and we'll be holding mass executions in a week's time. P.S. My son's betrothal is a farce and has likely only exacerbated said aforementioned issues with the rebels. All the love from Lithlinglau."

Gwyn cracked a small smile, though it was tinged with bitterness.

"You forgot the part where their niece was apparently sleeping with the enemy."

I winced. "We've all been there, Gwynnie."

"I haven't," Gallagher said with a shrug.

She shoved him, but her smile turned more genuine. They split off to go into their respective rooms at the top of the hall and I continued in the opposite direction to mine, nodding to Hamish when he came into view.

He returned the gesture, though it was punctuated by an expression I was too tired to decipher.

I didn't have to ponder it for long. As soon as I shut the main door, I smelled the perfume. Faint, floral, familiar.

Sure enough, when I pushed open the door between the sitting room and my bedroom it was to find Lady Fiona sprawled artfully atop my bed.

Naked.

I would have questioned whether she was concerned about anyone coming back here with me, but Fiona never had minded an audience.

If I hadn't been so tired, I might have even expected her after her display earlier. She wasn't the type to take no for an answer.

"Fiona," I sighed. "I already turned you down once tonight."

Normally, I would have felt badly about being so blunt,

but she could be stars-blasted persistent when she wanted to. Her feelings, if she had any, never came into play.

She trailed a hand along her skin, and I looked pointedly elsewhere. Not that the sight was offensive, in and of itself. Fiona knew she was gorgeous, from her sleek black locks to her well-proportioned figure, slim and curved in all the right places.

"I thought you were just being coy," she teased. "I know you were favoring Gracie for a while, but surely you've grown bored of her by now."

"I could have sworn I announced my engagement tonight. Pity you seem to have missed it," I said, looking around for her clothes.

She tilted her head, studying me. "Don't tell me this is about that—"

"Do not finish that sentence." I snapped my gaze back to her, then regretted it when I saw that she had moved to put her...assets on better display.

"Socairan, I was going to say." Her voice dripped with false innocence as she tilted her knees to the side and gently grazed her bottom lip with her teeth.

"I'm sure you were," I muttered, surveying the room again.

"Galina, then," she intoned in a singsong voice, drawing out the syllables.

I finally spotted Fiona's dress draped over the arm of the wingback chair next to my fireplace. I crossed the room to grab it but spun around halfway there at the sound of her footsteps. She was standing a mere foot from me, her expression oddly speculative.

"You know..." She tapped her finger against her bottom lip. "I thought that name sounded familiar, but it took me a while to place it."

I gritted my teeth against the memory that assaulted me. Copious amounts of whiskey. Fiona's lithe form reminding me of another perfect body I had held in my arms. Galina's name slipping from my lips with precarious timing.

"I've already apologized for that," I said sincerely.

Even Fiona didn't deserve to be called by another woman's name. She shrugged, the motion pulling at parts of her I tried not to notice.

"Oh, don't worry about that, Dav," she said, her deep-blue gaze drifting from my eyes down to my lips. "You know I always enjoyed a little roleplay."

She closed the distance between us, trailing her fingers along my arms.

"I know you've had a long night," she murmured.

Of course she knew. She was the biggest gossip at court. My parents were the collective spymaster of all of Lochlann, and still, Fiona Shaw rivaled them in the speed with which she gathered information.

"I have," I confirmed. "Which is why I'm ready to sleep now."

It was a lie.

My mind was a maelstrom. There was no rest to be had.

"Or," she countered, her hands moving to the top button of my jacket, "you could let me make it better. Do you want me to beg?"

She stretched up to purr that very sincere offer in my ear.

I let out a slow, controlled breath.

It would be so easy to cave, to bury myself in Fiona and let her temporary warmth chase away memories of questioning my own men in the dungeons. To work out some of the tension that thrummed through my veins. To enjoy the feeling of being wanted after a night of weathering Galina's icy courtesy and false smiles.

Galina, who had made me want things I shouldn't, then told me it meant nothing to her. Who had spent her evening subtly surveying her options for when our undesirable *arrangement* was finished. Who was across the hall right now, probably hating me.

I placed my hands firmly on Fiona's waist, and her lips tilted up in a victorious smirk.

Until I picked her up and moved her away from me before setting her back down. Reaching behind me, I grabbed her dress from the chair, handing it out to her.

"Good night, Fiona." This time, I left no room for argument.

"Fine." She rolled her eyes, more exasperated than offended. "You know where to find me when you change your mind."

I didn't bother responding. She dressed quickly and left without a backward glance.

Then I was alone, surrounded by the deafening silence and the weight of my mistakes, wondering if I was an idiot for wanting the closest thing I had felt to peace since Mac died.

Even if it had been mostly lies.

TWENTY-FIVE

Galina

As exhausted as I was, sleep did not come easily.

Or at all.

The night went by in a torrent of what-ifs, until the darkness threatened to swallow me and I could feel the ghost of Alexei's fingers grasping at my arm, gripping me closer to him. I could feel his breath on my cheek.

If you would behave, I wouldn't get so frustrated, Galina.

His voice morphed into a Lochlannian accent, the imprint of his hand transforming into an assassin's blade.

I threw my blankets off, practically running to the balcony. The burst of night air soothed me, cooling the thin sheen of sweat that had settled over my skin. I gulped in greedy lungfuls, letting the still, calm night wash over me.

It wasn't enough. I was still trapped with the wall behind me and the trees stretching out in front of me. I couldn't breathe. I needed to see the stars.

With Davin home, it was probably safe to venture onto the rooftop. Surely, if the soldiers on guard were suspicious, they would go to him.

I might have risked it anyway, with how I was feeling tonight.

After ducking into my room to throw on a dressing gown, I crept back out onto the balcony. The icy sting of the iron staircase bit through the silk of my slippers, but it was worth it for an unobstructed view of the sky.

Or, the view would have been unobstructed, had there not been a tall, broad-shouldered figure standing against the far balcony.

I froze as Davin turned to face me, cool blue eyes locking onto mine.

Even in the silver lighting, he looked nearly as exhausted as I felt, his hair disheveled from running his hand through it.

He didn't look surprised to see me, or maybe it was the familiarity of it all. Late nights under a starry sky with only each other for company.

Then again, he knew where my rooms were. As usual, I was the only one left in the dark.

"Your rooms are across from mine?" I surmised aloud.

Though he could have wandered up here from anywhere, the explanation seemed the most likely.

"Apparently," he muttered, his words forming a small cloud in the cold night air.

I could have turned around and gone back downstairs—should have, perhaps—but the alternative to being on this roof with him was being alone in my room with my own relentless thoughts.

Besides, it was hard to muster up any real anger toward him these days.

Though, if I was being honest with myself, I hadn't been strictly *angry* with him in some time.

I crossed over to the railing, resting my arms on the balustrade and taking in the endless sea of stars. The sky felt closer from the mountains back home, the world tucked away in safety. Out here, it was easy to feel exposed.

Vulnerable.

Or perhaps that was just the penetrating gaze of the

rooftop's other occupant. We stood for several stilted heartbeats before Davin's low tone eventually cut through the silence.

"It probably says something about our lives that the days when I was a captive and you were half-betrothed to Lord Hardly-the-worst-I-could-do feel like simpler times, in hindsight."

I couldn't argue that. Now, I was a fugitive from my kingdom, and he had spent his midnight hours questioning traitors amongst his own men.

"Ah, and now *you're* Lord Hardly-the-worst-I-could-do. My, how things come full circle."

The corner of his mouth tilted up. "Technically, that's *Laird* Hardly-the-worst-I-could-do."

"How silly of me," I said, my expression mirroring his. "You know, I suppose it was painfully apparent, in hindsight, what with your penchant for expensive beverages."

It was a risk, touching on things we rarely mentioned, but something about the hush of the night compelled me toward honesty.

He tilted his head like he was deliberating his next words.

"Is that how you put it together then?" he finally asked.

I sucked in a breath.

Somehow, he had realized that I found out long before the rest of my kingdom. He was wrong about how, though.

"What makes you think I did?" I asked anyway.

He turned his scrutinizing gaze on me, and I resisted the urge to look away.

Was he, too, thinking about the morning I left?

That was a day I would just as soon go my entire life without reliving, let alone while he was right in front of me, staring at me with the same discerning eyes that had made me set aside my better judgment to begin with.

Even now, I wasn't sure what was worse—that he had used me for information I would have given him freely, or that while I had been dreaming of a life with him, he had withheld the information that might have made that possible.

Perhaps that last part was my fault, though, for being foolish enough to want something when he clearly hadn't.

"So you didn't, then?" he pushed.

I debated hedging, but there hardly seemed a point now.

"No," I said shortly.

His expression shuttered, and I found myself offering an explanation I wasn't entirely sure he deserved.

"I didn't put it together by myself," I clarified. "I had a visit from your dear friend, the maid."

He let out a bitter huff of air.

"Of course you did," he said. "And did Aino happen to mention why she felt the sudden need to betray her own kingdom?"

He remembered her name. *How charming.*

"She claimed she felt that I deserved to know, under the circumstances." There was an edge to my tone I couldn't quite suppress.

He snorted in disbelief, and my lips parted in ire. Heat washed over me, chasing away the sting of the cold from the icy stone floor and the metal of my ring.

So much for not being angry with him anymore.

"You disagree?" I demanded, my voice only slightly less irritated than I felt.

Davin leveled a look at me. "I think we both know that's not why she told you."

He wasn't wrong there. She had told me because she was jealous, but I didn't especially love having that confirmed. Any lingering doubt that they had enjoyed...a relationship, effectively vanished.

"That's not an answer," I said evenly.

He shook his head, sighing. "It wasn't about what you did or didn't deserve, Galina. It was a lot more complicated than that."

It was my turn to scoff. "And here I thought I had left all the patronizing *svolochi* behind in Socair."

"I'm not trying to patronize you, Galina, or be a bastard." Davin sighed and ran a hand through his hair.

He went on before I could assure him that he didn't have to try to be a bastard. It was one of his many natural skillsets.

"It's just not as simple as a yes or no answer," he said. "Rowan was in danger, and I was in an impossible situation."

"And you thought I was a threat to her?" I wasn't sure if I was indignant or just genuinely curious at his faulty rationale.

He shook his head, not as much a denial as a show of frustration. "I *thought* you were loyal to your uncle, who could certainly have been a threat to her. Besides, you hated Rowan."

I tried very hard not to wince at the implication that I hadn't been loyal to my uncle, or that I wasn't now. Even though it was true. Instead, I focused on the second part of what he said.

"I didn't hate her," I corrected.

I just hated that she had waltzed into my life long enough to be more important than I was to my uncle, my almost-betrothed...and later, Davin.

"And I certainly didn't wish death on her," I went on. "If anything, I would have gladly helped you get her back to Lochlann and out of my life."

Tucking his hands in his pockets, he tilted his head toward the sky, releasing a slow breath through his nose.

"I know that now." If he had sounded frustrated before, there was only resignation in his tone now. "And for whatever it's worth, I am sorry for the way...everything went."

Sorry for lying? Sorry I found out? Sorry for our night together?

I found I wasn't brave enough to ask.

"Don't apologize for something you would do again," I told him, not sure which of those things I was referring to.

"I wouldn't," he responded, his gaze meeting mine once again.

Somehow, I didn't think even *he* knew which of those things he meant.

Complicated, indeed.

I took a deep breath, raising my defenses back up before Davin could demolish them completely as he had an unsettling tendency to do.

"It hardly matters anymore," I said as neutrally as I could manage. "Whatever happened in the past, we're allies now, at least for the next six months."

"Allies?" He peered at my face like it was a puzzle he couldn't quite solve. "Well, I suppose that's better than the alternative."

Was the alternative in this scenario being his enemy? Or being his future wife?

Storms. Davin was the only person who could make me question everything this way. And honestly, I wasn't sure being his ally was better than being his enemy.

At the very least, it wasn't easier.

I pushed off from the railing, straightening to my full height. "On that note, I should get some sleep. We have a long day of allying ahead of us tomorrow. Goodnight, Davin."

I was already halfway to the stairs when I heard his voice sound softly behind me. "Goodnight, Lina."

That one, simple word—a name I hadn't heard him use in ages—both twisted and released something inside me.

My steps faltered briefly before I continued down the staircase.

It wasn't until I was safely ensconced in my blankets that I realized I hadn't thought about Alexei or the assassin once on that rooftop.

The Breakening

GALINA

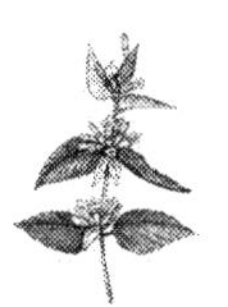

A Year and a Half Ago

When Rowan had burst into my life, effectively stealing the very satisfactory plan that was laid before me, I had been frustrated. Angry, even.

But I had never hated her like I hated the woman standing before me now.

"I'm sorry to be the one to tell you, My Lady," Aino said, her voice filled with false niceties.

No, she wasn't.

The maid hadn't displayed a single ounce of contrition since she barged into my room with her fake sincerity and her I-just-thought-you-should-knows.

But the worst part—the absolute ugliest piece of the entire encounter—was that she was right.

I should have known.

Should have guessed. Should have prodded. Should have done anything but trust Davin with his stupid laughing eyes and dimpled smirk and surprising wit.

My mind raced with a thousand different memories. The

casual way he referred to Princess Rowan. His expensive tastes. The cultured manner in which he spoke.

And what was it he had said that very first night on the roof?

The perils of being in a new court.

At the time, I had thought he meant *kingdom*. But he was halfway to a concussion, given to a rare display of transparency, only I had been too blind to see it.

Then there was the way Iiro treated him like a valued prisoner, the way Theodore respected him as an equal.

I wanted Aino to be lying, but the things she said added up.

Davin was a liar.

And I might have been able to move past that if it weren't for the fact that our every single storms-blasted interaction had been a ruse, designed to get information out of me, as she so gleefully informed me.

Aino couldn't have been lying about that. Couldn't have known about Iiro leaving, if Davin hadn't told her.

"Leave," I ordered her in a voice like ice.

She complied. Only when she was gone did I finally allow myself to consider the ramifications of everything she said, including the last little tidbit she had dropped with a malicious sparkle in her eyes.

He told me when I came to his rooms this morning.

I scoffed.

Did he now? To his rooms, or to his bed? The bed that I occupied only a few short hours ago. Did he also tell you that you were perfect? Did he murmur the words against your skin like he was praying to the only deity he had ever come close to believing in?

And did I have anyone to blame but myself for showing up at his door like every other *laskipaa* he managed to win over?

That wasn't the worst part, though.

The worst part was that she had told me knowing full well I wouldn't endanger her precious marquess. My feelings had been so appallingly obvious.

Even now, I couldn't bring myself to want him in danger. To run to my uncle with what I knew, knowing it would hurt him.

I wasn't sure how long I stood there feeling like my body was caving in on itself before an achingly familiar knock sounded at the passageway door.

Should I ignore him? No, he would only come back later.

With each measured step to the doorway, I schooled my features a little more, until I was outwardly serene when I answered the door. His mouth—his perfect mouth, the one that had slid across every inch of my body—was open, like he was already poised to speak.

I cut him off.

"Davin, I was just coming to find you," I said, because he wasn't the only one who could lie with a straight face.

He closed his mouth, then opened it again. "You were?"

"Yes. To tell you I'm leaving." That part wasn't a lie.

Or at least, it wouldn't be when I was finished talking to Theodore. Storms knew he owed me a favor since he called off our betrothal talks, twice.

Davin's shrewd gaze roamed over me. "Did something happen?"

"Nothing I wasn't expecting." I gave him a dismissive wave of my hand. "Uncle is finalizing my marriage contract, and I need to be off to meet my new husband."

Sadly, that was probably also true, or would be soon enough.

I shoved down the traitorous thoughts I had entertained about a different life with a husband I chose.

It was ridiculous, now, the things I had let myself picture. Fanciful notions for someone far less practical than myself. I should have known better.

Der'mo, but I *had* known better.

I should have realized that Davin would join the endless ranks of men who used me for their own ends.

Davin's eyes didn't leave mine, but I kept my face perfectly blank.

"Lina–"

The name was like a spear lancing into my gut.

"You know, that was never strictly appropriate, but it's even less so with my betrothal being finalized," I told him, my voice colder than I meant to let on.

"Tell me what happened," he said. "Is it your uncle? Because we can—"

"It's not," I interrupted him sharply, the concern in his voice making tears stab at the back of my eyes.

Was it feigned? Real? Was anything real?

Taking a deep, subtle breath, I continued in a milder tone.

"Honestly, we both knew what last night was." *Lie.* "You don't have to pretend otherwise for my sake. It's not like I was planning on marrying you. I just...wanted a bit of fun before I had to go back to real life." At his hesitation, I pushed harder. "Come now, Davin. We always knew it would end this way."

His features shuttered, his posture going ramrod straight.

"I see. In that case, I'm glad I caught you in time to say goodbye." There was something in his voice I couldn't—didn't want to—read. "For whatever it's worth, I meant what I said."

That prodded at my carefully held self-control. The hell he had meant anything he said.

"About the life debt," he expounded when I didn't ask.

"I doubt we'll ever see each other again." The truth of those words threatened to bowl me over, that everything ended like this.

I would never again see his smirk or banter with him on cold rooftops, or hear his low, sardonic chuckle.

It had all been lies to begin with.

"Well then," he said, his tone as hard as his deep-blue gaze. "Congratulations, and...have a nice life, Galina."

Pain lanced through my chest. "And you as well." *Laird* Davin.

I didn't wait for him to say anything else. Instead, I gently closed the door, waiting until his footsteps faded back down the passageway to finally let the tears fall.

TWENTY-SIX
Davin

Present Day

I WASN'T sure there was enough coffee in the realm to stave off the level of exhaustion I felt the next morning.

Only Blaine's disapproving stare kept me from drinking directly from the carafe he had brought with my breakfast. Even then, I had to practically bribe him to bring more while he fussed over the healthy amount of caffeine for an able-bodied young man and how I was wildly exceeding it.

Despite his quibbling, my manservant watched me with concern etched into his aged features as we went through my schedule for the day.

Blaine had worked for my family for most of my life, and he had happily taken on the role of my manservant when I came of age. He could read me nearly as well as I could read him, and he was one of the few people I allowed to see my unguarded moments.

Or rather, I just hadn't been able to hide them as well around him. Especially not when Mac died, or when Row left for Socair.

With a sigh, I stared at my cousin's name on the parchment in front of me.

Her letter was next to my blank one, and a fresh wave of guilt washed over me as I penned a response.

Dear favorite cousin,

Now that you mention it, I did happen to leave Socair in parallel to someone who was also leaving Socair, of their own volition and choice. We then happened to, by complete coincidence, slip and fall into a betrothal arrangement only once she was a solid five or so feet into Lochlann.

We both know there are laws on a woman leaving a betrothal in Socair, whether she wishes to be in it or not, and I, for one, am horrified to find that I have inadvertently played a role in such egregious behavior. I am only happy that you were far enough removed from it all to avoid being falsely implicated.

Since, under the terms of the treaty, no one can force her to come back to Socair now, I suppose we'll all have to lie in the bed we've made.

Your still favorite cousin,
Davin

PS Tell your husband to remember how much

I love him, and how fervently he has returned that affection.

I HOPED she understood the things I'd left unsaid. *I'm sorry I couldn't tell you. I wanted to protect you. I had to do this. We've got this under control. Forgive me.*

The postscript spoke for itself.

After sealing the letter and passing it off to Blaine, I downed one final cup of coffee before trudging back down to the dungeons for another round of pointless questioning.

Judging by the look on my father's face, it was clear he felt the same way.

But there were clearly more traitors among us. That much was painfully obvious, given the even more tight-lipped stance they all took this morning.

Even Dougal refused to look us in the eye, his expression far more hardened than it had been the night before.

Did Graeme remind them to keep quiet again? Or did someone else threaten them after we left?

A wave of fury overtook me at the realization that we were quite literally surrounded by enemies. How was I supposed to keep anyone safe if I didn't know who to trust?

Several hours passed while we tried every interrogation practice we knew. Some of them verbal, and others...decidedly not.

An idea began to form in my mind as we went through each one. It was clear—to me, at least—that we were done with the rebel soldiers. If we wanted to root out the real traitor, we needed to cut the head off of the snake all together.

The only way to do that was to draw him out of whatever hole he was hiding in.

I ran into Galina in the hallway on the way back to my

rooms. Ewan towered just behind her. He gave a subtle nod to indicate that everything was fine. No obvious threats.

That was something, at least.

"Good afternoon, My Laird," she said coolly, though I didn't miss the slight teasing expression in her pursed lips.

Her crystal eyes swept over me, lingering on the bags under my own and the tight set of my shoulders. She had a terrible habit of both seeing more than I wanted her to, and also less.

"Good afternoon, Lina," I greeted, and something flashed in her eyes.

I wasn't sure why I had used her nickname last night, but now that it was out there, it felt strange to revert back to her full name.

Taking her hand in mine, I brought her knuckles up to my lips, pressing a kiss there.

For all that I had trusted Ewan with the truth about the rebels, the lie of our betrothal wasn't something I was willing to share. There was too much at stake for us both, and no real benefit to anyone knowing.

A faint blush rose into her cheeks, and I could almost believe it was sincere. Her tone was even when she spoke, though.

"Did you learn anything new?" she asked, breaking eye contact with me.

I sighed and extended my arm to escort her down the hall, wishing the day was closer to being over. I still needed to clean up, and we had courtiers to entertain and traitors to suss out.

"No, but I have an idea on that front," I answered. "Something I'll need your help with, since we're allies and all."

Her fingers stiffened reflexively, and I wondered if she was thinking of our conversation from last night, too. But she only smiled up at me demurely, effectively hiding her thoughts behind her favorite polite mask.

"Of course," she agreed easily. "Isn't that why I'm here?"

Her tone was pointed enough that I wondered which one of us she was trying to remind.

IT WAS late afternoon by the time we found ourselves in the village market.

It had taken me longer than I planned to scourge the stench of the dungeons off of my skin and change into something that didn't reek of defeat and looming executions.

I met Galina and my cousins and our sizable escort of trusted—or as trusted as we could get at the moment—guards in the courtyard so we could walk down to the local village.

Being that market day was the busiest day of the week, it was a good time to introduce Galina to my people.

While we still had traitors to root out, we also had a vote to secure, and part of that meant selling the would-be betrothal to anyone who would listen. The people needed the stability and something else to focus on after word of the rebel traitors spread.

They would hear about it soon enough, if they hadn't already. Tomorrow, we would be posting the formal execution announcement. At least we could give them something positive, too, something to root for.

So, we set out to do just that.

On the way, we discussed my plan to plant misinformation among the courtiers. Lina already had some ideas on that front, and on how to keep track of the information we spread and to whom. How she had memorized the titles and pastimes of the entire Lochlannian court already was beyond me, but then, she had always been a quick study.

This particular market day was the perfect opportunity to implement the plan, too, since many of the local noble families were also in attendance. As I had predicted, the ladies had donned gauzy scarves over their shoulders.

Including Fiona, who I dutifully steered us clear of.

As we walked along through the village square, we stopped at each stall and shop so I could introduce Galina. While most of them were congenial, there were those who watched her with expressions of wariness, and a few who held downright contempt in their gazes.

The children showed no such hesitation. Then again, that might have just been because their desire for sweets outweighed their apprehension.

"Did you bring us sweets, mi'laird?" one of them asked.

"Jem!" his mother chastised with an apologetic look my way.

I waved her off, reaching into my pockets for the square of chocolate I had, indeed, brought. I broke a piece off for Jem, and he happily ran off, making way for the rest of the children.

A tiny girl with red hair bounded up after him. Ariana Fraser. I always remembered her because she reminded me of Avani when we were children, the way she would size you up in a single, probing glance.

As much as I loved all of my cousins, I found myself wishing she was here now, helping me deal with this unmitigated disaster. As the heir to the throne, she was the only one of my cousins who understood the subtle maneuverings of life at court. Or at least, the only one who cared.

Until she lost Mac, anyway.

I shook the thought away, directing my attention to the next child; Ariana's tiny brother hovered behind her, shooting terrified glances Galina's way.

"She doesn't *look* dangerous," the girl told him dubiously.

Galina appeared to be nonplussed, and I choked on a laugh, in spite of myself.

"Not to you," I assured the child.

Galina shot me a thinly veiled expression of annoyance.

I leaned in, talking in her ear. "Well, you'll never convince them like that."

When she glanced uncertainly at the children, I remembered that Socair had suffered a plague several years back that impacted the fertility of many of their people. Children were scarce. I had never seen any at court, which wasn't unusual in itself, but I couldn't recall many being mentioned either.

I pressed the next square of chocolate into Galina's hand. She took it gingerly, unwrapping the muslin around it and crouching down until she was closer to eye level with the children.

"You're pretty," a new boy said, his attention fixed solely on Galina. "Is that why mi'laird wants to kiss you?"

Galina flushed to her roots, and I decided to take mercy on her.

"It is, indeed," I told him.

He nodded, like that was the answer he had been expecting, and took her chocolate before running to catch up with the others.

"Where are they going?" she asked, her tone wavering between concern and curiosity.

"They aren't running away from you, if that's what you're wondering. On market days, they play games," I said. "You'll see them again, either playing knucklebones or horseshoes in that field over there."

I pointed to where they were doing exactly that, and her posture eased ever so slightly. Almost like she had enjoyed the interaction with them. I wasn't sure why I had taken note of that specifically, but I cataloged it all the same.

A few more children came, and Galina looked visibly relieved at the decided lack of further inappropriate questions. Or at least, overt ones.

She relaxed with each child, going so far as to smooth the hair from the forehead of the last girl who came. Which didn't give me any feelings of any kind.

Once we were done doling out chocolate, we made our way through the other stalls. Though there was still some suspicion, most of the villagers seemed to have thawed after watching Galina interact with the children.

Perhaps that's why I was foolish enough to let my guard down.

Or perhaps it was Galina, her calm presence, and the sheer amusement factor of watching her navigate the chaos she was so unaccustomed to.

Either way, my smile was coming a little more naturally by the time the sun began to set on the horizon.

And that's when the first explosion went off.

TWENTY-SEVEN
Galina

Boom.

I had the irrational thought that the smell reminded me of home, the way it had always accompanied the obsidian plumes that rose up into the sky from the mines in the mountains of Ram.

It was so familiar, in fact, that for a moment, I forgot to be afraid.

Then the screaming started.

Boom.

Davin's body covered mine, the hard muscles of his chest pressing me into the ground while his solid arms wrapped around me.

Boom.

Closer, this time. My ears rang, drowning out the frantic pounding of my heart, the cries around us...drowning out everything but the pervasive odor of black powder and smoke.

Boom.

The ground trembled, and Davin tightened his grip around me.

Somewhere beyond the smoke, beyond the chaos, I registered his scent of parchment and cloves and spiced bergamot.

I closed my eyes, wondering if that was the last thing I would ever smell.

Then finally, the world was still.

"Lina." Davin's voice was frantic in my ear, his fingers prodding along my sides and my head. "Are you hurt?"

"No." My voice sounded far away to my own ears. "Are you?"

He shook his head, getting to his feet and holding out a hand for me. Black ash rained down around us, but the screams had abated. Davin looked around until his eyes landed on Gallagher and Gwyn.

"Are you—" he began.

"We're fine," Gallagher answered, a very anxious Lady Fenella and one of the village children tucked in next to him.

Davin nodded, the motion dislodging some of the ash that had settled onto his black hair. "All right, then. Gal, check for wounded. Gwyn, see if you can find out who the hell is responsible."

In a louder voice, he called out instructions and reassurances to both the courtiers and the villagers, taking charge of the chaos more effortlessly than should have been possible.

Once the majority were headed back to their homes, he called for Ewan.

"Escort Lady Galina back to the cas—" he started to order.

"No." The word was out of my mouth before I could consider what I had just done—that I had just argued with Davin in front of his own men.

I braced myself for his reaction, but he didn't look upset, only confused. He moved his hands to my arms, then my face, like he was confirming I was still uninjured as his expression carefully searched mine.

"You'll be safe," he assured me, misunderstanding my objection. "I'll send enough men to ensure it."

I shook my head, and he dropped his hands back down to his sides.

I wasn't concerned about that. It didn't feel right to return safely to the castle when there was so much to be done here... and there was a small, unreasonable piece of me that wasn't ready to be parted from Davin so soon after...

"There are wounded," I said in a milder tone than before. "I can help...if you'll allow it."

He blinked rapidly. "It's your decision."

"Then I'll stay."

He looked like he wasn't sure what to make of that, but he didn't try to convince me to go. Not that there was time.

Before he could respond, Gallagher raced past us with the first of the wounded. His features were drawn in fury as he cradled the small body against his chest.

That's when I realized the chaos had only begun.

THERE WAS SO MUCH BLOOD.

The smell of dust and dirt and blood permeated the air, tinged with the scent of herbs and alcohol.

We had followed Gal to the local healer's house. In the back was a makeshift infirmary, but it was tiny, not equipped for more than one or two patients at a time.

The single bed at the back of the room was already occupied by a villager, so the rest were left to sit in chairs or be laid on tables, all of their injuries on full display for the world. Broken limbs and bleeding heads. Gouges and contusions and bleeding that couldn't be stopped.

Davin cursed under his breath, catching the attention of the girl from before—Maisey, the apprentice healer, I learned rather quickly. She was frantically at work on one of the villagers.

She called him over, gesturing toward fresh bandages on a

table that was just out of reach. He didn't hesitate before rolling up his sleeves, dipping his hands in a bowl of pure alcohol and passing her the needed instruments and bandages.

Within moments, I was also throwing off my cloak and repeating the same steps that Davin had to clean my hands before joining Gallagher.

Stretched on the small table in front of him was the little girl whose black hair I had smoothed back earlier. Her eyes were shut, her arms hanging limply over the edges of the table as Gal held his hands over a wound on her abdomen.

I didn't need to be a healer to know that the blood pouring from the gaping flesh was a bad sign. Something inside of me cracked at the sight of it. Of her.

"What do you need?" I asked, struggling to keep my voice steady as I surveyed the medicines and herbs that he had available.

He met my gaze for one solid moment, then dipped his head in an appreciative nod.

"Hand me the horsetail and yarrow. I need to make more coagulants to stop this bleed." He gestured toward the shelf behind us with a crimson-soaked hand.

I grabbed the vials from the shelf, selecting a jar of cayenne pepper as well. Not waiting for permission, I blended the herbs and spice together into some aloe before reaching out to apply it to the wound.

Gallagher hesitated for the briefest moment at the potent smell of the cayenne.

"Trust me," I said. "It helps."

Without a word, he moved his hands long enough for me to apply the mixture. I wondered if perhaps I had imagined just how bad the wound was before. While there was still a deep gouge and an alarming amount of blood, it didn't seem to be quite as severe as I had thought it was.

Small mercies.

We worked together applying the mixture, and eventually, the blood slowed enough for us to bandage her up.

Gallagher's hands were in constant motion, flitting from one wound to the next as I applied medicine and he wrapped her in bandages.

When her eyes fluttered open, we let out a collective sigh of relief. Her fair skin was sallow, and she was lethargic, but she was awake.

And more importantly, alive.

He called for Ewan to transport her to a more comfortable location while we moved on to the next patient.

After that, we fell into a steady rhythm, bandaging, cleaning, medicating, and healing one patient after the next as Davin and the other healer did the same on the opposite end of the room.

Hours passed, or days? I wasn't sure which.

Everything was a blur of cutting more cloth for bandages, grinding down the herbs I'd found in the garden outside to make more medicine, and doing whatever else Maisey, her father, and Gallagher needed to help the villagers.

When Davin wasn't helping with the injured, he was reassuring the villagers, checking in with the soldiers, and sending updates to his parents, who had stayed at the castle to take care of the courtiers.

The man never stopped.

By the time it was said and done, fifteen people had come to us injured from the explosions. Three had died before they could be brought here, and we lost two more after they arrived.

It was a miracle that there weren't more, or, more accurately, a mark of Gallagher's extreme skill. He had managed not to lose a single person once he started treating them, discovering and evaluating injuries faster than I would have thought possible.

Things were finally coming to a lull when the chime of the bell above the door rang.

In walked a tall, lean man with sandy blond hair, large brown eyes, and pale, aristocratic features currently carved into a show of concern.

I would have known from Gallagher's dark expression that the newcomer wasn't welcome, even before he muttered irritably under his breath.

"Fancy seeing you here, Laird Tavish."

TWENTY-EIGHT

Davin

TAVISH SURVEYED THE ROOM, his eyes lingering on Galina for long enough to make me clench my jaw.

Even after hours of rushing around the crowded infirmary and tending to the wounded, she was striking. The single strand of hair that fell from her braids only framed her delicate features, and her cheeks were flushed with exertion.

She was gorgeous, in an obvious way. So, of course, people looked at her, but there was something more sinister than simple ogling in his gaze. A speculative gleam I didn't like.

"Cousin," I called, forcibly pulling his attention from her. "Is there something we can do for you?"

"I believe that's my line. I rushed from Dewmire as soon as I heard," he said loudly enough for every villager in the room to hear.

The hell he had rushed anywhere.

I took in the pristine cut of his jacket and pants, pressed to perfection. His countenance was calm and lackluster, and not a single thinning hair on his head was out of place.

Not to mention, Dewmire Keep was several hours' ride away. He wasn't remotely disheveled or out of breath in the way that someone who had been frantically riding a horse would be.

"I wasn't aware you had any particular skill with healing," I said amicably, setting aside a tray of blood-soaked bandages.

He let out a light laugh, full of false self-deprecation. "My boy, I've become so accustomed to caring for the village, I was halfway here before I remembered you had finally returned from your holiday."

I reminded myself that everyone in this room had been traumatized enough today without watching me run him through with my sword. But stars if I was in the mood for his games after watching my people writhe in pain and die today, after seeing abject terror on the same small faces that had been filled with laughter only hours ago.

"It means the world to me that you were willing to come to support my people while I was seeing to the trade agreement, making sure that all of Lochlann had enough food in their stores for the upcoming winter." I managed to keep all traces of sarcasm from my tone. "If you're looking to help now, you can help bring water to the wounded. Or your wife can..."

I trailed off, making a show of looking for her.

His eyes barely narrowed before he smoothed his expression over. I practically watched the gears turn in his head as he decided how to play this.

Would he admit she hadn't cared enough to come check on them, when a Socairan had spent hours healing their wounded, or admit he had kept his wife safely away when the villagers were in danger, and again, the outsider had stayed to help?

A surge of pride went through me. Galina was a variable he hadn't accounted for.

I despised the part of me that was playing games in a room where at least one body was still growing cold, but I despised Tavish more for making it necessary.

"She went up to the castle to check on your betrothed," he finally said. "Since it was clear Lady Galina was the target of this attack, it didn't occur to me that she would still be here."

His words sucked all the air from the room. The only sounds came from where Maisey and Gallagher were washing up their tools, the soft scraping of metal and splashing of water sounding nearly as loud as the explosions had been.

"She's not one to cower from a threat," I assured him.

Galina glanced over in surprise, but Tavish didn't look nearly bothered enough at the implied slight to his wife.

"No, of course not," he said, a bit too amicably. "I just would have thought you'd be too concerned about her drawing another...incident, when your protective resources are already so depleted. But I admire your boldness, truly...and hers, refusing to falter even when the rebels have made it clear that they won't stand for this alliance."

The villagers had been hanging on our every word. With that one utterance, one single statement that I had no doubt would spread like wildfire, he had ensured that they blamed Galina for drawing the attack and me for not protecting them from it.

How very convenient for him.

In fact, all of this was convenient for him.

Once again, I considered his state when he had walked through those doors.

How could he have gotten the message so quickly? He could have been on his way to visit the market, but that's not what he said happened.

He hadn't been out of breath when he got here, even though his estate was several hours' ride away.

Pure murder surged in my veins.

"It was an unusual escalation," I said quietly. "The rebels have only attacked soldiers before now, and royals, but there were children playing in those fields."

Children who always played in those fields on market day.

They weren't collateral damage. They were the intended target. Perhaps not to kill, but at least for the scare tactic. What faster way to unite people against a threat?

"An unspeakable tragedy." Tavish didn't have a speck of remorse in his eyes.

Of course not. He didn't care who he hurt in his play for power.

"It would have been," I agreed, "if not for Galina's knowledge of medicine."

It was true. Gallagher couldn't have saved them all, even though I saw him risking exposing his fae abilities more than once to save someone today. He was barely standing as it was.

Even with Maisey and her father, it still wouldn't have been enough if Galina hadn't been mixing such potent salves.

"We're fortunate she was here," I went on. "Men who would stoop to hurt children will stop at nothing. If it weren't my betrothal, they would find another reason to be angry. But don't worry, because I can assure you our protective resources are anything but depleted. I've already had word sent to my uncle requesting additional soldiers, and in the meantime, my men will guard the village."

"Of course, an excellent plan. Only..." Tavish reached around me, grabbing the ladle from where it rested on the counter. "Are you certain that they are *your* men?"

Satisfaction gleamed in his eyes. He could have been baiting me over the arrests, but this felt like more than that.

He was too smug, like he knew something I didn't. Like he had the names of every rebel masquerading as a loyal soldier and would die for the chance to rub them in my face.

Any lingering doubt that he was responsible for what happened today effectively disappeared.

Whatever it took, I was going to win this vote.

And then, when I had won, when I had no discernible motive, when enough time had passed that everyone had finished gossiping about the little spat between me and my not-quite-cousin...

Then, I was going to end him.

When Galina got to the roof that night, I was already waiting with a glass of her favorite white wine.

It had been jarring to go from the chaos of the village to a ridiculously late dinner with courtiers in the same evening. From blood-soaked bandages to fine linens and crystal goblets.

The handful of nobles who had been in the village discussed the attack in low whispers, as if they were afraid the mere mention of it all would bring the rebels to the formal dining hall.

I couldn't say I blamed them, but it made for an ominous evening, nonetheless.

Galina took the glass of wine with an arch of her eyebrows. She said nothing about the fact that I had clearly anticipated her presence.

"White wine?" she asked, her crystalline gaze reflecting the stars above us.

"Well, I figured you hate me enough already without forcing you to drink hard liquor." My tone was light, like we hadn't both spent our day watching people die.

I needed five minutes to not think about that.

Galina surveyed me a moment before taking the glass, tilting it against her lips.

"I don't hate you," she said, her lashes fluttering as she savored the flavor of the wine. "I...*nothing* you."

Her tone, too, was more casual than the storms churning behind her eyes.

"You *nothing* me?" I played along.

She took another long sip from her glass, a delicate hip resting against the balustrade as she pretended to consider her response.

"Yes," she said. "It's a perfectly neutral stance wherein I have no feelings at all regarding your person."

There was a time I had believed that was exactly how she felt about me. A bit of fun, she had said. But *fun* had never really been her style.

I shook my head. "No. I understood the concept perfectly, but thank you for that slightly hurtful clarification."

She lifted a single slim shoulder. "I thought you'd appreciate the honesty."

I let out a low chuckle, taking a drink from my own glass, relishing the burn of the whiskey all the way down.

"Of course. You and your endless penchant for truth telling. Have any delicious crab soup lately?" It wasn't the question I wanted to ask.

I wanted to ask why she was here if she had exactly zero feelings regarding my person, but I wasn't willing to risk her leaving just to prove a point.

"I'm sure I would have, if you had anything to say about it," she shot back. "You do seem to enjoy making me miserable."

It was a joke, but it brought home the reality of our situation, of the way we had spent our evening. I sucked in a breath before asking my next question.

"*Are* you miserable?"

She turned to face me, her eyes searching my features. "Would it matter if I was? We have a deal."

I let out a disbelieving huff of air. "Yes, Lina. It would

matter. It does matter. And we made that deal before you spent your day up to your elbows in other people's blood, knowing the people who did that would have rather it happened to you."

She blanched slightly but didn't back down.

"You warned me about the rebels," she reminded me.

"It isn't the same," I bit back.

Another pause.

"And what about your vote?" she asked quietly.

The vote that would give Tavish everything he needed to fund his pet rebels. The vote I had to win if I didn't want the entire kingdom to go up in flames.

"I would find another way," I told her, not entirely untruthfully.

Galina coming here had been a last-minute idea. It hadn't even factored into my plans to win the vote originally. If she left, I still had as many options as I had before she showed up to my room that night, with the small added downside of having to explain away our failed betrothal.

So they weren't good options, necessarily, but it wouldn't be impossible.

"If you had another way, why did you force me into this charade to begin with?" She sounded more curious than angry.

Because the idea of you coming here and marrying someone else just as you'd come back into my life was unthinkable.

The thought barreled into me unbidden, surprising me with its veracity. I stumbled over my response.

"I didn't say I had another way. Just that I would find one. If you're miserable, that is."

She looked out over the moonlit grounds, then back at me.

"No, Davin. I'm not miserable." Her silvery blue gaze held mine. "But...thank you."

"For not wanting you to be miserable?" I tried for a teasing tone again, but she didn't smile.

Instead, she held my gaze seriously for several silent heartbeats.

"For not leaving me in Socair," she finally said, returning her gaze to the stars and resting both of her arms on the balcony.

I could have told her she left me no choice, with the life debt, but we both knew that wasn't strictly true. And I didn't want to lie to her. Not again.

Not anymore.

"You're welcome," I said, studying her controlled expression. "Thank you for staying, when I offered you a way out."

She wordlessly held her glass out for me to refill before she spoke.

"You're welcome."

Silence fell again after that, not tense, but not exactly comfortable either. We were both weighed down with everything that had happened today. Though somehow, it didn't feel quite as heavy in our shared quietude.

For all she claimed to *nothing* me, Galina didn't leave. I knew she would be here tomorrow, too.

We both would, because despite my very best efforts, I couldn't seem to *nothing* her either.

TWENTY-NINE

Galina

SEVERAL DAYS PASSED without another incident, without word from Tavish or the rebels that he was clearly conspiring with. But instead of being calming, it was as if everyone was holding their breath waiting for the other shoe to drop.

Somewhere between court dinners and afternoon teas and even short reprieves under a star-strewn sky, we all seemed to be waiting for the next disaster to strike.

And yet, I was still wholly unprepared when Anna brought an envelope in with my afternoon tea. My fingers trembled as I flipped it over to reveal a crimson wax seal in the shape of a ram's head.

Swallowing hard, I unfurled the letter, my pulse racing.

First, my eyes landed on the date.

It had been penned the morning that my wedding was supposed to have taken place.

Had they canceled it? Postponed it? Had Alexei been waiting at the end of an aisle that I would never walk down, his brittle pride assuring him that I would turn up in the eleventh hour?

The room swam in my vision, dizziness settling over me.

Dread only further pooled in my stomach when I beheld

my uncle's familiar slanted cursive, quashing any residual hope that the letter was from my parents. And I knew by the lack of endearment with the salutation that I wouldn't like what he had to say.

Galina,

I trust that this letter finds you well. I can only imagine that it does, since I haven't heard from you in some time. This is not the behavior that has been instilled in you, the behavior of a clan wife or a Socairan.

I assume I have at least instilled you with enough loyalty to know that your arrangement with the Lochlannian is not valid without my approval, which I have not granted.

Despite your exploitation of the loophole you found, I will ensure that Lochlann understands that as well.

One way or another, you will be returning.

It's time for you to fulfill your duties to your duke, your parents, your clan, and your betrothed. Your real betrothed.

You are rather fortunate Lord Alexei is still determined to have you as his wife. He has asked for leniency on your behalf, and I have graciously agreed to see our agreement through rather than remove you from the clan.

Do not take for granted this generosity that

is being bestowed upon you. I trust we will see you soon.

Your Devoted Uncle,

Sir Mikhail

WITH TREMBLING FINGERS, I placed the letter back on the nightstand. I wasn't sure what the worst part was, the reminder of how badly Alexei wanted to own me, or how clear it was that my own uncle would never take my side.

Or the guilt that tugged at my insides when I read words like loyalty and duty and knew that I was failing at both.

I mentally calculated the time it would take to get home.

Davin had said he had other options. He didn't need me here.

Perhaps I had built this up in my head. Perhaps it wasn't as bad as I remembered it.

Had I overreacted?

Maybe Alexei would have gotten better, in time.

Maybe my departure had only served to make our inevitable relationship worse.

If I didn't go back to him, would he come here and drag me back, twice as angry as he would be if I returned to him on my own? Did I want to risk that?

A light knock at the door pulled me forcibly from my thoughts. I didn't recognize the pattern, but Anna must have because she didn't look remotely surprised to see Jocelyn on the other side of the door.

"I can see to Lady Galina's hair this evening," the princess said, a polite dismissal in her tone.

Anna nodded, her concerned gaze going between me and the letter before she excused herself.

"You heard back from your uncle?" Jocelyn said once we were alone.

I nodded, still not trusting my voice to speak.

"Is there anything we should know?" she asked.

I had a suspicion that she was already aware of the letter's contents, even if it had been sealed when it arrived, but I shook my head anyway.

"More or less what we expected. Threats to return. Attacks on my sense of loyalty and duty." I tried to say that last part without inflection, but Jocelyn's sharp gaze told me I had failed.

"I see," she said in a deceptively casual tone, gesturing for me to face the mirror.

"Oh, you don't have to—" I began, but she shushed me.

"If I can tame a squirming Rowan's hair into submission, I'm quite certain I can manage yours." With gentle hands, she separated out sections of my hair.

"You spoke of duty," she said neutrally. "Yours to marry Lord Alexei?"

"Yes," I admitted. "All marriages in Socair are arranged, but of course, mine held special significance."

She grabbed a small pin from the vanity to secure the braid she had already finished. "Things weren't so different here when I was a girl. Even now, many families arrange marriages."

Something in my shoulders eased. I had been expecting judgment, to have to defend the ways of my kingdom yet again, but there was no censure in her words.

I nodded my understanding, and she went on.

"I wonder, though, if your duty is obedience, what is Lord Alexei's?"

"To shelter me, care for me...protect me." The words tasted bitter on my lips.

She nodded again, moving on to another braid. "And your uncle's duty in arranging your marriage?"

"To find someone who will do those things, I suppose, and in his case, also to serve his clan."

"And did he?" she pressed.

I might have wondered what she knew, but her tone was merely curious.

Perhaps that's why instead of defending him automatically, I took a moment to consider her question, to admit that the answer was a resounding no on all counts.

Some unshakable, long-held belief fractured inside me.

Where had my uncle's responsibility to me been when he all but sold me to a man like Alexei? Where had his responsibility to his people been when he used my marriage to secure a war that accomplished little outside of the slaughter of his soldiers?

And Alexei...

I didn't answer her outright, instead posing a different question. "But what does it say for my loyalty if it is contingent upon their actions?"

"A fair question," she allowed, braiding another golden strand of hair. "Did Davin ever tell you why I was not married to his father at the time of his birth?"

I hesitated, wondering if I had offended her with my talk of loyalty when this entire upcoming vote hinged upon the fact that she, by all accounts, had not been.

"No," I finally said.

She nodded, like that was the answer she had been expecting.

"My parents also raised me to believe in loyalty," she began. "To them and to my kingdom. So when I found myself expectant with the crown prince's child, knowing that he needed to marry another, I agreed to keep it secret. I was somewhat more reluctant to marry the late Laird Anderson, as he was solidly four times my age, and a lecherous monster. But marry him, I did."

The tight set to her mouth would have told me this story

was going nowhere happy, even if I hadn't known the man had died.

"When I arrived here, I found out about the things he inflicted on his servants, the things he would come to inflict on me."

Her navy eyes locked on mine in the mirror. "Tell me, do you think a man like that deserved my loyalty?"

I didn't need to think about my answer. "No."

"But he was my husband, and I had sworn obedience."

"But...he gave up that right when he hurt you."

The words sunk in just as soon as they left my mouth. Had Jocelyn seen the moment's hesitation as I digested them. Did she realize just how much they applied to me, as well?

"And what of my loyalty to my kingdom?" she continued. "Do you think Oliver deserved to have his son kept from him for the sake of his people?"

"I don't know," I admitted after a short consideration.

She shrugged one delicate shoulder. "I don't, either. Even now. I know that I have loved Oli for as long as I can remember. I loved him then, but I was not as loyal to him as I was to the things I had been brought up to be loyal to."

She waited until I nodded to go on.

"See, love can be blind, and often is." A soft smile crept on to her mouth. "You can't always choose who gets your love, but you get to decide who is deserving of your loyalty."

Those words struck a chord I hadn't been ready for, strumming along my mind and down into my chest as I allowed them to resonate fully.

"And you think my uncle isn't deserving?"

"That's not a choice I—or anyone—can make for you." The smile died from her lips. "But I will tell you this. I know what it is to be a captive in your own home, and it's not a life I would wish on anyone."

I wasn't sure how much she knew or had guessed about my relationship with Alexei, but it was like she was seeing straight through to my nightmares of endless years spent behind the towering walls of Wolf Estate, his shadow looming over me until I withered away to little more than a specter haunting the halls of the place that would never be a home to me.

"What if I have no choice?" I spoke the fear aloud before I could stop myself.

Jocelyn put the final pin in my hair, moving until she was standing directly in front of me.

"Let me be very clear about something." Her voice was pure, unrelenting steel. "As long as you are in Lithlinglau, *no one* will take you from this estate without your explicit consent. Not your uncle. Not the man who believes he holds some claim over you. The king of Lochlann himself would have to go through me to get to you, and trust me when I say, he has no wish to do so."

I blinked, not sure what to say to that. What to think.

"So if you wish to stay," she continued, "you don't need to marry. And if you choose to go, no one will force you to stay here against your will."

My lips parted, but still, no words came out.

"Do you understand?" she asked in a gentler tone.

No, I wanted to say.

I couldn't begin to understand why a woman I barely knew would stand between me and her own king for something that no one had ever offered me before.

But I had been raised to be obedient, so I cleared my throat until I could speak in a voice that didn't tremble.

"Yes. I understand."

Her shrewd gaze once again locked on mine.

"No," she said a bit sadly, "you don't. But in time, you will."

THIRTY

Davin

THE MORNING of the executions was appropriately gloomy.

Despite the cold front and overcast skies, villagers and courtiers alike came out in droves for the event. Between them and the larger army we had with the new soldiers from Alech joining our ranks, it was a sea of bodies pressed in on each other, leaving little room to move around.

Lina's arm was threaded through mine as we walked to the outskirts of the estate. Right off of the road, next to a towering oak tree and surrounded by a large crowd already, were Lithlinglau's brand new gallows.

The macabre edifice that promised nothing but death was apparently prime entertainment, if the expressions of some were anything to go by.

Unfortunately, some of those expressions belonged to children.

Even though we had our reasons for a public execution, it made me want to be sick. A few were propped up on the shoulders of their parents, while others ran around in the grass just on the outskirts of the crowd, playing games and laughing as if this were market day.

"Last chance to go back," I whispered as we moved closer, the crowd finally taking note of our arrival.

Some of the children ran up to us, already asking for sweets or trying to speak to Galina, which only cemented my previous feelings.

She expertly navigated the exchange, pulling out treats that she had apparently brought with her, as if she had expected them to be here and planned ahead.

As soon as they ran off again, she tucked her arm in mine once more and leaned in close enough so that only I could hear her.

"I already told you no, Davin," she murmured. "It's nothing I haven't seen before. We have public executions back home. Besides, this is what they expect of the Lady of Lithlinglau."

She gestured behind us toward my mother standing resolutely at my father's side, and I nodded reluctantly.

She was right. It wouldn't be a good look for her to stay behind.

"I'm not as delicate as you seem to think I am," she added a moment later, punctuating the statement with a challenging expression.

"Lina, love," I said quietly. "Delicate would not be the first word I used to describe you. Or the second."

She let out a short, disbelieving breath before raising her eyebrow. "So what would be, then?"

We locked eyes for a single charged moment before the oppressive crowd pressed in once more, truncating our conversation. It was probably for the best, since I wasn't sure either of us wanted the answer to that question.

I forced my attention back to the people around us.

Given the amount of courtiers present, one might think that today's mass execution had replaced tomorrow's ball to kick off the social season. The thought shouldn't have made me as bitter as it did.

That had been the point, after all.

To remind the villagers and nobles alike that we wouldn't tolerate this rebellion any longer.

I scanned each face as we passed, taking note of them. Lady Fenella spoke with her nieces near the Campbells and Stewarts, while Lairds Gray and MacFarley stood off to the side, barely deigning to acknowledge any of the commoners surrounding them.

Our current path, though, led us directly where Laird and Lady Buchannan were speaking with the MacBays and Lady Fiona.

Since her impromptu visit to my room, Fiona had given me the space I asked for, and Gracie had been rather subdued since my return. Still, given my history with both of them, I was more than a little eager to steer us away from that side of the crowd.

Which, unfortunately, meant that we nearly plowed right into the Andersons.

Tavish's narrowed gaze was fixed on me and Galina, fury rolling off of him in waves. I wasn't sure if I should take it as a personal victory that he was so angry, or if I should be offended that he felt he had the right to be angrier than I was.

What I wouldn't give to add a noose to the stage for him.

"Laird Davin," he seethed.

"Tavish," I responded curtly, choosing not to use his title. "I do hope you enjoy yourself today."

His face reddened, his lips parting to respond before Galina cut him off.

"Darling, I think they're waiting for us," she said smoothly, pointing toward the stage. "Always a pleasure to see you, *Lord* Anderson, Lady Anderson."

The corner of my mouth twitched in response as I led her to where my cousins and parents were waiting.

It was telling that the gallows were preferable to Tavish's company, even if they were chilling to look at. Tall wooden beams towered above us while five ropes hung idly from the main rafter, swaying in the breeze.

With a sigh, I signaled to the hangman to proceed.

A heavy weight sank to the pit of my stomach like a stone sinking to the bottom of the loch. These weren't the first deaths I'd been forced to order, but it was the first time I had been forced to order a mass execution.

I clenched and unclenched my gloved fists, steeling myself as the first five men were led up the steps and to the center of the stage where the row of nooses awaited them.

Scottie stood proudly in the middle, black eyes narrowed over his broken nose, his expression still haughty. His death wasn't one I would mourn.

But the others...

I couldn't understand why they were so ready to die rather than give us even the slightest bit of information. The name of their leader, the location of their base camp, their plans... anything to help us prepare for whatever was coming next.

They had stayed resolutely silent on all of it, even up to the morning of their deaths.

The only thing I had gotten from any of them was a single sentence, repeated from man to man.

"The Viper is everywhere."

It didn't sound like something Tavish would call himself, but then, I wouldn't have guessed that nearly thirty of my soldiers would rather hang than see my cousins and me take over as the stewards of Lochlann, so what did I know?

Viper was a clan in Socair, as well, but we didn't have any particular enemies there that I was aware of. I couldn't devote any more time to unravelling that mystery right now, though, because it was time for the formal sentencing.

Galina and I climbed the stage where my family was already waiting, and I cleared my throat to begin.

As soon as I formed the words, "hanging until death," Scottie's countenance faltered slightly. His smug expression faded while his throat bobbed up and down. There it was, fear coming in at the eleventh hour.

For a single, unreasonable second, I wondered if he would break, if this was the moment that he would change his mind and tell me what I needed to know. I stepped forward, ready to halt the hangings just as his gaze locked on to someone in the crowd.

His expression hardened, and he squeezed his eyes shut.

I scanned the crowd, already knowing it was an exercise in futility. There were too many familiar faces there, too many faces in general, staring ahead or lost in conversation with someone at their side.

Of course, it would have been too easy to ask for a sign to be nailed to their foreheads with a formal admission of guilt.

When it was clear that the men's minds were still made up, I gestured for the hangman to continue.

Time sped up and slowed down all at once, passing in a series of disjointed moments. The creak of a lever, followed by the groan of the floor giving way. The snap of a rope pulled taut and the crack of a breaking neck, echoed five times over.

Their bodies swayed for several long moments before the village healer checked them for a pulse. Once each of their deaths were confirmed, they were cut down.

And five more took their place.

I hadn't realized that my hands were balled into fists until Galina adjusted her hold on my arm, her fingers threading between mine. Her grip was firm as she kept her eyes fixed straight ahead.

No. Delicate was certainly not the word for her.

I didn't allow myself to look away from the stage, but I grounded myself in the feeling of her thumb tracing an arc back and forth over mine.

There was another sentencing and another hanging, making a grand total of fifteen executions in under an hour. Then another.

That made twenty. Then twenty-five.

But the last group was the worst to come.

Gwyn shifted uncomfortably to my left, her hazel eyes fixed on Dougal's form as he joined us on the stage, along with the remaining two traitors.

It took everything I had not to wrench my gaze from the noose around his neck or the unshed emotion in his eyes when he traded one last look with his wife.

Once again, the lever was pulled, the floor gave way, and the rope pulled taut with the weight of the dead.

THIRTY-ONE
Galina

THE FIRST BALL of the season arrived just a single day after the execution.

It wasn't anything new for me, going from death to politics. Storms, it wasn't even new since my arrival here. Wasn't that what had happened after the explosions?

Still, it was a strange contrast, from a crowded field that smelled of death to the spacious ballroom that dripped in opulence.

Especially when my night had been plagued with visions of the gallows, only it was me hanging from the noose, branded a traitor while my family looked on. Then it was my parents.

Then Davin.

And so on, it had gone.

Anna worked even harder than usual to cover the dark circles under my eyes while I worked to put my nightmares back in the box where they belonged.

So, I focused on the things that were real. The ones I could control.

Like picking out the jewelry I would wear that night, and mentally preparing myself to watch the ladies of court take every excuse to press themselves further against Davin and lean up to whisper in his ear.

Not that they needed an excuse.

Not that my preparations would keep me from actively wanting to shove some of them into the nearest lit fireplace, either.

These things felt small and frivolous in light of everything else, but they were easier to cling to.

And clearly, I wasn't the only one in need of a distraction.

When Davin and I entered the ballroom, it was already filled to the brim with courtiers desperate to either make light of yesterday's hangings, or to forget about them entirely.

There were candles everywhere, suspended from the ceiling to look like stars. Flowers and silks and fountains of sparkling wine adorned the room, as an orchestra guided the dancers with their music.

I had been to elegant events before, but Jocelyn had truly outdone herself, giving us something we could all focus on instead of the chaos of the world around us.

Since Davin had hosting duties, we didn't dance the first dance together. Or the second.

Or any. Which was fine, since I needed to be focused on my prospects. My very, very appealing prospects.

Like Laird Humphrey, who had only tried to accidentally graze his thumb above my ribcage two or three times.

Disrespect for the boundaries of betrothals was apparently an epidemic in Lochlann. As much as it galled me to admit it, Davin had been right when he said our betrothal would only enhance my prospects.

At least, I assumed that was why, when I had to field several comments about "leave it to Davin to go to another kingdom to make sure he has the very best," followed by proposals of varying subtlety.

Not all of my potential future husbands were terrible, though.

A few were downright congenial, their grips light and polite as they led me around the dance floor, their questions curious without being ignorant. And though it was frustrating, I reminded myself it was why I was here.

I wanted them to be making proposals I could follow up on when the time was right. At the very least, I needed them to.

Still, the dances were endless. In fact, only an hour into the evening, it seemed as though the only laird in the entire storms-damned room who hadn't tried to claim my hand was the one I was betrothed to.

Not that I cared, since he wasn't the one I would actually be marrying.

He was probably just giving me the chance to meet my eventual real fiancé in a way that wasn't remotely awkward with my current fake fiancé's scrutinizing gaze so often finding me, even over the heads of his own dance partners.

When I finally got a break, I headed over to the refreshment table, steering clear of the warmer beverages in favor of light sparkling wine.

Immediately, I was joined by three other figures.

Gallagher was the first to speak, his tone kind but teasing. "How are your toes faring after Laird MacCallum?"

"Decidedly worse for wear," I admitted. "But he was nice enough."

"And he has an enormous—"

"Penchant for gambling?" Davin interjected helpfully.

Though I knew he hadn't slept much more than I had—he couldn't have, when we were on the roof even later than usual—his face didn't show a single sign of fatigue. None of him did. He was perfectly put together in a silver and pale blue outfit that complemented mine to perfection.

And judging by his outwardly calm expression, he, too, had locked his demons in the box where they belonged.

"I was going to say," Gal glanced from his cousin, back to me. "He has an enormous vineyard down south."

I bit back a sigh.

This was not new, Gallagher attempting to point out something helpful whilst Davin was markedly less so. It had been happening with increasing frequency since Davin returned, as every new day brought a new batch of courtiers.

Gwyn sipped at a glass of iced pumpkin cider, surveying the crowd with a critical eye. "Well, tell me which one you're leaning toward so I make a show of picking someone else for Auntie Jocelyn's sake."

Her brother made a face, and she shot him a look of sympathy. "You, too, Twinsy. It's *our* turn to face the hangman's noose now."

I choked on my wine.

While most of the room had been trying to avoid mentioning of yesterday's executions, Gwyn, apparently, had no such compunctions.

Gallagher shook his head mutely, giving me a slightly horrified glance when Gwyn looked away. Whether because of her off-color joke or because Maisey was going to murder him, I wasn't sure.

"Perhaps you'll be able to rope one of the lairds in with your overwhelming sensitivity, Cousin," Davin remarked.

Gallagher coughed. "Went right to *roped*, did you?"

Gwyn snorted, and Lady Fenella shot her a judgmental glance.

"Now, Laird Gregory is a decent option." Gallagher gestured vaguely in their direction.

I eyed the kind blond with the slightly crooked nose who was escorting his mother through the ballroom, trying to see him in a favorable light. Though Jocelyn had said I was welcome to stay here, it would be easier for everyone if I had another arrangement when this was all said and done.

Easier for me, also, to move on rather than stay here and

watch Davin once he was no longer encumbered by a need for discretion.

Besides, I did want to get married. I wanted children. Just...not with Alexei.

And, if I was being honest, not with Laird Gregory, either.

"He has a comfortable estate along the eastern border," Gal went on. "His family is very close, too—"

"A little too close, really," Davin interrupted from my right, his posh tone sounding more high-handed than usual. "But if you don't mind your husband having an unhealthy relationship with his mother or their thirty indoor cats, then he's a real winner."

I attempted to hide my expression behind my wine glass, mostly because I wasn't sure whether it would be a grimace or a smirk. *Damn him.*

"Not to mention, Lady Fenella would be your mother-in-law," Gwyn tacked on, her eyes widening in warning.

I tried very hard to keep to keep the horror from my features, swiftly moving down the list.

"Well then, what about Laird Gray?" I asked, subtly gesturing toward the man with the piercing green eyes. "He's attractive and witty."

"He's got a great arse, too," Gwyn added with a not-so-subtle look at said bodily region.

Davin scoffed and shook his head. "Every brothel this side of Alech agrees with you. Though they do say he's a generous tipper, so high marks for that."

"You would certainly know, wouldn't you?" I bit out, irritability winning out over amusement.

It was bad enough contending with the sinking feeling every time I thought about putting myself at the mercy of another stranger without his oh-so-helpful running commentary and the unwelcome reminder of his extracurricular activities.

Davin raised an eyebrow at my tone. "While brothels are

an excellent place to find gossip, I have never seen the need to patronize those particular services. Having to pay someone takes all the fun out of things."

Gwyn snorted, but I only raised my eyebrows.

Strangely, though, I believed him. Stranger still, something inside me, something that shouldn't matter at all, eased at the admission.

Gallagher made another valiant attempt to steer the conversation back around.

"Laird Gibson has—" he began, but of course, Davin cut him off.

"Halitosis and a drinking problem."

"MacConnel—"

"Anger issues."

"Ferguson—"

"More gambling."

"O'Doyle—"

"Foot fetish," Gwyn interjected with a shiver, and I decidedly did not need to know more.

Davin eyed the stocky man who was bellowing with laughter in the corner before he turned to me with a wicked gleam in his eye.

"Though, I would never judge you if that was something you—"

"Porter?" I interrupted, staunchly refusing to allow him to continue that line of thought.

"He's..." Davin trailed off, and Gallagher gave him a challenging look.

My fake betrothed looked beseechingly at Gwyn, who shrugged with a rueful expression.

"He's fine," Davin finally admitted, looking like he had swallowed something sour.

"Well, good," I said lightly. "He's headed this way."

Davin made a tutting sound.

"That's unfortunate, since I require your presence making

rounds." He sounded as though it was anything but unfortunate. "Don't worry. You'll have plenty of time to meet him later."

Gallagher shook his head while Gwyn chuckled under her breath, and I took Davin's proffered arm with something strangely close to relief. There *was* time to meet Porter later, and I had a job to do at Davin's side.

At least, that's what I told myself, steadfastly ignoring the voice in my head that told me I would rather be politicking with boring courtiers at Davin's side than dancing with the man I should want to marry someday.

The Contingency Plan

DAVIN

A Year Ago

The brothel in Hagail was as busy as ever.

Half-dressed women flirted and laughed to music that was just this side of too loud, and the heavy scent of perfume and cigar smoke permeated the air.

But all of my attention was focused on the man in front of me, a Socairan guard I had paid an otherworldly sum of gold to bribe his way through the tunnels to bring me back information on the brewing war.

"Last I could find her, the princess was traveling with the soldiers, but she's not fighting." He spoke in an accented undertone, though no one was paying us any mind.

That was why we met here.

I wanted to be relieved that Rowan was safe, but the word *yet* lingered in the air. She wasn't fighting yet.

"And...the other?" I asked.

"Lady Galina is safe behind the walls of her family's estate," he said. "Clan Ram has not yet entered the war, but even if they do, the soldiers there would never hurt a lady."

I scoffed at that, my thoughts drifting to Rowan.

"A Socairan lady," he amended.

Nodding, not entirely reassured, I passed the man a heavy coin purse.

He weighed it before looking at me shrewdly.

"It's getting more dangerous," he said. "It will be double next time."

Normally I would have argued, but he was my only means of information. I couldn't even go myself. There was no way through the battalion standing guard on the other side, and my skin was far too pale to blend in.

"I don't care what it costs," I told him, getting up to leave. "Just get the contingency plans in place and tell me when the pass opens."

"Who is she to you?" he asked curiously.

Obviously, he wasn't asking about my cousin.

"No one," I replied, turning to leave.

It wasn't even a lie. I hadn't so much as spoken to her in a year.

Perhaps she had only thought of me as a bit of fun—or used me to understand what her wedding night would look like—but we had been friends once. She might have been able to walk away from that without so much as a backward glance, but I couldn't turn off the part of me that cared about her.

Stars knew it would be easier if I could.

THIRTY-TWO
Davin

Present Day

UNFORTUNATELY, it was only a matter of minutes before another laird swooped in to claim a dance with Galina.

It was like the entire court had been holding their breaths, waiting for the moment they could get their hands on her.

Eyes had followed her from the time we arrived, even more so than usual.

It wasn't hard to guess why.

Galina had finally relented to getting her gowns made the way she wanted them, starting with tonight's.

Rather than a straight Socairan style, she had blended the fashions of her kingdom and mine into a brocaded silk gown that was equal parts elegant and alluring, the pale blue shade mirroring her eyes and providing a sharp contrast for her olive skin.

The neckline was high, but wide, leaving just the tops of her collarbones exposed before the fabric met at a single point on each shoulder and draped down into long, split sleeves. Her golden locks were artfully arranged around a circlet of diamonds and sapphires, a combination of her usual braids and the half-up fashion that was popular in the court here.

She was stunning on an average day, but tonight, she was absolutely devastating.

Every laird in a fifty-mile radius had signed up to escort her around the dance floor, all of them eager to speak with her. To test her out on their arms.

I had known this would happen. Hell, I had told her myself that she would have her pick of nobles by the time this was over. So I had no reason at all for the way my heart clenched every time a laird led her to the dance floor.

Away from me.

And I knew…I knew I could have stopped them by choosing to dance with her myself, but hadn't I promised her I would help her find a suitable husband while she was helping me to win this vote?

Of course, I also knew that wasn't the only reason I avoided dancing with her, but the others didn't bear thinking about.

So instead, I watched while one laird after another spun her around the room, her graceful whirls and lithe motions captivating the entire room. It was Porter now, friendly bastard that he was. I couldn't tell if she was falling for his gentle charm as she smiled up at him, all politeness and demureness.

But he was sure as stars smitten with her.

Thankfully, he was too upstanding to act on those feelings. His smile remained genuine and respectful as he held her as close as propriety would allow, and not a hairsbreadth closer.

A tugging motion at my arm interrupted my thoughts, and I looked down to see Gracie MacBay's narrowed eyes following my gaze.

She let out a noise between a laugh and a huff as I led her into the next dance move. "You nearly missed our turn. I would ask where your head is tonight, but I think that's obvious."

"Apologies," I said sincerely.

While we had a history, one that I didn't intend to revisit, Gracie didn't deserve to be completely ignored during our dance.

She peered up at me, something indecipherable churning in her eyes. I spun her away from me before pulling her close again.

"You really are going to marry her." She said the words like they were an epiphany, like someone who had only just heard of our engagement for the first time tonight.

"Did you think I was announcing the betrothal for fun?" My tone was light, but it was concerning that someone already thought we were lying.

She shrugged unapologetically. "Considering the sheer volume of times you told me you didn't want to settle down, it did occur to me you were merely playing games with the vote coming up."

I kept my face as neutral as I could, torn somewhere between not wanting to hurt her feelings and not being able to tell her the truth.

"Gracie, I meant it at the time. I wasn't trying to use you—"

"No, I know that," she interrupted, her brown eyes turning rueful as she continued. "You never looked at me the way you look at her. Hell, Davin, you never look at anyone that way. Except possibly yourself in the mirror."

"Well, can you blame me?" I joked back, happy to take the out she was giving me rather than focus on her rather unwanted assessment.

We moved through the other dancing couples, and it was an effort not to turn at the scent of lavender and rosemary.

"No," Gracie said, her tone quieter and more serious this time. "But I wouldn't expect that much grace from the other ladies. When they realize you're serious, they'll likely bring out the pitchforks."

She paused long enough to spin out and back to me before adding in a warning tone, "Especially Fiona."

She wasn't wrong about that.

Ever since the surprise nudity debacle, I had upped the guard to our family wing, going so far as to tell Ewan and Hamish to watch both of our doors to keep unwanted company far, far away.

"So why aren't you bringing out the pitchforks?" I finally asked, meeting her copper gaze.

It wasn't that I wanted her to be upset with me. But considering all the time we spent together, I couldn't help but wonder why she hadn't wanted to string me up on the gallows along with every other traitor we knew.

She took a breath, holding my stare.

"You were always honest with me. You never pretended to want anything else. I can respect that, at least." She gave another graceful shrug, spinning out once more. "Which is why I'm going to be honest with you now," she added in a low tone. "You need to be careful."

I bristled. "With Galina?"

She shot me an exasperated look. "With Tavish."

His name barely left her voice on a whisper, her eyes darting around the room to ensure no one was listening to us.

"I'm handling the vote," I assured her just as quietly, hoping it was true.

"Are you?" she asked pointedly.

The song finally came to an end, and I dipped into a bow while she curtsied, as was common for the end of a dance. Before the music could start up again, or another lady of the court approached and tried to commandeer my time, I held out my arm for Gracie to take.

It wasn't until we were at the mostly empty end of the refreshment table, drinks in hand, that I spoke again.

"What do you know?" I asked, keeping my expression congenial.

"I know that he paid my father a visit yesterday, and he's looking awfully smug today," she said from behind her glass. "Something you would have noticed as well, were you not so distracted."

"He always looks smug," I scoffed, though I filed that information away for later.

MacBay was one of the lairds on the Lochlannian Council, as well a major player in the Assembly that would be voting. It was no secret why Tavish might want to meet with him now, of all times.

"But does his wife always talk to the docket master's wife like they're old friends?" Gracie pressed.

I subtly looked in the direction she was indicating, swearing under my breath. Sure enough, there was Edith Anderson with Laird MacArthur's wife.

Stars damn it all.

Gracie was right. I should have noticed that myself.

When Laird Gray invited her to dance, she excused herself from my company, but not before casting me one last warning look.

Once she was gone, I quietly ran through several different scenarios, along with potential contingency plans for them.

Though grateful for the information, I was still surprised Gracie had volunteered it. We were no strangers to a late-night dalliance, but hell, we had never precisely been friends. As Gwyn had pointed out in the carriage, I didn't have close friends outside our family. Not after Mac, especially.

At least, I hadn't thought I did.

But then, it would hardly be the first time I had lied to myself about the nature of a relationship.

AFTER MY DANCE WITH GRACIE, I tried to make a few subtle inquiries as to the nature of Tavish's interactions. It would have been nice to banish him for the entire social season, but sadly, not feasible and not conducive to my overall new look of maturity.

I was regretting the necessity of that right now.

Gracie was right. He was looking especially smug. When I couldn't glean what I wanted to, I made my way over to my parents where they were chatting with Gallagher.

Even then, with the need to focus on the political games afoot, I couldn't resist looking in *her* direction. Galina was dancing with a different partner. A smile graced her lips, her face lit up with the exertion of the dance.

"Did you have some damning evidence on him as well?" Gal asked, his words pulling my focus away from Galina.

Gal was watching her, too, his expression more amused than I felt.

I took a sip of my whiskey, perhaps a larger one than was strictly necessary, before answering. "Forgive me if I want her to have all the facts up front. I'm trying to be a good...ally."

He made a mock thoughtful noise. "And yet, I seem to recall Laird Gregory only having three cats, not thirty."

I cleared my throat.

It was possible that I exaggerated on that front, with Gwyn's assistance. "How am I supposed to remember the exact number of cats a man has?"

My parents both coincidentally suppressed coughs at the exact same time.

"Well, this dance is ending if you want to step in yourself." There was a challenge in Gal's words, but I brushed them off.

"I can't now," I said, glancing back down into my glass before finishing it off.

"Then I suppose I'll have to be the one to save her before old Laird Henderson steps in." He still didn't move, waiting for my reaction.

I smiled through my gritted teeth, waving a hand toward the dance floor. "Don't let me stop you."

Gallagher shook his head before heading in that direction, muttering what sounded suspiciously like a Socairan insult under his breath. I set my glass down with more force than was strictly necessary, eliciting raised eyebrows from both of my parents.

"Something the matter?" Da' asked mildly.

"Tavish is the matter," I answered darkly, decidedly not noticing the way that Galina's smile widened, her shoulders easing when Gallagher stepped in to take her partner's place.

My parents wore twin expressions of neutrality.

"Yes," Da' said evenly. "That does seem to be the problem."

"He's cozying up to the docket master's family," I told them.

"So we noticed," Mamá said.

Of course they had. Only *I* had been lacking in my observations this evening.

"You're not concerned about that?" I demanded, turning to face them, though the dance floor was still very much in my periphery.

"I didn't say that," my mother corrected. "But there's nothing that can be done about it tonight, which is more than I can say for your other problem."

I held her steady gaze with my own.

"I don't have another problem," I lied.

She rolled her eyes, something she had perhaps done three times in my entire life.

"Indeed," she said flatly. "My mistake. Then, I, for one, am glad you're handling it with such grace."

"As am I," my father added, all false heartiness. "I think it's delightful how well they're getting on."

"And it will be lovely to have her in the family," she went on. "Don't you think, Oli?"

"Absolutely," Da' agreed.

"For the last time," I said, pinching the bridge of my nose. "We aren't actually—"

"Oh, darling," my mother interrupted smoothly, her eyes fixed on the dance floor ahead. "I didn't mean you."

"No, of course not," Da' chimed in. "I think you've removed yourself from the running with an efficiency I might go so far as to call impressive."

"Stunning, really," Mamá said.

This time, there was the slightest edge to her tone. I motioned to one of the servants to refill my glass.

"I know what you're doing," I said, trying to ignore the vicious feeling churning in my gut.

She hummed noncommittally, her brow arching in amusement as she took a sip from her glass. "Then, why is it working so well?"

I sighed, wondering the same thing. Then, the song came to an end and the next one began. Gallagher and Lina didn't switch partners.

"If you'll excuse me," I added. "I have appearances to keep up."

"By all means, if that's what you want to call it," my father called after me, and I ignored him.

With each step I took, I tried to remind myself that I was getting in too deep. That all of this was supposed to be for show. A carefully crafted ruse that helped us both get what we needed.

I told myself that regardless of her stalwart presence at my side over these last few days, or the conversations on rooftops where the rest of the world faded away, we were not real.

She was still the girl who walked away, and I was still the boy who lied to her.

The ruby on her finger glinted under the candlelight, a shining symbol of yet another lie we were telling the world. Ourselves. Each other.

And just like when I had been stuck in Socair, this ruse was a necessary one.

That was the only reason I crossed the room, barely acknowledging the other dancers as I stepped between them, making my way straight to Galina.

It was for my people. My home. And not at all because I had a sudden visceral need to touch her, to hold her in my arms. To be the only man she was looking at.

"I'll take it from here," I said, tapping my cousin on the shoulder.

My cousin dipped into a short, slightly mocking bow before leaving the floor, an amused expression on his face that I didn't deign to acknowledge.

In fact, I ignored everything except for the woman in front of me.

The pink that tinged her cheeks from the exertion from dancing. The life that glimmered in her starlit gaze. The way her hand fit seamlessly in mine as I pulled her nearly flush against me.

I didn't waste any time before leading her into the next step, guiding her across the floor around the other couples just as smoothly as if we had been dancing together the entire time. Our entire lives.

Several times, Galina's full lips parted as if she were about to say something, then closed just as quickly. I didn't blame her.

Tension pooled between us, binding us together by a single, fragile thread. Usually, I would find a way to break it, severing that feeling, or any other, with a glib remark or a humorous comment.

But words failed me as I stared into her eyes and found that she was staring right back. The longer we danced, and the longer she held my gaze, the more her expression softened until it morphed into something almost vulnerable.

Something I had only seen on her once before.

Eventually, the sounds of the music and the chattering court were eclipsed by the pounding in my chest and the gentle breaths escaping her lips.

Nothing else mattered anymore. Not my corrupt cousin. Not the vote or the rebels or the fallout of every bad decision I had ever made.

It all fell away.

Instinctively, my fingers flexed around her back, pulling her closer to me, as close as this dance allowed. Her breath hitched, but she didn't pull away. Instead, she melted into me everywhere we touched.

This was why I had avoided dancing with her all night.

Because for all that we both claimed to be pretending, nothing about this moment felt like a lie.

THIRTY-THREE

Galina

THE DANCE SHOULDN'T HAVE CHANGED anything.

It wasn't the first time Davin had put his hands on my waist or laced his fingers in mine since we started our whole charade.

But the memories had come flooding in of a different dance on a snow-covered rooftop.

He hadn't spoken then, either, and hadn't taken his eyes off mine.

Not for the first time, I realized that Davin's rare silences said far more than his never-ending stream of sardonic words did.

In fact, he had been uncharacteristically quiet the rest of the night. While he had gone through the motions of dancing and hosting and bantering with the other courtiers, it had been markedly more subdued than usual.

Even when he escorted me back to my rooms, he had said nothing but a charged "Good night, Lina."

So I knew it was a terrible idea to go to the rooftop, but I couldn't seem to stay away. My feet carried me up the familiar winding staircase like I was being pulled by an invisible string.

Davin stood where he always did, a glass of wine waiting

in his hands. His stance was casual, but the air thrummed with tension, just as it had during our single dance.

He looked over at me, and his gaze seemed to linger a little longer than usual before he turned back to the sky, wordlessly holding out my glass. Stepping up to the railing, I took the proffered glass, trying desperately to ignore the way warmth shot through me when his fingers brushed mine.

"I'm surprised to find you up here tonight." Immediately, I wanted to take the bitter, telling comment back.

It wasn't even true.

After all, wasn't that why I had come up to the roof tonight? Because I was expecting him to be here?

That line of questioning led to another, more dangerous one about why it was that I was even seeking Davin out in the first place.

Hadn't I learned this lesson once before?

He raised an eyebrow, either at my words or my tone, and I had no choice but to explain my ill-thought-out statement.

"I just meant with the sheer volume of women vying for your...attention this evening." *Every evening*. "In a less than subtle manner."

Though, I supposed there had been time enough for that between when he left the dance and when he found his way to the roof. Maybe he had already enjoyed someone's company. We hadn't made any promises of chastity to one another.

The thought made my stomach twist uncomfortably, and I raised the glass to my lips to hide my scowl.

A short huff of air escaped him, but there was no humor in the sound. He turned to face me, his expression closed off.

"Do you honestly think that I would do that to you?" he demanded.

I forced my voice to sound casual when I responded.

"It's not as though I have a legitimate claim on you." I couldn't bring myself to say that I had no claim on him. "It would be ridiculous of me to be upset by that when I spent my evening searching for my future husband."

Davin moved imperceptibly closer to me, a muscle working in his jaw.

"Ah, yes. How is that going? See anyone you can't live without?" There was an edge to his low tone that I couldn't quite decipher.

Storms, maybe I didn't want to.

I swallowed hard, shifting so that I was facing him as well.

"If you're trying to rub in how limited my options are, there really is no need." I never should have danced with him.

His gaze narrowed, ocean eyes raking over me in disbelief.

"I would hardly call the entire Lochlannian court *limited*," he shot back.

He was right. I knew he was. So why did it feel that way?

"Indeed," I said drily. "Then who would you pick?"

He furrowed his brow. "For myself?"

"For me," I said flatly. "As my *ally*, Davin, who would you choose?"

My grip tightened around the stem of my wine glass, frustration surging through me at both my insistence on pressing this issue and whatever he was about to say in response.

His eyes blazed into mine. He opened his mouth, then closed it, before finally parting his lips to utter a single name.

"Gallagher," he said, looking out at the moonlit countryside.

Was I imagining the slightest hint of challenge in his voice?

I froze, blinking several times. Of all the names he could have mentioned, he chose his cousin?

"He is the highest ranking, aside from me, obviously, and the kindest," he continued on. "He doesn't have a weird set of quirks—at least, not bad weird. He would be faithful. Why wouldn't you want to be with him?"

That time, I was certain there was a dare hidden in his words, certain that the smug arsehat knew perfectly well why I wouldn't want to be with his cousin or anyone else at this court.

I finally found my voice. "Gallagher doesn't want that."

Davin huffed out an imitation of a laugh. "Don't be ridiculous. He just thinks it would upset me."

Would it? I wasn't brave enough to ask.

"That's not it," I said, unwilling to say more on the subject lest I out Gallagher's secret lady friend.

Davin leveled a look at me. "You can't honestly think that anyone could look at you and not want you, Galina."

He said it like it was obvious. Like it was an indisputable fact, like the sky being blue or the sea being wet.

Years of carefully honed self-control once again turned to dust because of this single, infuriating man. So instead of brushing his comment off the way I should have, I tilted my head up, looking at him with pure, unveiled challenge.

"We both know that isn't true."

His lips parted. One heartbeat passed. Then another.

"Is that what you think?" Davin stepped closer, close enough that his breath was warm against my lips. "I told you once before, that's the problem, Lina. Sometimes, it's *all* I want."

Then his perfect mouth was on mine, cutting off my stream of consciousness and any objections the more rational part of me may have made. I melded my body with his, taking his breaths for my own, scraping my nails along his scalp, and swallowing the groan he let out in response.

He pulled me against himself, a gesture that was equal parts possession and need. His lips trailed from my mouth, down to my neck, and lower as he pressed me up against the cool stones of the castle wall. For the first time since I got here, I was grateful for the dipping neckline of these stupid Lochlannian nightgowns, grateful for the access it gave him to my exposed skin.

I gasped, gripping him tighter to me, desperate to feel him

closer still. He pushed my dressing gown off of one shoulder along with my nightgown, his mouth chasing the fabric as it slid along my skin.

Storms, I wished he would just take it off.

That thought stopped me short.

Der'mo.

I had been here before. *We* had been here before, and I couldn't believe I was stupid enough to let us wind up here again. Hell, to goad us into this very moment.

"Davin," I breathed, barely able to force his name past my lips.

He made a noise in the back of his throat, and I realized that saying his name was in no way the deterrent I needed it to be.

I tried again. "I... We should stop."

There was barely a moment's hesitation before his hands disappeared from my body and he straightened to his full height. I already mourned the loss.

Our panting breaths filled the silence until he finally spoke.

"Galina?" he asked, wariness coating his tone, as though he already knew what I was going to say.

"We can't do this," I said with more confidence than I felt.

My heartbeat was thundering so loudly, I wondered if he could hear it, too.

He swiped a thumb over his lip, his expression morphing into his indifferent mask as he considered my words.

"Because you want to be with Gallagher?" he finally asked.

I shot him an exasperated look. "Don't be a *laskipaa*. No, I don't want to be with Gallagher."

He scoffed, shaking his head. "Then what?"

What did I want? What was the problem?

Weren't those things rolled up into one?

For the second time tonight, I spoke without thinking. "I

want someone who wants me for more than a single fleeting moment, Davin."

A rare emotion crossed his features, darkening his eyes even in the moonlight. *Anger.*

"Single. Fleeting. Moment?" He bit out each word. "You don't get to put that on me when you're the one who called it *a bit of fun* and then walked away, like it was nothing to you."

"Nothing to me?" I demanded. "I'm not the one who made you believe that we were...friends when all I wanted was your information."

"If I had wanted information," he said, his voice rising, "there were a hell of a lot easier ways to get it than spending hours every night on a stars-damned freezing rooftop."

His words felt true, but they didn't soothe the old wounds like I expected them to.

All this time, I had thought that his lies were the worst offender, but for months after he left, every time I closed my eyes, all I could see was that witch in his bed, the bed that still smelled like us.

"If it wasn't *nothing* to you, why was she even in your rooms that morning? Why were you telling her the things I had told you in confidence? A little pillow talk?"

"She was there because she was checking in as a spy for Lochlann. And yes, when I had information to help Rowan get out of Socair alive, I used it." He ran a hand through his hair, frustration making the motion jerky. "But I did *not* sleep with Aino—or anyone, for that matter—after that night you saved me on the rooftop. Which you would have known, had you bothered talking to me about it instead of running away the second things got the least bit complicated."

Anger ignited in my veins as I took a single shaky breath.

Bothered talking to him about it? Like we had talked every storms-blasted night about his home and his family and his life as a guard and all the other things he lied about?

Like I could have just asked him and expected an honest answer.

Even now, I wasn't sure how to process everything he had just said, wasn't sure whether or not to believe him.

"The least bit complicated?" I was as close to yelling as I ever got, white, puffy clouds of furious air billowing out between us. "What the hell do you call our situation up until that point, Davin?"

He opened his mouth to respond, but I barreled over him.

"And if you had wanted more between us, you wouldn't have sat on the information that you were in a position to—" I clamped my lips shut before I could give him that final piece of myself, the piece that I hadn't been able to get past.

His eyes widened, and I cut in again before he could say anything else.

"It doesn't matter, Davin. At least that was one thing you never bothered to lie about. You weren't under obligation to want something just because I did."

"I don't think you knew what you wanted, Galina." Davin took several steps back, clasping his hands behind his head as he furiously looked up at the stars. "I think you came to my rooms that night believing that it could change nothing between us, and the moment you realized that wasn't true, you looked for any reason to walk away from it."

Silence fell, heavy with the weight of everything we had said and everything we hadn't.

Was he right?

I hadn't expected to feel quite so much with him that night. That much was true. Even when I left breakfast early, I hadn't gone back to him. Instead, I had returned to my rooms to think, to ponder whether I could actually leave the family and the clan I was loyal to, for Davin's sake.

Whether he would even want that.

And I hadn't come up with an answer to either question before Aino knocked on the door.

Had I been looking for a reason to walk away? A way to make an impossible decision easier? Because Davin had withheld the option that would have made that choice wholly unnecessary.

If he had wanted to marry me, he could have asked for my hand as Marquess of Lithlinglau, and my uncle would have jumped at the chance for that alliance. But he hadn't, and I hadn't been sure I was willing to part with my life in Ram for a guard.

When he finally met my gaze again, I shook my head, my anger dying like the final embers of a long-forgotten fire and leaving only icy resignation in its place.

"In the end, we both had choices to make, and what matters is that we didn't choose each other. You can't honestly tell me that you think that's a basis for..." I trailed off, because I didn't even know what, if anything, he was getting at with all his confessions and accusations. "For anything."

Davin looked away, shaking his head. "No. I suppose not."

It was unreasonable, the way my heart dropped into my stomach. Had I wanted him to argue?

Yes. Of course I had. Stupid, stupid *girl that I was.*

"Well then," I said as briskly as I could. "Let's just go back to being allies and forget this ever happened."

He made a bitter sound in the back of his throat. "Sure, Galina. We'll just tuck this utterly forgettable moment in the backs of our minds with the rest of them, shall we?"

Davin took a step closer, closing the gap between us once again, his eyes full of a challenge I didn't know how to answer.

"I'll help you pick out your husband while you pretend you don't want to stab everyone who so much as looks at me and we both go on like we don't know what it is to watch the other one come completely undone."

His hand came to rest on my face, his thumb brushing against my bottom lip. "Is that what you want?"

No. That's the farthest thing from what I want.

But I can hardly handle the idea, the hope, of anything else, only to see it turn to ashes in front of me again.

"Yes," I lied, the word breathier than I meant it to be. "That's what I want."

One heartbeat passed, then another, my chest rising and falling in sync with his.

"All right, then." He straightened up, all trace of emotion gone from his tone. "I'll see you in the morning at breakfast."

Though it was Davin who walked away this time, I couldn't help the feeling that he had been right. That somehow, I was still the one running away.

Then again, he had never really given me a reason to stay.

THIRTY-FOUR

Davin

It was rare I let myself miss Mac, but tonight his ghost haunted me.

Or perhaps I just wished it would, that I could have any piece of him at all.

That I could go back to the days of lounging around a lake with him and having the nerve to think the worst thing that could happen was him having kids that would interfere with our nights at the tavern.

That I could go back to not understanding what it was to lose someone, when lately it seemed that was all I did.

Sometimes I wanted to punch that version of me in the face.

Then again, right now, I wanted to punch tonight's version of me in the face, as well.

What was I thinking?

That was a ridiculous question. I had been thinking about the way Galina's skin felt against mine, about her perfect, full lips and her wry sense of humor and all the best parts of us while I ignored every last body we had buried in the backyard.

For all that I had accused her of not knowing what she wanted, was I really any better?

The thoughts whirled relentlessly in my head, refusing to let me sleep. So I stayed awake, researching laws and answering invitations on behalf of myself and the woman I was trying and failing not to think about.

The one I could still taste on my lips, even after my second glass of whiskey.

All in all, it was a relief when there was a light knock on the servant's door to my room. I looked up, surprised to find gentle rays of sunlight already creeping through the heavy curtains.

Blaine entered the room just behind his knock, bringing a breakfast tray along with several pieces of mail. His usually unflappable expression twisted into something close to concern as he looked me over.

It was fair, if I looked anything like I felt.

Though, the frequency with which I was seeing this expression on him lately was becoming rather alarming.

While he sent for a bath and an entire carafe of coffee, I picked at my breakfast tray and began reading through the stack of mail he had delivered. One piece caught my attention with an official-looking red wax seal. Apprehension churned in my gut when I beheld the crossed swords and scroll sigil.

It was from the Assembly.

I braced myself as I unfurled the letter, scanning the page. I read it once, then twice before my mind wanted to comprehend the innocuous-looking script.

In light of recent events with the rebel attacks, we feel it would be prudent to expedite the decision regarding Lithlinglau estate and the surrounding territories.

The vote will take place 29 Samhain, 307.

THE AIR WHOOSHED from my lungs.

The vote had been moved up.

Instead of the four months I was supposed to have to win the Assembly over, I was now down to five short weeks.

I CALLED my family and Galina to my private study, spending the few minutes before they arrived racking my brain, trying to figure out the motive behind moving up the vote.

Was it because of the executions? The attack on the village? Had Tavish accomplished what he set out to do with those things, making me look weak?

Or was it the opposite? Was this an underhanded move on Tavish's part because he was scared that he was losing favor?

His wife had been talking to the docket master's wife.

And I hadn't been paying attention.

Stars damn it all.

My father arrived first, followed shortly by the twins. My mother and Galina were right on their heels, escorted by Ewan, who stayed to guard the hallway.

Galina, of course, showed no signs of the fatigue I felt. Her hair and cosmetics were done to perfection, her pristine gown another blend of the styles in our kingdoms, this time in gold.

She was calm. Collected. A polite smile adorned her lips as she nodded in greeting.

I might have even believed her façade, if not for the way she avoided meeting my eyes.

Not that I was trying either. I wasn't sure I actually wanted to read whatever was churning in her icy gaze.

It was too much to hope that no one would notice, but at

least my family didn't outright comment. Even Gwyn was uncharacteristically restrained, exchanging only a subtle—well, subtle for her—look with Gallagher before turning back to me.

Once everyone was seated around my desk, coffee in hand, I delivered the news.

"The vote has been moved up." Despite my best efforts, frustration edged my tone.

A silence descended over the room like a dense cloud of fog.

"Tavish?" my father asked.

I took a deep breath, considering what I knew. "I strongly suspect."

"How the hell can he do that?" Gwyn exclaimed. "We have spies everywhere. Surely we would have heard something before now."

She wasn't wrong. Spies everywhere should have included mine, and those of my parents. It was concerning that we hadn't heard a single word about the timeline move before getting the official notice.

"Apparently not." I gritted my teeth. "It would seem that Gracie was right about him winning over the docket master. She seems to believe Tavish is working on the other lairds, as well. Her father included."

Galina's otherwise calculating gaze wavered slightly at the mention of Gracie's name before she schooled her expression once again.

I tossed the letter on the table before explaining our new timeline. Gal pulled the parchment over, his auburn brows furrowing as he skimmed it.

"*...For the purpose of a fair vote, it is imperative to exclude lairds with bias, including, but not limited to; family members...*" His tone was incredulous as he read. "So, he's not only gotten the date moved, but he's also managed to stack the Assembly?"

Gwyn's knuckles went white as she clenched her fists, leaning over her twin's shoulder to read the rest.

"That's a bold move, severing our entire family from the vote," she said.

"Well, it's paid off," I muttered darkly.

Tavish and I were already excluded for obvious reasons, but preventing our families from voting affected me far more than it did him. I might have understood the stipulation, except that the vague wording could mean that even the distant cousins were out, which was solidly half of our allies.

"Actually," my mother said, a small smile creeping onto her face, "he might come to regret the way that was worded. They didn't say immediate family. The Andersons have many distant relations, by marriage or blood, several of whom are his allies."

My breath came just a bit easier.

"But their votes don't count for as many," I said, mostly for Galina's sake. At her questioning look, I explained. "The votes for the Assembly are based on several factors, including the number of people under your purview. It's one of the reasons Lithlinglau is so influential. We, along with the MacBays, have more votes than anyone aside from the King and Queen."

"Who are now excluded." Galina said the words neutrally, but the subtle pursing of her lips told me she understood how bad that could be for us.

"Still," Da' interjected, "it's a start, getting the Andersons' family removed as well."

We launched into a discussion on strategy after that, throwing out suggestions about which lairds we could potentially still sway, alliances we might forge or favors we could call in. Obviously, we knew my aunts and uncles would help where they could.

We weren't out of options, at least.

It wasn't until lunch was over and the others prepared to file out of the room that Galina looked directly at me.

She had remained relatively quiet through the meeting, though her attention hadn't wavered. I was sure she had some ideas of her own taking root.

"Any court can be won over," she offered in an undertone. "We can still fix this."

I arched an eyebrow at her casual use of the word *we*.

She sighed, not pretending to misunderstand. "We are still allies, are we not?"

Allies. I was beginning to hate that word, but I supposed it was better than nothing.

"That we are," I agreed.

Galina left then, followed by the others, but my mother lingered at the doorway, a rare bit of hesitation in her stance.

"Whatever happened," Mamá began.

"I know, Mamá," I cut her off. "Don't worry. We'll still put on a perfect show. Just. Not here."

She crossed the room to me, concern softening her features. Lifting a hand up, she pushed the wayward hair back from my forehead like she had when I was a child.

"I wasn't worried about that. But I hope you know I've always wanted more for you than the mere appearance of love." She shook her head sadly.

"I do know that," I assured her, taking her hand in mine. "But we both know how important this vote is."

"The fate of the kingdom does not rest on your shoulders alone, Darling. If you lose this vote, we will find another way to protect our people. We always do."

A bitter huff of air escaped my lips. "You love Lithlinglau."

After whatever had happened with Laird Anderson, something she rarely spoke of, she had rebuilt this place room by room and turned it into our home. The people were my primary concern, but it was adding insult to injury, knowing that the family of the man who had hurt her would try to take this place away.

"I love *you*," she corrected. "And I am tired of watching the people I love hurt by politics."

I didn't have the heart to tell her that I wasn't sure politics were the problem this time. At least, not between me and Galina.

AFTER OUR MEETING in the study, my mother went to find Galina to prepare for the afternoon's tea with the ladies. Gallagher was waiting for me in the hallway when I emerged.

"Spar?" he said. It was less of a question than a demand.

I started to tell him I had too much going on today, but he gave me one of his obnoxious *I know what's best for your health* looks, and I relented.

"Fine."

We walked to the private sparring ring in silence, then wordlessly removed our coats and picked up our practice swords.

The clanging of steel rang out for several tense minutes before Gal finally spoke.

"Anything in particular that you want to talk about, Cousin?" He raised an eyebrow.

Though he was being slightly smarmy about it, it was true that I had been unfair to him. I sighed.

It wasn't like I had really ever doubted his loyalty to me. This situation with Galina was between her and me. It really had nothing to do with him.

"Do you need me to spell out an apology? Write you a sonnet about it, perhaps?" I asked, parrying his sword away. "I could trace it out for you, right here in the sand."

I gestured to the sand lining the ring, and he huffed out a laugh.

"That won't be necessary," he assured me. "I take my apologies in the form of vodka. Don't think I didn't see that Rowan put extras in your trunks."

I nodded once, grateful to be done with the subject. "Consider it done."

"Notice she didn't put extras in my trunks. She always did like you best," he remarked a moment later. "That's why I'm not forcing an apology from you now."

So, it wasn't done. Lovely.

"For Rowan's sake?" I asked, furrowing my brow as I went on the offensive.

"No." He blocked my attack. "Because I know it was harder than you'll ever admit that she left so soon after Mac died."

My next blow landed a little harder, and Gallagher made his irritable face.

"And I can only assume that's why you're being so patently ridiculous about this."

He didn't need to expound further.

I blew out an exasperated breath. "I said I was sorry, Gal."

He dodged the next blow with ease, in a move that reminded me of how often he practiced with his sister and father in the ring. He had been holding back before, but he wasn't anymore.

"You didn't, actually, but that isn't the point." He lunged at me then, and I narrowly avoided the edge of his blade.

"What do you want me to say? I know you wouldn't..." I trailed off, not sure how to finish that sentence.

He wouldn't what? Court someone who was looking for a husband? Someone who was gorgeous and brilliant and even, very occasionally, fun? Someone who I had absolutely no claim over?

He raised his eyebrows, and I shook my head, going on the offensive again.

"I *am* sorry. I just can't seem to think straight where she's concerned." The admission cost me more than a little of my pride.

"I know that feeling," he said.

My next hit was deliberately to the side of his ribcage.

"Ow," he said, grabbing his side with his free hand. "Not about her."

"Then who?" I asked, needing to hear him give me a name, any other name, more than I was willing to admit.

"Maisey."

I wasn't sure why that caught me by surprise, but I hesitated long enough that he got the upper hand once again.

"The healer's apprentice? I didn't think that was serious."

"It's...getting there. Maybe."

I thought back to Galina's scoff when I suggested Gallagher, the way she had hedged.

I narrowed my gaze at him, feigning a thrust to the left before attacking on the right. "Is there any particular reason you told Galina before you told me?"

He shrugged, easily compensating for the feint. "I *like* Galina."

I leveled a look at him.

"Oh, fine," he relented. "I just didn't feel like dealing with the implications yet, and by the time we got back here, I was having too much fun watching you make an arse of yourself over this Galina thing." His expression sobered. "But for what it's worth, I didn't mean to cause any actual problems..."

"You didn't," I told him truthfully.

I thought back to our conversation last night and every loaded accusation that we had hurled at the other with expert precision.

No, the problems had been all ours.

"Besides, I'm not sure why I thought it mattered," I said darkly. "If it isn't you, it will just be someone else."

Gal gave me a disbelieving look. "And you're all right with that?"

I pictured Galina dancing with the other lairds, their hands on her waist, their warm breath whispering in her ear. The visceral part of me that wanted to set them on fire for having the nerve to look at her at all.

Then I remembered the ice in her eyes when she told me she was leaving to marry someone else, her words last night. The entire time I had known her, it had felt like she was a bird, perched on the edge of a rooftop, half a wrong move away from taking flight.

Yes, that's what I want.

Maybe she wasn't lying. Maybe I was only hearing what I wanted to.

"I have to be," I finally said.

THIRTY-FIVE

Galina

FIVE WEEKS.

The words repeated like a mantra in my head, a countdown I couldn't ignore. Five weeks until the vote, then another month until my charade with Davin was over.

Until I married someone else and saw him in passing at functions and pretended... What was it he had said?

Pretended we had never watched each other come undone.

Der'mo.

On the other hand, perhaps my uncle would come to cart me back to Socair. Then I could see Davin at the Socairan court while I stood silently at the side of a man who relished the sight of his hand imprinted on my skin.

Since I had stopped going to the rooftop for obvious reasons, I had plenty of time to think of the many potential scenarios every night.

During the day, I worked in a frenzy to win over the ladies of the court, and through them, their husbands. Only two ladies were directly on the Assembly themselves: Lady Fenella...and, to my eternal dismay, Lady Fiona.

When I wasn't hosting teas or making appearances on

Davin's arm at other estates for grand balls and parties, I was helping out in the village, dropping comments about Davin's initiatives—which were very real—and trying to show the people that I wasn't something entirely *other*.

It wasn't unthinkable that Davin could earn the vote. The people were sympathetic toward him, and slowly, me. The ladies loved him, and not just in the obvious way. He seemed to have more actual friends at court than he realized.

But I saw other things, too. The jealousy over everything Davin had and the power his family held. The resentment of giving one of their own royals to Socair, rather than retaliating.

A low murmur of conversation pulled me back to the present, and I graciously accepted another compliment on my ring. Today's tea was at Lady Fiona's estate, which was less than a day's ride away.

It was nice that she was so close.

And not only was she strikingly beautiful, but she was also the sole owner of her holdings. A single woman in possession of an estate and vast fortune.

No wonder she was the envy of the court.

She didn't need to marry. Her future was already secure.

Vaguely, I considered whether or not I was envious of that life. Perhaps I would have been before I met Davin, but what I wanted couldn't be obtained through the freedom or the wealth of owning my own estate.

The grating voice of the woman in question pulled me back into the present.

"Lady Galina, you've been so tight-lipped about the wedding, one might think you weren't planning to marry at all," Lady Fiona said, stirring a lump of sugar into her tea.

Gwyn stiffened next to me, her delicate china teacup frozen just in front of her lips at the thinly veiled jab, but I gave a polite laugh.

Fiona Shaw was one of the few ladies I had not yet been able to win over.

She didn't seem to have any particular attachment to Davin as much as she had an attachment to being the center of attention.

I played into that.

"There's hardly been time to plan around the social season, and of course, Davin would be devastated if we couldn't marry in his family home, but as soon as we have plans, you'll be the first to know," I said conspiratorially to the small group of ladies at my table.

Fiona's lips pursed like she was either satisfied or amused by my answer.

I decided to opt for the former, since the latter would have made it harder to refrain from accidentally spilling my hot tea in her lap.

"But surely you have some preferences," Lady Gracie spoke up next, not unkindly. "Even if you married at one of the other castles, things you would want."

Gracie MacBay was perfectly nice.

She was also, I had gathered, somewhat of a...former favorite of Davin's. In fact, I suspected that if I hadn't come along and he had needed to marry, he would have chosen her. Perhaps he still would, when our arrangement was over.

All of which made it difficult for me to want to talk to her...or look at her.

Especially when every time I did, I wondered if that was what he really wanted; petite and brunette and easy-going and a thousand things I would never be.

The table had fallen silent, though, waiting on my answer. Jocelyn's eyes were on me, and I didn't want to force her to intervene.

"There is one thing," I began. "In Socair, women wear dresses the color of their clan, or the clan they're marrying into. Since I would technically be staying in Ram,"—*if my uncle hasn't had a chance to unclan me yet*—"mine would be red."

A few of the ladies looked intrigued, others scandalized.

"Like your ring," Gracie commented.

I nodded.

"And Laird Davin?" Fiona chimed in again. "Is there anything he wants? He doesn't strike me as the type to stand back and let someone else plan his entire wedding."

Like everything she said, her words were a challenge, wrapped in a polite query. And though I bristled at it, she wasn't wrong. He would undoubtedly have opinions.

"Well, if I know Davin," I started out with a self-deprecating smile.

The ladies laughed like it was a joke, because of course they didn't realize how well I *didn't* know him.

Then again, perhaps I did, because suddenly it wasn't so very difficult to imagine the kind of wedding he might want. Loathe though I might be to consider it, I soon found myself describing everything I thought he would love.

"He wants the ceremony to happen at night, just to be difficult," I said, and a few giggles sounded in response. "But mostly because he wants to see the stars."

I could picture it then, his face at the end of a moonlit aisle. Candles floating on the lake as a tribute to Mac. The guests in black and white, a contrast to my crimson gown and the matching accents in his ensemble. The soft hum of a lyre playing in the background while we danced until sunrise.

I laid it all out for them, the wedding we would never actually have. By the time I was finished, a rare stab of tears pricked at the backs of my eyes.

When I finished speaking, I noticed Fiona's smugness had, if not vanished, at least abated. Gracie was smiling softly while Jocelyn looked almost...sad, before donning her usual court mask.

But Gwyn...Gwyn was looking at me like she had never seen me before.

The next few weeks were a blur of moving from estate to estate for one function after the next.

I spent the events doing what I had promised Davin I would—accidentally letting information slip, so he could track where it went. It was more exhausting than I could have imagined, especially with the threats that hung over all of our heads.

And that was before factoring in the show we had to put on.

It was so much worse now that I remembered how it felt to have his lips against mine. Now that I recalled with startling clarity the way it felt to believe, for a single fleeting moment, that we could have something we never would.

I forced myself to consider potential suitors. But every time one of them took my hand for a dance, I heard the echo of Davin's voice in my ear, telling me a doubtlessly exaggerated version of their flaws.

At least with the new lairds, there was no history, nothing holding us back from a...perfectly functional relationship. Perhaps I would actually study medicine.

Surely that would be worth putting up with Laird Foot Fetish.

Of course, every ball, just as I managed to convince myself how wildly content I would be in my new life, Davin would ask me to dance. It wasn't his fault, necessarily. It would have looked suspicious if he hadn't.

Still, I dreaded each spin and turn that would put me close enough to feel his body heat.

All in all, it was a relief when we finally headed back to Lithlinglau for a break.

Rather, it would have been, if there hadn't been a letter

waiting for me when I returned. My heart dropped into my stomach when I remembered that I still hadn't heard from Alexei.

He had plenty of faults, but he wasn't the type to stand by idly while someone else dealt with his problems.

When I turned the letter over, though, it was to find the familiar crimson ram's head seal. I wasn't sure if that was better or worse. Had Prince Oliver's letter been that persuasive?

Alexei's silence was almost more ominous than my uncle's threats.

Almost. But not quite.

Galina,

My patience is running thin, and so is Lord Alexei's. This will be your last warning. If you refuse to care about your honor or your clan or your family, then know that I have given Lord Alexei permission to see to your punishment in my stead if you continue to delay.

He didn't bother to sign it. He didn't need to.

My fingers trembled as I curled the letter back up. It was a small mercy that we had been gone when this letter came through, that it had been delivered directly to my rooms. At least Davin wouldn't see it.

Shame pooled in my gut.

Delicate is not the first word I would use to describe you.

If only he knew how the mere whisper of a threat of being

back in Alexei's furious clutches could turn me into a quivering mess.

Though, fear wasn't the only thing making the blood pound through my veins.

For all that I had seen my uncle's ruthlessness with the people around him, some part of me had wanted to believe that he wouldn't apply it to me. I had made excuse after excuse for him.

But he had known.

He had known how Alexei had treated me.

He must have, or he wouldn't have realized that the threat of my future husband's punishment was so much worse than the duke of my clan's.

My conversation with Jocelyn came rushing back.

You can't choose who you love, but you can choose who is deserving of your loyalty.

I couldn't ignore the part of myself that loved my uncle, the man I remembered from my childhood who had been generous and funny, at least when it was only our family.

Loyalty, though...that, I could finally acknowledge he had never deserved.

Perhaps that's why I felt no guilt at all when I threw his letter into the fire, watching the last vestiges of the obedient girl I had been go up in flames.

Not that it mattered how I felt.

If my uncle followed through on his threats, loyalty would not be a choice I was given.

I wasn't sure it had ever really been a choice. Not for me.

The Cost of an Alliance

GALINA

A Year Ago

Would anyone hear me if I screamed?

Would it make a difference if they did?

I glanced around at the room of clansmen surrounding me and decided that it wouldn't. So instead, I stood tall, forcing a smile while the churning sea of congratulations and well wishes threatened to drag me under.

Of course, they wished our union well.

Our betrothal meant a victory in this war. It meant more death and bloodshed and the beginning of a new era.

Or so my uncle claimed.

All I could do was hope that the care packages of salves I had sent to the soldiers I knew—from "my father," obviously—would be enough to save their lives. Some of them. Any of them.

My uncle stood proudly next to my betrothed, soaking up the praise and power that this new alliance promised. With one move, one marriage contract, he had secured his place at the right hand of our would-be king.

And now Clan Wolf was right behind him.

Alexei's possessive grip on my hand tightened, and I belatedly realized I had failed to respond to the latest well-wisher quickly enough.

I fought to keep from wincing, even though one more ounce of pressure could crack the delicate bones in my hand.

Did no one notice?

I supposed that was better than if they saw everything but said nothing.

At least there was still time before the wedding.

One of my uncle's terms was that we wait to finalize the betrothal until the war had officially begun. He made up a story about wanting us to marry in the Obsidian Palace once victory was assured, but I knew it was because he was hedging his bets, in case the war hadn't taken place and he wanted different prospects for me.

A glass of vodka was thrust into my hands as someone raised their cup to toast us. I stared down at the offending liquid for several long moments before Alexei's grip tightened again.

"Is something wrong, *Radnaya*?" he asked.

It was impossible not to contrast his patronizing tone with Davin's teasing one, to not remember the victorious smirk on Davin's lips when I admitted I didn't like the drink.

It was impossible not to wonder, all the time, if I had made a mistake in leaving before he could explain himself.

But then, what could he really have said? It wasn't like the maid had been lying. Theodore had confirmed that much.

It was just more wishful thinking on my part, imagining a life that was anything but the one I had now. Forcing a smile to my lips, I peeked up at Alexei through my lashes.

"No, My Lord," I said quietly. "I apologize."

He smiled, nodding approvingly when I raised the glass to my lips.

"To the handsome couple!" Sir Nils called.

"To victory!" Mikhail added.

To Alexei dying on the front lines, I thought hopefully.

Then, I drained the glass.

THIRTY-SIX

Davin

Present Day

My favorite thing about traveling was the roughly seventeen thousand letters I had to look through when I returned. Normally, a missive from Rowan would be a rare reprieve from the world around me, but that was yet another thing I had ruined.

Dear Former Favorite Cousin,

It would seem that this arrangement of yours is still something of a problem for Sir-ArseFace-Mikhail.

He has taken up camp here at the Obsidian Palace, which is…just delightful. Especially since he's even more pleasant than usual.

And he's determined to get his niece back.

THE LETTER CRUMPLED SLIGHTLY beneath my grip, and a muscle ticked in my jaw.

I informed him that such an action was a bit premature. Then I dutifully added that he should know all about doing things prematurely, and how much such moves were frowned upon, much to my husband's displeasure.

But, I digress.

He's decided to come to Lochlann himself to discuss the nuances of the treaty, and as much as I would very desperately like to, we apparently can't simply decline a diplomatic envoy on reasons of general dislike.

To me, the wording of the treaty seems fairly clear, considering I wrote a rather large portion of it....

I COULD PRACTICALLY SEE Rowan rolling her eyes as she penned that, and it made me miss her more.

...but I've written Mamá and Da', and they're concerned he may have a small leg to stand on. Or at the very least, that he may find one.

Sorry to add to your fun, but not that sorry to be rid of him for a while.

Love,

Row.

P.S. My husband says that he did not survive a war just to suffer your unrequited affections.

P.P.S. I have included another case of vodka with this letter. Not because I'm happy with you at the moment, but because I feel like you could all undoubtedly use a drink right about now.

I GRINNED AT THE POSTSCRIPTS, but it was fleeting.

Mikhail was coming here. Or at least, to Castle Chridhe.

Worse still, he may have a point. Did that mean Galina would need to find a husband sooner? Would she want that?

Well, it would take him a few weeks just to get to the castle, and no one could drag out negotiations quite like the Lochlannian Council. So we had time yet to think about that.

Tucking the letter into my pocket, I joined Galina and the rest of my family for brunch.

She greeted me politely as I sat down next to her, just as she always did. Though we spent nearly every waking moment together, there was nothing personal about it anymore—no clever remarks or inside jokes, just the never-ending divide between us. An endless chasm of politeness and neutrality.

I would have preferred her ire.

"I see you received mail today as well," my father said, interrupting my thoughts and gesturing toward the paper in my pocket.

I arched an eyebrow in question, and Da' held up an envelope with the royal crest on the seal. I groaned, pouring myself a cup of coffee.

"What did they say?"

Da' scanned it, his lips parting to respond, before Mamá cut him off.

"Mostly, your uncle argued with your father about the need to come down here himself." She rubbed her temples, exasperated as if she were tired of having this argument. "Between the vote and this situation with Mikhail, he's concerned."

"That's really the sum of it," Da' added. "Not to mention the Uprising, the attack on our villagers, and their suspicious lack of action since then. He and Charlie are walking a very fine line with very little information."

The lack of information was the most frustrating part, and perhaps the most alarming. Why were we hitting so many dead ends?

We still couldn't even definitively link the village attack to the Uprising, and we couldn't link either to Tavish. There wasn't so much as a whisper in the wind about The Viper.

"Aren't we all?" I took a deep breath, steeling myself to relay the contents of my own letter. "Rowan wrote something similar. She also mentioned that they were forced to approve an envoy for Mikhail to come here to argue the finer points in the treaty language."

If I hadn't been studying Galina for her reaction, would I have noticed the way the blood drained from her face?

Her mask shot into place, but her fingers moved to anxiously trace one of the charms on her bracelet. It was the wolf's head, presumably a gift from her former betrothed.

Charm bracelets were important in Socair. Every woman I had ever met there had worn one, though the maids' had been made of braided leather, rather than silver. So I understood why she didn't take the bracelet off, but Lithlinglau had its own jeweler, one she knew she had access to.

Why not have that charm removed?

This wasn't the first time I had seen her toying with it. Was it a source of comfort for her? Something to remember Lord Overbearing by?

When Galina saw me noticing, she froze, her back going ramrod straight, her hands returning to her lap.

"Apologies, my lo–aird," she murmured, uncharacteristically stumbling over the word.

Fortunately, or possibly by design, Gwyn chose that moment to say something ridiculous to Gal, creating a steady back and forth of banter so Galina didn't have to feel quite so scrutinized.

"For what?" I asked neutrally, keeping my voice just as low as hers had been.

Was she apologizing for thinking about him?

"Fidgeting." Her cheeks flushed, and she raised her cup of coffee to her lips to try to hide her expression.

I blinked several times, putting together her excuse with the reason she had nearly misspoken.

My Lord, she had been about to say.

Like it was a reflex for her. Like she was used to being chastised like a child for something as innocuous as displaying her anxiety on a rare occasion, in relative privacy.

Mikhail was an arse, to be sure, but she didn't call him *My Lord*. She called him Uncle.

An overwhelming surge of anger rushed through me, and I fought to keep it from my expression.

"You're fine," I told her, trying and failing not to picture Alexei's head on a pike for ever making her question herself.

"It's just...not proper," she explained quietly, smoothing out some imagined wrinkle on her skirts.

Strictly speaking, she was right. As a child, Mamá had often covered my hand with hers to still my movements. But it certainly wasn't an apology-worthy offense.

"It's just us here," I reminded her gently. "And if propriety was that important to us, Gwyn would have been ousted from the family years ago."

I said the last part a little louder, and my cousin didn't miss a beat.

"To be fair, if propriety was that important, none of us would have been born to begin with," Gwyn added with a shrug, before taking a large bite of pastry.

"Gwyndolyn!" Mamá cut in, exasperation lacing her tone, while my father and Gal laughed.

Galina had a ghost of a smile on her lips, but she still looked far away.

"Lina," I said softly, pulling her attention back to me. "We haven't come close to exhausting our options, and we still have time. No one is going to take you from here...unless you want to go back."

I wasn't ready to think about what those options were.

Would she pick from among the lairds whose only redeeming qualities were that they allowed her to fidget and allowed her to study medicine? The thought twisted in my gut, but not as much as the one that followed on its heels.

Did she want to go back, even in spite of everything?

She clenched her jaw, determination replacing whatever dark emotion had taken hold of her.

"I won't ever want to go back," she said definitively, her steely blue eyes meeting mine.

I held her unwavering gaze for a solid minute before responding.

"Then that's settled." I said the words casually, like I believed them.

I wished I could.

But after Rowan's letter and the letter from Chridhe and Galina's wolf charm and our stupid last stars-damned night on the roof, nothing felt even remotely close to being settled.

THIRTY-SEVEN

Galina

TICK, tick, tick.

I had grown to love nearly everything about this room. The vast space that had been overwhelming at first was now open and peaceful. But I still hated the tall, gilded clock that sat innocuously in the corner.

Every night, it marked the endless hours of tossing and turning in between nightmares. Since I had stopped going to the rooftop, even the few hours of sleep I had been eking out before were steadily slipping from my grasp.

The bags under my eyes were getting harder to hide by the day, and tonight was worse than usual.

Mikhail was coming here.

My uncle was leaving his kingdom for the second time in his entire life with the single, solitary purpose of bringing me back to Socair. To Alexei.

Every time I closed my eyes, that's what I saw.

Alexei looming over me, his breath on my face, his triumph at finally owning me in every possible way. Mikhail raising his glass in a toast while Alexei enforced his right to a public consummation...

My eyelids flew open.

An empty cup of chamomile and valerian tea sat at my nightstand, as useless now as when it was full. Even the steady drizzle of rain on my windowpanes wasn't enough to calm the thunderous beat of my heart.

Finally, I couldn't take it anymore.

I threw a velvet dressing gown over my nightclothes and slid my feet into a pair of slippers. I wasn't even sure what I was doing until I found myself out on the balcony.

Of course, there were no stars tonight. Still, I inhaled the earthy smell of the damp stone, letting the cold, stinging pellets of rain wash over my skin.

It wasn't enough.

So up I climbed to the rooftop.

Of course I did. Hadn't this been my destination all along? It was empty, which wasn't really a surprise, considering we hadn't been up here since that night.

I shouldn't be here now, either. Shouldn't be wishing he was here, too.

I should go back down to my rooms, dry off, and force myself to get some sleep.

That was the only rational thing to do.

But I knew what awaited me in my rooms. Thoughts of Alexei and Uncle Mikhail and white-hot brands searing into my flesh. More importantly, I knew what didn't await me there. Or rather, who.

Before I could talk myself out of it, I was descending a different set of stairs on the other side of the roof, doubting my sanity with every muffled footfall.

What in the storms am I doing?

What if he's sleeping?

Worse, what if he has company?

That last thought might have stopped me in my tracks if I weren't already on the bottom stair. As it was, I looked up to see Davin, seated in a chair by his fireplace, very much alone.

I was rooted to the ground like one of the statues in the

courtyard, remembering the words he had half-hurled at me on the rooftop.

Do you honestly think that I would do that to you?

Honestly?

I hadn't thought he was capable of being chaste, let alone that he would want to. According to him, though, this wouldn't have been the first time he had forsaken company for...my sake?

I did not sleep with Aino—or anyone, for that matter —after that night you saved me on the rooftop.

Der'mo. Why was everything so confusing where he was concerned?

Even now, he was...unexpected.

There was a half-empty glass of amber liquid in his hand and a book balanced on the arm of the chair. I watched, somewhat mesmerized, as he dipped his quill in an ink pot on the table to his left before scrawling something in the margins of his page.

It was jarring, realizing I had never before seen him hold a quill, would never have guessed he wrote with his left hand. *What else didn't I know about him?*

Why did it feel so unspeakably wrong that I was running out of time to learn?

Only when he paused to run his fingers through his hair was I pulled back into the moment. The armor I usually kept in place lay in pieces on the ground around me, my emotions running wild in the chaos of my fatigue.

I knew it was a tremendously terrible idea to raise my hand and tap on the glass balcony door, rather than turn to walk away while I still could.

Davin always had brought out the reckless side of me.

It only took two taps for him to snap his head toward the window, sitting forward so rapidly he nearly spilled his drink.

Then he was at the door in a matter of seconds, pulling it open and searching my form with an inscrutable expression, almost like he was checking me for injuries. Perhaps he was only taken aback by the sight of my damp locks falling limply from my braid and my overall disheveled appearance.

Either way, he recovered himself quickly.

He stepped back, casually allowing me entrance like it was commonplace for me to show up at his rooms in the middle of the night. Then again, considering our history, perhaps that was truer than I wanted it to be.

He left the room, disappearing behind a door before returning with a towel. I took it and began to wipe the rain from my face as he spoke again.

"I'm afraid I don't have any wine in here," he said, turning to a liquor shelf. "But I do have several bottles of excellent whiskey."

"I wouldn't say no," I replied.

He surveyed them for a moment before pulling down a tall bottle with squared edges and pouring me a glass. My heart was still pounding, so I took it from him gratefully, prepared to hide my distaste as I took a tentative sip.

He watched me, the corner of his mouth tilting up when I widened my eyes in surprise. It was smoother than I expected, sweeter and richer, but with an almost crisp finish.

"This is...good," I told him truthfully.

At that, he smiled outright. "I thought you might think so. It was aged in a white wine barrel."

He gestured for me to sit down, and I did.

Several beats of silence passed before Davin casually re-opened his book, dipping his quill in the inkpot once more. It didn't feel like he was ignoring me. More like he was giving me space to speak if I wanted to, without the obligation if I didn't.

Since I had no idea what to say, I appreciated the lack of scrutiny. I took the time to gather myself, willing my heartbeat to slow in my chest while I sipped absently at my drink. I wasn't sure if it was the whiskey that had such a calming effect, or merely Davin's presence.

I was hoping the former, but when the minutes ticked by and I realized the only thing missing was Davin's low, bantering tone, I knew I was probably lying to myself.

Finally, I broke the silence.

"What were you working on?" I asked.

He finished the note he was making, dipping the quill in the ink once again before responding. "Looking into laws that might be pertinent to the vote."

"You write with your left hand," I blurted out.

What was wrong with me?

Davin's gaze flitted to the glass in my hand, which was, apparently, nearly empty. Well, then. Vaguely, I recalled that I had been too anxious to eat dinner, and it had been a couple of months since I had any liquor, since no one here seemed particularly offended by my preference for wine and champagne.

"I do," he confirmed.

His tone was suspiciously neutral, like perhaps he was fighting back a laugh. I pictured his scabbard, on the left side for a right-handed pull, and the way he had uncorked the whiskey with his right hand.

"Do you do anything else with your left hand?" I asked curiously.

He made a choking sound, and I played back the words in my head.

I hastened to explain. "I meant...because you wear your sword on your left hip, and—"

"Obviously, that's what you meant," he said, mirth sparkling in his cobalt eyes. "What else would you mean?"

"I hate you," I told him flatly.

"I know." His voice was lower then, more serious.

Silence fell again, more charged this time, punctuated by the gentle scratching of his quill against the pages.

"Aren't you going to ask why I'm here?"

The feather on his pen stopped mid-swoop, and he raised an eyebrow. "Would you give me a real answer if I did?"

No. Maybe.

"You could at least give me the opportunity to artfully hedge the question," I said with a half shrug that felt far less graceful than usual.

He shot me his signature stupid perfect gorgeous smirk. "By all means, then."

I gave him honesty instead. "I'm tired of doing that."

"I know," he said again, the smirk falling from his features. "Not much longer now. Only a handful of weeks."

My stomach sank. It was an effort to breathe.

"That isn't better," I said, my voice sounding hollow, even to my own ears.

Davin took a long sip of his whiskey, setting his quill aside and closing his book.

"I know," he said for the third time.

It took finishing the rest of my whiskey to dredge up the courage to ask him what I really wanted to know.

"Did you mean it, when you said you weren't with anyone after that day on the roof?"

His eyes met mine, something like a warning in them.

"Not while I was in Socair."

An unreasonable sting of jealousy flared in my gut, even though it was the height of hypocrisy.

"But when you got back?" I pushed.

He clenched his jaw, the firelight dancing in his eyes as he visibly braced himself to respond. "When I got back, I thought I would never see you again, and I looked for any distraction I could find."

My mind was fuzzier than it should have been, processing his words slowly.

"Did it work?" The words came out a whisper.

"No," he said flatly. "It didn't."

"It didn't work for me, either," I admitted.

His eyebrows climbed into his hairline, either at the admission that I had missed him, or the more obvious one, that I hadn't been chaste after our night together. I had needed to know if it would be the same, if I was building up what Davin and I had shared, because I had never experienced it with anyone else.

Getting the answer to that question had almost been worse.

Of course, it wasn't the same. Nothing was the same.

"Alexei?" Davin asked the question like he already knew the answer.

The sound of my former fiancé's name, coupled with the idea of giving him that kind of control over my body, sent a shudder through me.

For a moment, my whiskey-addled mind considered telling Davin the truth, but I didn't want Alexei invading this space, this part of my life, any of it. At least, not yet. Not tonight. Not like this.

So, I swallowed the words and answered his question instead.

"No." I shook my head for emphasis. "It was before our betrothal was finalized. Just a lord in Ram."

I was unreasonably satisfied to see the same jealousy I had felt sparking behind Davin's eyes now.

"Not a guard?" His tone was equal parts teasing and... almost possessive.

"No. I've never slept with any guards, as it turns out," I said pointedly.

After all, Davin had never been a real guard.

He gave an acknowledging arch of his brows, looking down at his whiskey glass for several moments before he spoke again.

"Would it have changed anything?" he asked. "If you had known?"

I thought about that—really thought about it. Hell, I had

considered it often in the endless nights this past week alone. I still wasn't sure. With the state of our kingdoms, I would have either had to betray my family to be with Davin...or worse, let my uncle use him as leverage.

And would it really have mattered, knowing the truth, if he hadn't wanted more?

Missing someone when they were gone wasn't the same as wanting to marry them, and Davin had never actually said that he did want to marry me. He had never said anything more than vague half-comments.

Neither of us had.

"I suppose we'll never know," I finally said.

He nodded like that was the answer he was expecting. We were quiet then, accompanied only by the sounds of the crackling fire and the rain pattering on the window outside.

Eventually, between the warmth of the whiskey and the flames and the comforting scent of parchment and cloves, I finally fell asleep.

THIRTY-EIGHT

MY EYES FLEW open at a familiar rap on the door.

It took me a moment to orient myself, to register the amount of light streaming in through the window...and the body melded against my chest.

I had started my night on the chaise lounge, but after her fourth or fifth round of nightmares, I wound up on the bed with her. On *my* side of the bed, hoping my nearness might calm some of whatever had her sleeping so fitfully.

But apparently, she had seen fit to wrap herself around me at some point in the night.

After that, she hadn't stirred again.

There was another knock at the servants' door before it cracked open, Blaine poking an apologetic head around the corner.

Galina shifted, blearily opening her eyes.

"What time is it?" she asked, her voice raspy from disuse.

"Nearly noon, My Lady," Blaine answered from the other side of the room.

She startled at the sound of his voice, clutching the covers. Pink bloomed on her chest, winding all the way up to the tips of her ears.

"Der'mo," she whispered, darting a glance toward the balcony.

It was raining even harder than it had been last night.

"You might as well use the front door." I answered her unspoken question. "While Blaine is the epitome of discretion—"

"Thank you, My Laird," he interjected as he poured two cups of coffee.

"It's very unlikely at this point that the castle doesn't know you slept here last night."

Lina looked to Blaine for confirmation, and he offered her an apologetic expression.

She shook her head then, climbing out from the covers. The bed was immediately colder without her in it. I told myself that was the only reason I wanted to pull her back down to me.

Blaine crossed the room with our cups of coffee, holding them out for each of us as I reluctantly climbed out from my side of the bed.

She thanked him, the blush in her cheeks not fading as she avoided meeting his eyes.

I followed her to the door and then out into the hall to her rooms, sipping on my coffee the entire way. The guards on duty that morning arched curious eyebrows in our direction. It wasn't until Hamish pointedly cleared his throat that they went back to focusing on anything else.

Unfortunately for Galina, there was no way word wouldn't spread about our sleepover now, if it hadn't already.

A part of me registered that it would only work in our favor, helping us sell this love story we were so desperately perpetuating. Another part of me was disgusted for thinking so practically. It tainted the moment somehow.

Then again, I wasn't sure if there had even been a moment.

"Thank you," Galina said quietly, pulling me from my thoughts.

She had turned to face me in the doorway, her body only a few inches from mine. "For last night."

"Any time," I said, offering her a small smirk.

She returned it, easing backward into her room before closing the door behind her.

It took me several long moments before I finally did the same.

I HAD to practically sprint from one appointment to the next for the rest of the day. Sleeping in had thrown off my schedule just enough that everything turned into a mad dash.

My father had made my excuses for being late to the morning hunt with the local lairds, but he didn't seem concerned about my tardiness.

At least I finally garnered something useful at the hunt. For all Laird Campbell was pretending to be on our side, the information Galina had leaked to his wife was the first to make its way to Tavish.

But Laird Campbell had no discernible ties to the rebellion, either. Certainly not the Uprising. Not that I could link anyone definitively to the Uprising.

That was the problem. They were smoke and mirrors, a rebellion that was everywhere and nowhere with a leader that may or may not have been made up, for all the information I could find.

Even the barman who had warned me in Hagail had mysteriously disappeared, though rumors reported corpses with black veins being burned in the tunnels.

It made me wonder, briefly, if Tavish actually had ties to the rebels.

Had I misread him? Had he only been taunting me? Was I letting my reluctance to part with Lithlinglau and my general dislike of the Andersons cloud my judgment?

I pictured his face when he had come bursting into the healer's house. There had to be something there.

And if he wasn't spearheading this damned rebellion, who was?

Of course, in the spirit of information traveling, my father was already well aware that I had spent my night in Galina's company, a fact he looked far too giddy about.

I didn't have the heart to explain to him that... Well, I wasn't sure what there was to explain. Nothing had happened. It felt like something had shifted, but I wasn't sure what.

Certainly, none of our issues had magically disappeared.

I reminded myself of that fact no less than twenty times over the course of the hunt, when my mind drifted back to the way she fit so perfectly against me. How soundly I had been sleeping surrounded by her lavender and rosemary scent.

And again over scotch and cigars with the lairds before dinner.

I was grateful when the lairds finally filed out of the room, heading down to meet their wives for dinner. The forced grin fell from my face, and I massaged my cheeks, prepping to play these games all over again just as soon as we joined them downstairs.

Before I could leave, though, my father closed the door to the smoke room and poured us both another finger of whiskey.

"So..." He drew the word out. "About Galina."

My eyebrows darted up to my hairline as I took a long inhale from my cigar, the taste of cinnamon and wood smoke filling my lungs before I blew it out into a ring in front of me.

"Da', if you think now is a good time for *the talk*, I hate to inform you that you're several years late. But if you would like any pointers, as long as we pretend we're not discussing Mamá, I'd be happy to—"

"No, you daft child." He narrowed his eyes at me, but a grin tugged at the corner of his mouth. "I think by now we are both well aware of the experience you have in that particular area. The entire kingdom is fairly aware, in fact."

I shrugged, wondering where in the hell he was headed with this.

"I was more wondering how things—outside of that area—are going," he said, taking a sip from his glass.

I chuckled, the sound coming out more bitter than I meant it to. "I can assure you, Father, that they're not going. Not in any area."

He shook his head and took a long puff of his cigar, holding the smoke in his lungs before letting it billow out between us.

"Have you talked to her about it?" he pressed.

I was about to give him a glib answer, but his pointed glare told me that he was being serious. Sighing, I set down my cigar and leaned back in my chair.

"We have talked, yes," I acknowledged. "And she made her feelings on the matter very clear."

"She said she didn't want to marry you?" He didn't bother to hide his surprise.

I considered that for a moment. Had she said that?

Back in Socair, yes. But since then, she had mostly said... that she didn't want something temporary.

"Not exactly, no," I finally admitted.

My father narrowed his eyes. "Did you offer marriage?"

Our conversations on the rooftop came back to me. The accusations we had both hurled around, the way we had seemed to talk in circles about everything except what actually needed to be said.

Had I ever actually told her that what I wanted wasn't

temporary? No, because I hadn't been sure of that. Wanting something more with Galina was dangerous, considering our past.

I hedged, brushing nonexistent lint off of my pants. "Again, not exactly."

Da' nodded, as if this made complete sense to him. "Ah. Why not?"

"Things are complicated with Galina," I explained. "She's always on the verge of running away, and I never can seem to feel settled. She said...that we didn't choose each other when it counted, and she wasn't wrong."

I stared at the floor, at the flames in the hearth, at the clock on the wall. At anything other than back at my father's assessing gaze.

"And you think that's it?" He raised his eyebrows. "That you only get one chance at that, and all the choices you make after that don't matter?"

"I think that if we were right for each other, we would have chosen one another."

"Of course. Like your mother and I did." He said the words so matter-of-factly that it took me a moment to realize he was being sarcastic. "We're all wrong for each other, naturally. Can't stand the woman most of the time."

I rolled my eyes, smiling in spite of myself.

"Let me ask you something, Dav," he said in a more serious tone. "Do you think that after all this time, she's the same person now that she was then? That you are?"

"No," I allowed. "But it doesn't change what happened between us."

"You're right, it doesn't. And it probably won't be as easy for the two of you as it would be if you were starting with someone new." He paused, letting that sink in. "But as your Grandfather Rowan always said, a man doesn't deserve anything he isn't willing to fight for. It's not too late to choose each other now, if you're willing to fight a little harder for that choice."

I met his gaze then, the twin to my own. I wanted to believe him. I really did, but I had been burned by hope before. Obliterated by it, really.

"And if she leaves again?" My voice was quieter than I wanted it to be.

"You have to decide if she's worth the risk." He clasped me on the shoulder. "But for whatever it's worth, she's had plenty of chances to run away, and she's still here."

I pictured Galina up to her elbows in blood and medicine after the village attack. Her thumb brushing mine at the executions. Her steady features when she reminded me that we were allies.

Her rain-soaked silhouette on my balcony because she had come to see me. On a bad day, when she needed someone, the woman who could hardly force herself to ask for help had sought out comfort from my presence.

He was right. She had stayed in every way it counted.

Now, it was up to me to decide what I was willing to fight for.

THIRTY-NINE

Galina

I COULDN'T FIND it in myself to be embarrassed about last night.

The few hours of sleep I had eked out in Davin's arms had helped to clear my head. So for the first time in what felt like ages, the world and the situation with my uncle didn't feel quite as overwhelming.

Even if things with Davin were more confusing than ever.

I hardly had time to contemplate the nuances of our conversation, or the way I had woken up entangled in his arms, or even what it meant that I had sought him out again in the first place.

My day had started out impossibly late and been filled to the brim with activities. Tomorrow was finally the autumn festival, so there was even more to be done than usual.

Jocelyn walked me through the village preparations, *so I would know for next time,* and I looked at her askance.

"It will be important to know, no matter what estate you wind up with, Darling," she assured me, continuing with her explanations.

She had carefully avoided the subject of my betrothal to her son all afternoon, though something in her countenance made me wonder if she'd heard the rumors about last night's sleeping arrangements.

Still, I was relieved when she didn't ask me any questions about it, or make any comments regarding the nature of my relationship with her son.

Our work carried us through to dinner, and I only just had enough time to freshen up and change before meeting Davin to greet the incoming guests.

Several of the noble families were staying at the castle again for the festival. Including, rather unfortunately, Laird Tavish.

His insistence on staying at the estate had been yet another way for him to throw down the gauntlet. Public opinion of him was waning, but he was determined to be seen as Laird of Lithlinglau.

Though his constant attempts at undermining Davin were frustrating, they weren't necessarily surprising. Per usual, he planted his seeds, sowing rumors among the courtiers while Davin and I systematically worked to uproot them.

What did surprise me, though, was when Gwyn spoke up after dinner when Davin made to escort me back to my rooms.

"I'll take her."

Davin's eyes widened in suspicion, and he arched an eyebrow. "Gwynnie?"

"I'm headed to my rooms anyway," she insisted. "Besides, you have to go make nice with the lairds." She gestured toward the men who were once again headed toward the smoking room.

"It's fine," I assured him, though I wasn't sure that was true.

The duchess wasn't exactly my biggest fan, so I had trouble believing that her reasons were as transparent as she was trying to make them appear.

"Perfect," she said with a wide, false smile, pulling me from the dining room out into the hall.

Gal let out a low whistle as he watched us leave, shooting me an apologetic glance as we rounded the corner out of view.

Neither of us spoke until we got to my rooms.

"Best check for assailants," she announced, ducking into my closet.

I resisted the urge to roll my eyes but didn't argue. She wasn't exactly swimming in patience, so I knew she would get to her real reason for being here soon enough.

"You should wear this tomorrow," she said, pulling out a deep purple gown and laying it on the bed. "It feels like autumn and will give off subconscious vibes of royalty."

Royalty vibes or not, it was stunning, with golden brocaded stitching along the hem and corset, and long, trailing sleeves.

Ducking back into my closet, she returned with a simple necklace, one from home. A golden strand with an amethyst dripping from the center, and earrings to match.

Once she was finished choosing my ensemble for the festival, she made her way around the rest of the room, keeping up a string of advice about the festival tomorrow, expectations, things to look out for, things even Jocelyn hadn't thought to mention.

"That's...helpful of you," I commented, raking my fingers over the soft fabric of the gown.

"Why wouldn't I be?" she asked, pulling my attention back to her.

I scoffed, giving her a disbelieving look, and she shrugged a slim shoulder in false innocence.

Apparently, I would need to go a blunter route. "Well, I was under the impression that you didn't particularly like me."

"You weren't wrong," she said simply.

I sighed, stepping away from the gown and taking a seat by the fire. "Then my question stands."

There was a beat of silence that stretched out between us before she spoke again.

"Aren't you going to ask why?" she inquired.

"I can guess why," I said. "You think I'm useless, that I came to Lochlann and put your family in danger when I couldn't even help defend myself."

She arched a sculpted brow, toned arms crossed over her chest.

"You think I don't like you because you can't fight?" She almost sounded amused.

"I think you don't respect me because I can't fight," I clarified.

Gwyn huffed out a humorless laugh. "Well, I'm sure Auntie Jocelyn would be fascinated to hear it."

I tilted my head, taking that in. That was...fair. In the short time I had known Jocelyn, I hadn't seen her so much as pick up a butcher knife, let alone a sword, and Gwyn had no problem respecting her.

"Then why?" I asked, genuinely curious now.

She surveyed me carefully, leaning against the wall in that casually intimidating way of hers.

"You mean after it was clear you had a convoluted history with my cousin, then you promptly cozied up to my brother?"

Oh.

A flush rose to my cheeks. I had never considered my actions from that angle.

"Then what changed your mind?" I asked.

She shrugged. "We both know you *don't* want Gallagher. We both know you *do* want Davin. What only you know is why you insist on taking him out of the running when it's so painfully obvious that you would choose him."

My lips parted in equal parts surprise and irritation.

"I didn't take Davin out of the running," I countered. "He took himself out. He doesn't want to get married, and according to him, he never has."

She let out a long breath, shaking her head ever so subtly.

"That's not strictly true. In fact, he was already calming down a bit before...Mac died." Pain flashed across her features before she covered it.

"Well, he hasn't since I have known him," I finally responded, wondering just how different Davin had been before the death of his friend.

"Of course not." She narrowed her eyes, looking at me like I was some obtuse creature. "Mac was like a brother to him. Growing up, I had Gallagher, and Avani had Rowan, and Davin had Mac. Then he lost Mac, and he grew closer to Rowan. Then he lost her, too, in a way. Can you honestly blame him for not wanting to be close to someone again?"

No, I couldn't. But... "Whether I blame him isn't the issue."

She blinked slowly, her fingers coming up to massage her temples.

"Stars, I get it now, why the two of you run in circles. Look, tomorrow is the autumn festival. It was their favorite—his, Mac's, and Rowan's. If you want to be stubborn, fine, but do me a favor and just don't spend the entirety of the day talking about all your other prospects."

I nodded solemnly, ignoring the way my stomach clenched at the idea of all my stupid *other prospects* I had been trying so hard to ignore.

She moved toward the door but turned back at the last minute.

"Listen, I know what it is to look ahead at the rest of your life and realize you won't be able to spend it with the man you love, and I wouldn't wish that on anyone. Not even you," she added with a ghost of a smirk. "But that doesn't have to be your life."

Then she was gone, leaving me alone in my room with the crushing weight of her final words. I paced my floor for hours, avoiding getting into bed where I knew a sleepless night awaited me.

Avoiding the niggling part of my brain telling me I knew exactly how to come by decent sleep. All I had to do was follow the thread that endlessly tugged at me.

It wasn't nearly long enough before I lost the battle with my self-control, but I didn't get a chance to act on those feelings. Instead, a tapping sounded from my balcony doors.

I hadn't needed to seek Davin out after all.

This time, Davin had come to me.

FORTY
Davin

My first stop had been the roof. When Galina wasn't there, I couldn't resist the urge to descend the stairs to her balcony, just as she had mine the night before.

There was a part of me that wanted to make sure Gwyn hadn't—well, hadn't done anything *Gwyn-like*. But there was another part of me that just needed to see Galina again.

My conversation with my father had left me with the barest edge of possibility, and I needed to know if it was all in my head.

In spite of our time together last night, I wasn't entirely sure Galina wouldn't shut the door in my face.

My gamble paid off, though.

As soon as her gaze snapped up to meet mine through the glass-paned doors, her shoulders eased, an uncertain expression crossing her perfect features. She had changed for bed already. Her hair was pulled into a loose golden braid that hung over one shoulder, her slim figure accentuated by a simple silk nightgown that left perilously little to the imagination.

Suddenly, I was finding it hard to breathe.

"I just came to see if my cousin had given into her more murderous urges," I said when she opened the door.

That was markedly better than saying, *I just came because I wasn't sure I could sleep unless I talked to you tonight.*

"Surprisingly not," Galina responded drily, stepping back to allow me entry.

"So I see. Dare I ask what she did want?" I set the bottle of whiskey I had brought down on a side table before scanning her room.

She scoffed, some inside joke playing out in her mind before she spoke again. "To help me pick out a dress for the festival, apparently."

That seemed...unlikely. I wondered what Gwyn had actually wanted, but Galina was a vault when she wanted to be. There was no use asking her about it if she didn't want to tell me.

My gaze finally landed on what I was looking for. I crossed the room to her bed, pulling her velvet dressing gown off one of the posts and holding it out to her.

"Here. Put this on," I said, trying and failing not to notice the way the silk hugged her curves, or the way it dipped low on her chest, revealing perfect olive skin.

"Really, Davin?" she sounded amused.

"Yes, really, Galina." I shook the proffered clothing until she took it, a wry smile on her lips.

While she was throwing the robe over her shoulders, I took the liberty of pouring us each a glass of whiskey.

"Better?" she asked when I turned around.

She was now a shapeless velvet lump.

"Much," I assured her.

Once we both had our whiskey and were seated by the fire, her eyes flitted over to mine. I noticed she was taking much smaller sips tonight, which made sense. She rarely made the same mistake twice.

I thought back to what my father had said. Had she changed?

I certainly had.

Looking at her now, I could see traces of the woman who stood on the rooftop in Elk with me all those months ago, arguing about loyalty and choices.

But I also saw the woman who had risked her life to make her own choice, to walk away from her uncle and her betrothed. She had fought for her right to walk alone into the tunnels and had done so with her shoulders back and her head high.

And she was still here.

Despite our estrangement for weeks, she hadn't left. She hadn't taken the out that I had given her to secure a betrothal sooner with someone else. She had stood by my side, even on the days she hated me, helping with this mess I was in. That my people were in.

No. She wasn't the same.

And I thought perhaps I hadn't given her the choices I should have, then or now.

I sure as hell hadn't given her the honesty I should have. That, at least, I could rectify.

"You were right, you know," I finally said, breaking the silence that had fallen over the room.

"Obviously," she joked, curling her feet up underneath her on the chair. "But do go on..."

"About why I didn't tell you the truth," I said, settling into the chair.

The smile faded from her lips, but she didn't look away.

"I *was* worried about Rowan," I continued. "And terrified of doing anything that might hurt her. By the time I realized I could trust you, though, I wasn't ready for what telling you might mean."

There was a brief, stilted pause before she responded.

"Were you that afraid that I would want to marry you?"

Her tone was edged with disbelief, and worse, hurt. "Did you think that if I knew, I would just throw myself at your feet and never let go?"

It was an effort to keep from laughing. That had been the furthest concern from my mind.

"Of course not," I assured her. "Half the time, I wasn't even sure you liked me. You truly do have a resting Socairan face."

A half-hearted smile tempted the corner of her lips.

"Then what was the problem?" She sounded more curious than angry this time, so I took that as a positive sign.

"The problem wasn't what you wanted," I admitted. "It was what I wanted. I've never had to try with anyone before, and there I was, waiting hours on a freezing rooftop just to talk to you. You were the only person I had been able to stand the silence with since Mac died."

I paused, shaking my head. "It was...a lot, especially when the people I was closest to had a history of disappearing."

When I looked back up, she was watching the fire, taking a long sip of her whiskey.

Did she hear what I didn't say? That she had, in fact, disappeared. That she had walked away without so much as a backward glance over something she never let me explain to her.

She turned her gaze back to me, visibly steeling herself. "So you were never going to tell me?"

I suppressed a wince, barely. It was an effort, forcing myself to tell her the truth when I knew it would only hurt us both.

"I was coming to tell you that morning." I delivered the words as evenly as I could, but she still squeezed her eyes shut, no doubt realizing what I already had.

That all it took was half an hour and one spiteful woman for everything to go to hell.

If I had told her sooner or she had bothered to hear me

out before leaving, we would have avoided all of this, but that was a game of blame that led nowhere.

She opened her eyes and set her glass down on the table next to her, but still said nothing.

I cleared my throat. "You told me not to apologize for something I would do again, and I need you to understand that I wouldn't. If I had it to do over, I would handle everything differently, and I never would have let you find out that way."

The seconds ticked by while she evaluated my face for veracity.

"And if you had told me?" she finally breathed. "What then?"

This was the part I had been bracing myself for, what I had been working myself up to say. So why did my mouth suddenly feel so dry?

A man doesn't deserve anything he isn't willing to fight for.

I took a deep, fortifying sip of my drink.

"Then I would have asked you to come back to Lochlann with me."

Her lips parted, her eyes widening in a rare display of vulnerability. "Oh."

I would have almost smiled at the sight of her speechless, except that she was giving me exactly no indication how she felt about that.

But then, hadn't she already?

You weren't under obligation to want something just because I did.

The question wasn't really what either of us had wanted then. It was what we wanted now. So I met her eyes solidly, finishing what I had to say.

"To be clear, I still want that," I told her plainly.

She blinked several times. "What?"

I thought about everything I could tell her, but ultimately, I settled on the simplest version.

"I want you to stay. Not as my fake betrothed, but as my real one. I don't want to play any more games with you. At least," I added with a smirk, "not unless they're the fun kind."

She huffed out what might have been a laugh, or might have been a slightly hysterical sob.

"I'm sorry," she finally said. "I just need a little bit of time, to process all of that, if that's all right?"

She said it like she thought it wouldn't be, because she wasn't used to being given a say at all, let alone time to make that decision. I wouldn't pretend it was exactly what I wanted to hear, but it was more than fair.

"Yes, Lina," I said firmly. "There's no rush, and there's no obligation. Take all the time you need. I'll just...head back to my rooms."

Though leaving her was the absolute last thing I wanted to do, I stood to go, turning toward the door.

"No," she said quickly.

I paused, spinning back to face her.

"I mean, we have a big day tomorrow, and we could both use some good sleep." She was avoiding my gaze, and I couldn't help the relieved smile that spread across my lips.

"Lina, Love, do you want me to sleep here?" My tone was teasing.

She heaved a small, resigned sigh, the barest hint of a smile on her lips. "I don't *not* want you to sleep here."

My grin widened. "Well, with that overwhelming endorsement, I wouldn't dream of being anywhere else."

And I meant it.

If a little time was all it took to finally start building something real with her, that was a price I was more than willing to pay.

FORTY-ONE

Galina

THIS TIME, I wasn't surprised to find myself wrapped around Davin when I woke up.

I was, however, unwilling to let kindly old Anna come in on us this way. When her second knock sounded at the door, I all but shoved him out of the bed.

"One moment, Anna," I called. "Go out the balcony," I hissed, practically throwing his coat at him.

"I see how it is. You get to sleep in until noon and go out the front door, and I get treated like your dirty little secret." His tone was mock offended, but his features were pure amusement.

"That can't possibly feel like anything new to you," I said flatly, though the corner of my mouth threatened to turn upward.

"Just for that, I think I'll stay." Davin's eyes were still heavy with sleep as he gave me a half smirk.

His hand came up to run through his disheveled midnight hair, somehow made even more attractive by its disarray. I tracked the movement, following it down to the open laces on his wrinkled shirt and the taut muscles they revealed.

I hadn't realized I was staring until a deep, sleepy chuckle pulled my focus back up to his devilish smirk. Der'mo. No one should be this attractive so early in the morning.

Shaking the thought away, I grasped for a half-hearted threat.

"If you do, I'll tell your cook that you've suddenly become allergic to that crustacean soup you love so much. She'll never make it again."

His eyes went wide with mock horror. "You wouldn't dare."

"Do you really want to find out what I'm capable of?" I challenged.

Davin raised an eyebrow, mischief sparkling in his wicked gaze. "As a matter of fact—"

Heat ignited low in my abdomen, spreading like wildfire the longer I looked at that grin. Ocean eyes skated from mine down to my lips before slowly wandering even lower.

All at once I heard him telling me he only wanted to play the fun kind of games, which then brought forth the rest of last night's conversation.

"Out!" I hissed, shoving him through the open balcony door, not quite trusting myself to let him stay, even if Anna hadn't been right outside the door.

He left with a last, lingering chuckle.

With my next breath, I finally called for Anna to come in.

"Good mornin'," she said cheerfully, her curious gaze going directly from me to the disheveled bed.

Of course, the pillows were sunken in on both sides, but she didn't so much as make a tutting sound before gesturing for me to sit down.

Even if her smile did get a bit wider.

I dutifully sat at my vanity, letting her steady stream of conversation keep me from overthinking last night.

Which was good, since I still had no idea how to feel about anything Davin had said.

I wanted to say yes, unequivocally, but storms if I didn't

know what it felt like to be broken by him. This wasn't something I could just jump into on an hour's notice, and there was hardly time to think about it today.

As I sipped my coffee, I remembered Gwyn's warning. This festival was important to Davin. And whatever else may be true, Davin was important to me.

I resolved to set everything else aside, at least for today. After all, compartmentalizing was my specialty.

Excitement thrummed through Anna as she twisted my hair into ornate braids, the movements careful and practiced. She looped through small sprigs of the purple flowers I had seen growing on the hills around the castle. Heather, she had called them.

I hadn't been prepared for their woodsy scent. It reminded me of home and my father's *herbery* in a visceral way that made me homesick. Not that I wanted to be back in Socair.

But I missed him. Both of my parents, really.

Focusing on my rosemary charm, I remembered this was what he had wanted for me—a life away from Alexei and out from under my uncle's thumb.

That would have to be enough for now.

When I was finally ready, I stepped out into the hall where Davin was waiting. His expression was halfway between surprised and expectant as his gaze raked over me.

I was strikingly aware of the space between us, and each heartbeat as it pulsed loudly in my veins. It wasn't just his attention on me that had time standing still, it was also just...*him*.

Somehow, in the hour since I shoved him out onto the balcony, the man had completely transformed. I had seen him clean shaven with freshly pressed clothes and perfectly tousled hair before. He was always attractive.

But this was different.

His suit jacket was a deep shade of evergreen with golden striping, and a sprig of heather rested in his pocket. The jacket itself was cut a little tighter than his usual style, emphasizing his trim waist and broad chest.

Perhaps the best part of all, though…instead of trousers, he was wearing one of the skirts that some of the lairds here preferred. I hadn't thought they were attractive at all until this one. Perhaps it was the man in the skirt that made it attractive?

Until this very moment, I would never have dreamed that calves could be…appealing. But I had been wrong. So, so wrong.

The flames from earlier returned, and a wave of heat spread through me. I swallowed hard as Davin cleared his throat.

"Eyes up here, Lina," he said.

His voice was deeper than usual, which was not helping my current situation at all. Worse still, the cocky bastard was perfectly aware of his effect on me.

He shook his head, a smirk teasing the corner of his full lips. "It's called a kilt."

I raised my brows and nodded, keeping my features carefully neutral. "Mhmm."

"They're very manly," he added, a playful edge of defensiveness to his tone.

"I can see that," I said, nodding with mock seriousness.

"Well, if you're all done ogling me, we should probably get going," he said, offering me his arm.

I took it, suppressing a smirk of my own.

We met his family near the front doors where Jocelyn gave everyone a onceover and a speech about how important impressions were at the festival.

It wasn't hard to remember that we needed to put on a show. After weeks of doing just that, it was practically ingrained in us.

But after last night, it didn't feel like a show anymore.

It felt like a small taste of the life we could have.

It made sense now, why the Lochlannians chose this week to have their festival. The leaves were painted in vibrant hues, displaying an array of oranges and reds, yellows and purples, and everything in between.

Colorful lanterns hung from the trees, and pumpkins were artfully arranged along each street corner around the booths and games that spread throughout the entire village.

I suspected, though, that the soldiers lined around the village were new this year.

We hadn't heard a whisper about the rebels in weeks. But that didn't mean they weren't still lurking close by.

"There are so many people here," I commented as we passed a large crowd lined up around a stall selling hot cider and spiced pumpkin treats. "It's hard to believe there are any left for the festivals at the other estates."

Davin's brow furrowed, his head tilting slightly. "There's only one other festival, and it's up at Castle Chridhe."

I thought back to my conversation with his mother, rather certain I hadn't misunderstood her.

"None of the other lairds host them?" I clarified.

"No." He shook his head, leading me to the center of the village square. "Chridhe for the north, and it used to be Alech for the south, but Aunt Isla and Uncle Finn were happy to let us take over the social events since Lithlinglau is more centrally located down here."

I turned and caught sight of Jocelyn, smiling graciously at the villagers, not looking half as devious as I knew her to be.

It will be important to know, no matter which estate you wind up with.

Well played, Jocelyn.

After plying me with a delicious hot spiced wine called

hippocras and a caramel-covered apple that was decidedly less so, Davin looped my arm through his and pulled me toward a gathering crowd.

I had mostly seen the courtiers in opulent ballrooms, so I was surprised to see them mingling so casually with the villagers.

Even the ever-lofty Lady Fiona risked dirtying the hem of her ballgown as she wandered with the MacBays through the gaming fields and cramped streets.

Up ahead, Gallagher was already waiting for us, standing a casual distance away from Maisey and looking like he was debating the merits of just closing that gap and being done with the entire façade.

She didn't look like she was far from the same decision.

I could relate.

When we got closer and Gal turned to join us, I invited Maisey to come, too. At least they could have a relative degree of proximity if they were with us.

He shot me a grateful look, and the four of us made our way to the front of a growing crowd where there was a sparring ring of sorts. Instead of the traditional ring that we had back in Socair, this one had a single giant log raised up several feet off the ground between two posts.

Anxiety settled into my stomach as I considered his mother's words from earlier. That we all had to participate in an event. Storms help us all if this was mine.

"Did one of you sign up for this competition?" I asked, and they both laughed.

"No," Davin dragged out the word.

"Gwyn humiliates us in private with alarming regularity," Gal said. "No need to make it a public affair."

Maisey chuckled, and I couldn't help but join her as the woman in question appeared.

The crowd went wild, several of the surrounding onlookers calling out bets to a man with a discreet black book.

Even though I'd seen her reflexes firsthand, it was still hard to wrap my head around the idea that a woman could openly compete in something like that.

"Does she usually win?" I had to practically shout over the din of voices.

"Not usually," Davin said with a wide grin. "But she's hoping that changes today."

"We'll see," Gal smirked, mischief dancing in his eyes.

At first, I thought their laughter was because perhaps her prowess had been overstated, though that seemed unlikely when she could catch a dagger out of thin air.

Sure enough, she bested opponent after opponent with her carefully honed skill and lightning-fast movements. I noticed with no small amount of awe that she didn't even seem to tire. She might be frustratingly overconfident at times, but at least now I could understand why.

When there were no more contenders waiting in line to fight her, Gwyn's expression turned victorious. She raised her sword in the air, celebrating her win—a little too soon, it would seem.

The loud, windy groan of a bagpipe rang out, silencing the cheering crowd. Gwyn glanced around in confusion just as a new challenger emerged from the tent. Her mouth dropped open in indignation as the crowd let out a deafening roar.

Davin threw his head back in laughter, and Gallagher let out a piercing whistle of support as the man raised his arms, making everyone cheer even more. Gwyn shot her brother a look of betrayal before locking eyes with the man in front of her again.

It was clear who he was even before the announcer made a dramatic announcement about the reigning champion facing off against the captain of the guard.

Prince Finnian. The twins' father. What was it Gallagher had said?

No one can best her in a fight besides their father. That explained her reaction.

"When did he get here?" Davin asked.

"This morning," Gallagher called. "Mamá stayed home, but Da' wanted to *surprise* Gwyn."

With the vote coming up and the constant threat of rebel attacks lingering over us, I was sure there was more than one reason for the captain of the guard to be here. But, for now, Prince Finnian did seem to be relishing the standoff against his daughter.

Immediately, I could tell this fight was different. I knew little and less about sparring, but the crowd watched in a hush as he countered every move his daughter made.

"Is he—" I began.

"He's toying with her a bit, yes," Davin confirmed.

"Or more accurately," Gallagher chimed in, "letting her get a few hits in so she's not quite as furious when she loses."

Maisey and I exchanged a wary glance. Gwyn's fury wasn't something I ever wanted to witness. Judging by the look on her face, it wasn't something Maisey was ready to face, either.

She took a small, pointed step away from Gallagher, who only grinned and closed that distance again.

"He's that good?" I asked.

"He's the best," Davin said simply.

Sure enough, the prince let a few more moves go by before switching to the offensive, going on the attack. It was over in a matter of minutes, with Gwyn letting out an irritable string of curses as her sword clattered to the ground below.

"And that's our cue to leave," Davin said, pulling me urgently toward the back of the crowd. "She'll be impossible for the rest of the day."

"Won't she be more upset that you're ditching her?" Maisey asked.

"No." Gallagher shook his head. "She won't even notice.

She'll spend the next two hours making Da' break the fight down move by move while he buys her consolation snacks."

I smiled at that. It was rare I saw her without some sort of food in hand.

"Does this happen every festival?" I asked curiously.

Gallagher sighed. "It does, indeed. Four times a year, Gwyn publicly gets her arse handed to her, and she takes it with less and less grace each festival."

I shook my head.

With what I knew about the duchess, that sounded about right.

After the sparring event, Davin led me through the festival, telling occasional stories as he went. I would have known this was his favorite even if Gwyn hadn't told me, but I might not have understood the way his features went distant when he pointed out the corn maze or the haggis stand.

He pressed another mug of hippocras into my hands.

"More magic drink?" I hummed over the tankard, inhaling the intoxicating scent of cloves and cinnamon.

His eyes sparkled with mirth. "I thought you might like it."

And he was right. So far, he seemed to have made a game of discovering what I actually liked versus the things I merely tolerated. Because of this, I was currently stuffed, having tried nearly everything the festival had to offer.

Though, there would always be room for more hippocras.

"Careful, though. It goes to your head."

I thought he might be right about that.

Or perhaps the spinning sensation was about more than the drink.

A gust of cool air whipped through the street, sending a shiver down my spine and rooting me more in the moment. Though, I was thoroughly unrooted just as quickly when Davin stepped closer, his warm hands going up to my hood as he pulled it over my head.

He lingered there, his eyes locking on to mine. For a moment, he was the only person in the crowd, everyone else entirely forgotten.

I breathed him in, the faint scent of bourbon and spiced wine on his breath. He was right, the wine must have gone to my head, because, regardless of the people undoubtedly watching, I suddenly found myself wanting to close the distance between us. To see if he tasted even better with the remnant of hippocras on his lips.

"You looked cold," he explained as his hands returned to his sides.

I nodded, taking another long sip from my mug, not trusting myself to speak.

A deep chuckle rumbled up from his chest at whatever he saw in my expression, and I was powerless not to return his smile.

He stepped away then, pulling up his own hood as another gust of wind blew in from the west, bringing with it the faintest scent of wintergreen.

My smile abruptly fell from my face, and my stomach churned.

"Lina, Love?" Davin's tone was concerned, pulling me back to the moment. "Are you all right?"

Instinctively, I glanced around, my heartbeat thundering as I scanned the faces of the crowd.

My gaze flitted past a self-satisfied Lady Fiona before landing on Laird Gray and Lady Gracie playing a game of darts, and finally a rather confused-looking Lady Fenella as she tried and failed to figure out a blacksmith's toy that some of the children were showing her.

Finally, my eyes landed on the branches of a birch tree, rustling in the breeze just overhead. They were notorious for smelling like wintergreen.

Not Alexei. Just a tree.

I considered Davin's question.

Was I all right?

Davin's grip was light on my arm, a stark contrast to Alexei's bruising hold. Children were laughing at the games nearby. The hippocras was warm in my hands.

And I was safe.

I laced my fingers in Davin's, pulling myself closer to his side before nodding.

"Yes," I answered him.

Alexei had haunted enough of my past. He didn't get to have this day, too.

FORTY-TWO
Davin

A PART of me had been dreading this day. Between concerns about another attack and having to face the festival without Mac or Row, it had lost the appeal it used to hold.

I was surprised by how quickly I lost myself in the distraction of leading Galina through the stalls and introducing her to every food and drink the festival had to offer. It had taken me all the weeks she had been here, but I finally figured out she didn't like things that were overly sweet or rich, and she was much more susceptible to delicious beverages than she was food.

The more she smiled and clung to my arm like she wanted to instead of just for show, the less acutely I felt the loss of the best friends who weren't here with me.

"It's almost time for our event," I said, leading her to the edge of the village.

Her hands froze with her mug of hippocras halfway to her wine-stained lips.

"I thought you were joking about that," she said, her eyes wide as she scanned the field.

"Nope. Mamá makes sure that every member of the family

joins every year. Says it's good for our image and public relations." I said the last part in my mother's brusque voice, and Galina snickered. "She's over there, throwing darts with my father."

Lina nodded warily, her icicle eyes scanning the gaming booths. Unmitigated horror seeping into her expression as she took in the potato sack races and the caber toss.

"You're not going to make me do anything embarrassing, are you?" she asked, suspicion lining her tone.

I shook my head, wrapping an arm around her back to lead her over to our game. It felt right, having her tucked against me.

"Of course not," I assured her, and her shoulders relaxed slightly. I pointed to a long lane with nine pins set up at the end, picking up a heavy wooden ball to show her. "This is *Skittles*. It reminded me a bit of *Gorodki—*"

A laugh escaped her, the sound almost lyrical. "So, it was yourself you were trying to embarrass, then?"

I rolled my eyes, thinking back to the times we had played the game in Socair and how very few wins I had sustained. My losses had begun unintentionally, but the longer we played, the more I just liked to see her having to bite back a laugh in front of all the courtiers.

"Something like that," I said, handing her the ball. "Besides, I may not be as competitive as Gwyn is, but that doesn't mean I don't want to play to our strengths. We'll ease you into the other ones," I added, watching her expression.

Sure enough, a dusty pink blush rose to her tan cheeks, her gaze turning thoughtful.

She didn't hate the idea of being here with me next year. That much was certain.

When the gamemaster announced that it was our turn, she stepped up to the lane, watching the team next to us and studying the technique they used before taking her place. She lined up just so before rolling her ball toward the pins, knocking over four on her first try.

Then it was my turn, whereupon I only took down one pin on the very end. Which, of course, made her laugh again.

"Which games do you usually play?" she asked, lining up for her next turn. "Perhaps we should play to your strengths instead."

A visceral memory washed over me.

Rowan, Mac, and me, sprawled out in the mud. Rope burns on our hands from where we tried and failed to beat the twins and Avani in a game of tug of war.

Gwyn raising her arms and shouting victoriously.

Avani's laughter ringing out freely as Mac pulled her into the mud next to him, smearing it on her face before he kissed her.

Rowan pretending to gag at the sight of their affection. Gallagher and I slinging mud at his sister.

Everyone happy and alive and here...

Galina's fingers laced through mine, her delicate touch pulling me from the memory. I shook my head as she searched my eyes. For the first time in a long time, thinking of those days didn't hurt quite as much.

"A little bit of everything, really," I told her truthfully.

She accepted my answer with a hesitant nod before launching her next ball down the lane and knocking down the rest of the pins. The grin she shot my way was mischievous and wider than usual. I suspected she knew where my mind had gone.

We played two more rounds before our team was announced as the winner. The gamemaster handed her a small pin engraved with the date as a trophy. She held it up proudly, her expression adorably smug.

"Only the best for the future Lady of Lithlinglau," I said.

She shook her head but didn't argue.

Even though we were the only ones close enough to hear.

LINA HAD FUN TODAY, if the glow in her cheeks and her easy smile had been any indication.

But none of that compared to how she looked now.

She was dancing with Gwyn and Maisey, her hair coming loose from her braids and cascading over her face as she spun in time with the music.

And she was laughing.

I couldn't look away from her bright eyes and her head thrown back, face to the autumn sky. The others were keeping up well enough, but Lina was grace in motion. She was the most captivating thing I had ever seen.

As the music went on, so did she.

The others kept up for as long as they could, dancing until their feet gave out and they fell into a pile of laughter and exhaustion. And all the while, Lina kept going, taking this dance that my people practiced all their lives and turning it into a work of art.

The crowd was nearly as enthralled as I was, cheering her on until she and Gwyn were the last two dancers on the floor, easily keeping up with the fiddler.

When the music finally ended, a round of applause went out, and both the ladies and the villagers who had participated in the dance rushed to congratulate them.

"It would seem that your little plan here is working," a drawling voice sounded beside me, making my skin crawl.

"Tavish," I greeted, without looking away from Galina. "I'm not sure what *plan* you're referring to, but yes, it does seem to be working, doesn't it?"

"It's a shame it won't last," he said.

I narrowed my eyes, wondering where he was going with this.

"I heard she isn't long for this kingdom. Her uncle is planning to drag her back, isn't he? In fact, I heard that she was never really yours to begin with."

"Galina isn't going anywhere," I said darkly.

Something sinister danced in his eyes as he looked from me and back to Galina, her cheeks flushed and her skin shining with a thin sheen of sweat.

His tone morphed into something seedier. "I think I'll offer to escort her back myself. I'm sure we could use the time in the carriage to—"

In a single swift move, my sword was out of its sheath and at his throat.

"Let me make something very clear," I gritted out, distantly aware that the crowd around us had fallen silent. "You will not touch Galina. No one will touch Galina without her express permission, and if a single hair on her perfect head is harmed, I will make it my personal mission to ensure that person no longer has the necessary appendages to touch anything ever again."

I pressed the blade further into his skin until a thin red line appeared.

"You might think that *The Viper* is everywhere, but let me assure you, so am I." I still wasn't sure if The Viper was Tavish, or merely someone he worked with.

But I was absolutely sure that I was finished letting people threaten Galina, regardless of who we were to each other.

The blood drained from Tavish's face. When he spoke, I realized it wasn't merely my threat that had him scared.

"What do you know about The Viper?" he breathed.

"I know enough," I lied.

Tavish huffed out a humorless laugh, his dark eyes flitting nervously around the crowd.

"No, you don't," he hissed in an undertone. "If you did,

you would know enough to be a hell of a lot more afraid than you are."

I opened my mouth to question him further, but a delicate hand on my arm alerted me to Galina's presence at my side. She positioned herself so that I could see her face, her eyes pleading with me to stop.

Several heartbeats passed before I lowered my sword.

There was no more music or dancing. No more games happening around us. All eyes were on the three of us, and I wondered if I had just ruined everything, rising to the bait he had so carefully laid out in front of me.

Gwyn was next to us then, along with Gal and Uncle Finn. The latter stepped between myself and my least favorite pseudo-relative, putting a hand on each of our shoulders.

"The sparring contest was hours ago, My Lairds, and I'm afraid I've already won. Best save this for next time then?" His tone was no-nonsense, every inch the captain of the guard in this moment.

"Of course, Uncle. Just a bit of fun," I said, sheathing my sword.

Tavish raised his eyebrows.

"Well, I'm not sure I'm as much fun as the youth these days," he said, getting his dig in for the sake of our onlookers. "But understandable, all the same."

Lina trailed her fingers down my arm until she could curl them around mine, which was just as well since it kept me from punching him in the face.

"Well, we'll have a different sort of fun, now. My Laird has promised me the next dance, after all. Unless you've changed your mind," she added with a coy smile.

"I would never miss a chance to dance with you," I said, bringing our entwined fingers to my lips.

Still, it took everything I had to turn my back on Tavish, leading Lina away to the floor.

All the way there, I felt eyes on me, like a phantom dagger between my shoulder blades. I couldn't shake the feeling that I was missing something important.

Something that might cost me more than this vote.

FORTY-THREE

Galina

My mind spun the entire walk back to the estate.

The festival had been a dizzying combination of highs and lows, but mostly the former. After Davin's altercation with Tavish, we had lost ourselves in dancing until the shadows faded from his eyes.

His cousins had joined us out on the floor, and eventually, the villagers, too, seemed to forget all about the thirty-second incident. Davin was still a bit more subdued than usual, but he eventually managed to enjoy himself again.

And now we were walking back, arm in arm, while I faced the prospect of the decision I had put off all day.

I imagined the life he was offering me. Waking up in his arms each morning. Juggling court politics with him during the day. Falling asleep next to him each night.

Davin stopped outside my door, leaning in to kiss me on the forehead.

"I'll see you later?" he murmured quietly.

Yes, I wanted to say. *And every night after that.*

But I hadn't been given the luxury of feelings for most of my life, nor choice, and I found that I was unaccustomed to dealing with either. Indecision warred within me, the hope I wanted to give in to facing off against the memories of how Davin had systematically dismantled my defenses until I was left with none to deal with the crushing, encompassing devastation that overtook me when Aino came to my rooms.

I wanted to trust him now. I *did* trust him now. But I wasn't sure I trusted myself with that feeling.

"I'm…not sure," I said.

He examined my features before nodding. "All right."

And I could see that it was. That though he was disappointed, he would never be angry with me for changing my mind, for telling him no.

Take all the time you need, he had said.

As Anna helped me undress, I forced myself to take deep breaths, sorting through everything I knew.

Davin was not the same person he had been then, and neither was I. For the first time since I saw him at the Obsidian Palace, I allowed myself to leave the past behind, shutting it firmly away where it belonged.

What did I know about who Davin was *now*?

He had threatened someone tonight, for me. Not for his pride or any sense of ownership or duty. Just because he cared. About me.

He had confided in me when he didn't have to.

He had lain in my bed and chased away the nightmares and expected nothing of me in return.

Then there was the matter of his unflinching loyalty to the people he loved.

Some things hadn't changed since my original perception of him. He had always been charming and witty and gorgeous. And yes, he was still cocky and downright spoiled, when he wanted to be.

But I loved those things about him, too.

Slowly, I pulled on my robe and my slippers. This time, when I headed to Davin's rooms, it didn't feel reckless or impulsive.

It felt right. A carefully reasoned decision wherein I weighed the risks of taking a chance on him against the reality of letting him go, and knew the latter was never really an option at all.

He was in the massive wing-backed chair again, his obsidian locks still wet from the bath and falling artfully across his forehead.

I didn't knock this time before I eased open his balcony door. He glanced over at me, his expression guarded.

"You were right, too," I said as soon as I closed the door.

"About what?" His voice was rougher than usual, not quite as teasing, as he took me in.

"All of it," I admitted, shrugging one shoulder. "I should have stayed to hear you out. I didn't know what I wanted, and I was utterly unprepared for what I was getting into when I showed up at your door that night. It was the first time in my life I didn't bother to think something through."

"You said you wanted to take it for yourself," he reminded me quietly.

I had said that, but had it been entirely true?

"Not it," I corrected. "*You*. I had never wanted to choose anything for myself the way I wanted to choose you, but it still felt like it was impossible when it meant betraying my entire family in the process. I thought... I don't know what I thought. That we could have that night for ourselves and walk away from it?"

It sounded ridiculous now.

"Is that why you left so quickly the next morning?" He asked like he already knew the answer, but I expounded anyway.

"I was trying to get perspective. I didn't know... I thought maybe...it was always like that." A flush rose to my cheeks as I tried, badly, to explain that I hadn't understood the way that night would change everything.

Davin's eyes darkened, tugging at something low in my abdomen. "It isn't."

"I know that now." My voice was barely above a whisper.

And I did know.

Whatever magic had been there with Davin had been entirely absent in the single night I spent in a man's company after that, but hearing him confirm that it was the same for him was like having a bandage put on a wound I didn't know was still bleeding.

"And honestly," I went on, "I wasn't sure what you wanted. I'm not the only one with a...resting Socairan face. But it was never just a bit of fun for me."

A ghost of a smirk crossed Davin's mouth before he was serious once more.

"We made a mess of things," he said.

"We did," I agreed. "And we've run in circles ever since. But I don't want to keep living in those mistakes."

I stepped closer to him until I was standing between his knees.

He looked up at me, his cerulean gaze equal parts wariness and hope. "You'll stay?"

I didn't know if he meant tonight or forever, but my answer was the same. "I'll stay."

FORTY-FOUR
Davin

I'll stay.

Galina's hands came to tentatively rest on my shoulders, her face leaning down until she was so close, I could feel her breath on my lips.

I was terrified to move, to break whatever spell we were under.

It seemed impossible that after everything, she was here, telling me she would put the past behind us, but I damned sure wasn't going to waste it.

So I placed my hands gently on her waist, pulling her closer to me until her lips met mine. When I kissed her on the rooftop, it had been impulsive, driven by need and want and jealousy.

This was nothing like that.

This kiss was slow and exploratory, like we had all the time in the world. Her lips were soft and warm, and she tasted like...everything.

She tasted like home.

She sighed against my mouth, pressing herself in closer, and the sound tugged at every part of me. However I had survived eighteen long months without her, I knew I never wanted to do it again.

"I missed you," I murmured against her lips. "Every single day after I left," I added, skating my mouth across her jaw.

She tilted her head back, giving me access to her neck, and I promptly took advantage of it, kissing every bit of exposed skin I could find. *Stars*, I had missed the way she tasted, the way her soft skin felt against my lips.

"I missed you, too," she said breathlessly, her fingernails dragging lightly against my scalp. "*Storms*, I missed your stupid, arrogant face."

"What else did you miss?" I teased, smiling against her collarbone.

She leaned in, balancing her knees on either side of mine.

"Not your incessant need for praise, that's for sure," she joked.

I hummed against her skin, dragging my mouth back up to her jaw.

"Nothing else comes to mind?" I froze, the threat of stopping clear.

"You're. Insufferable." Her insult didn't land as hard when she could barely get the words out.

"That's not an answer, Love," I taunted.

Her breath hitched at the endearment, her eyes going wider than before as she settled into my lap a little further.

"Fine," she breathed. "I missed your lips. Are you happy?"

"Very," I assured her, continuing my ministrations. "I missed your lips, too. And the rest of you. I did not, however, miss this robe."

I tugged at the belt of her thick velvet monstrosity, untying it.

"No, no," she teased. "You love this robe. You insisted I wear it just yesterday."

She didn't make a move to stop my hand, though. If anything, she arched closer against me.

I deftly untied it with one hand while I ran the other up and down the lapel, slowly, my knuckles grazing her skin. "Do you want to keep it on?"

She sucked in a breath.

"No," she admitted, tilting back until the robe fell to the floor.

She was in another of those maddening silk nightgowns, one that left very little to the imagination.

She paused, then, looking down at me with her lips swollen and her pale eyes blazing like the hottest part of the fire.

"I don't want to have to miss you again," she said, her tone more serious.

I moved aside her hair to press a kiss to her shoulder.

"You won't," I said. "You're stuck with me now."

"Good. I can live with that," she responded, leaning back into me.

Gently, I reached up to pull the ribbon from her braid, letting it flutter to the floor by her robe. Then I ran my fingers through her hair like I had wanted to do every moment since she came to my door in Socair, until it fell in golden waves around her face.

My heartbeat stuttered in my chest at the sight of her, cheeks flushed, hair undone, and firelight playing along her skin.

I pulled her in for another kiss, one arm wrapped around her waist, the other tangled in her silky strands. She made a small noise, and I tugged at her hair until she angled her head, giving me the vantage point I needed to kiss my way down the side of her neck.

"Perfect," I murmured the word against her skin. "And mine."

"What?" she choked out.

"The first two words I would use to describe you."

She went still, and I prepared myself for her to pull away

again. Then she melted into me, her fingers digging into my biceps, her lips pressing against mine with a renewed fervor.

"Yes," she said in between kisses. "Yours. Only yours. Always yours."

She said it like a promise, like the vow she had all but agreed to make with me one day.

And it was a promise I had every intention of holding her to.

FORTY-FIVE
Galina

When I woke up tangled with Davin for the third morning in a row, I quickly decided that it was my favorite place in the world to be.

Perfect, he had said. *Mine*.

I had expected to balk at the word, but it sounded entirely different on the lips of someone I trusted.

His.

It felt right. It felt like everything.

I tilted my head up to examine the man in question. His eyes were still closed, dark lashes kissing his cheeks as his breaths came slow and even. He was sleeping on his stomach, one arm slung around me and the other tucked under his pillow.

I reached up to trace the lines of the tattoo that spanned from one muscled shoulder to the other. I had only seen glimpses of it our first night together, and my memory hadn't remotely done it justice.

On the surface, it was a black dragon with its wings spread wide. It made sense now, that he would have chosen something to represent the family name that meant more to him than it would to a person who hadn't had to fight for their right to bear it.

On closer inspection, though, there were thousands of intricate arcs and whorls that made up the shape, forming smaller images within the large one. He had explained some of them. Roses for his mother, a wicked-looking sword for Gwyn, a flame for Mac, all deftly woven into the serpentine scales.

It made sense. Davin protected what was his.

His. I savored the word once again.

My fingers traced the lines of his ink, my lips chasing the motion.

Something pulled low in my stomach, unfurling like tendrils of smoke and warming every part of me. Suddenly, I wasn't close enough to him. I needed to feel his skin against mine, against every part of me.

But when he started to stir, I realized there were pressing needs to attend to.

I needed a lavatory, and I needed desperately to freshen up.

Carefully, I slid out from under his arm and out of the warm bed, already regretting the necessity. For a moment, I watched his sleeping form, hoping I had time to slip right back where I had been before he woke up.

After retrieving my robe from where it was still pooled on the floor by the chair and securing it around my waist, I crept quietly out onto the balcony. The crisp autumn air washed over me, several degrees cooler than it had been at the festival.

I practically sprinted up the stairs and across the roof to my balcony, shivering and grinning like a fool the entire way, already thinking about exactly how I would spend my morning with Davin.

Perhaps that was why it took me longer than it should have to notice that something was wrong.

I was already halfway across my room with the door shut behind me when I froze in my tracks.

Wintergreen.

The smell assaulted me, violently bursting the bubble of peace I had been stupid enough to let myself fall into. A shadow cast over me from behind, blocking the gentle rays of light from the window.

Before I could turn around, before I could run, one massive hand came over my mouth while the other tugged me backward until I hit a solid chest. I sucked in a breath, choking on the familiar, pervasive smell.

The worst part was that the feeling coursing through my veins like poison wasn't shock. It was resignation.

Hadn't I always known that Alexei would come for me?

His breath was hot on my cheek, his voice a low growl in my ear as he pulled me against his body, tight enough that I struggled for air. It was almost a relief when I couldn't smell the wintergreen anymore.

"You've had your fun, *Radnaya.* It's time to come home."

FORTY-SIX

Davin

It was freezing.

I groaned and stretched, abruptly realizing how alone I was in my bed. My very soft, very warm companion was noticeably absent. Which was rather unfortunate considering the dream I had just woken up from.

Propping myself up on my elbows with a grin, I scanned the rest of the room for Galina, but she wasn't there.

I climbed out of bed, throwing a robe over myself. The doors to the lavatory were open, and she wasn't inside.

"Lina?" I called, checking the study and the balcony next.

Both were empty.

An uneasy feeling crept up in my chest. I knew it was ridiculous. She wouldn't have left after last night. I hadn't asked her what plans she had today.

She had probably just gone down to breakfast, or to subtly throw our very real relationship in Fiona's face at tea.

Surely.

I pulled open my door to ask my guards if they knew where she was, stopping short when I saw Ewan standing sentry outside of her rooms.

It should have been a relief, but my stomach twisted.

"Has Lady Galina come out this morning?" I asked as casually as I could.

He furrowed his brow. "No, mi'laird. I thought..."

"Yes?"

"I thought she was in your rooms, to be frank," he said slowly.

That was fair, all things considered.

"Not at the moment." I tried for a smirk, but I was sure it fell flat.

Crossing the small distance, I raised a hand to knock at her door.

There was no answer.

"Lina?" I called.

Still nothing.

The unease morphed into something closer to panic. Even when she hated me, she had always answered the door.

I tried the handle, and it moved easily, the door opening with a deceptively quiet click. Something in my expression must have betrayed my concern because Ewan stood a little straighter, his hand going to the hilt of his sword.

There was no need for his diligence, though.

This room, too, was empty.

My heartbeat thundered in my ears. I called for her again, though my voice was more alarmed this time. Frantic footsteps led me from her closet to her attached bath before I circled back to the main room.

That's when I saw it.

A prism of crimson light danced on the marble surface of the vanity, reflected from the deep red ruby of the ring I had taken far too long to pick out.

And underneath the ring, a single sheet of parchment.

I ripped the letter from the vanity, my eyes skimming along the slanted cursive.

"Mi'laird," Ewan spoke up cautiously.

"Hang on," I muttered, trying and failing to comprehend the words in front of me.

They couldn't mean what I thought they did.

"Davin." This was a different voice, unexpected enough that I spun around.

Uncle Finn stood in the doorway, his expression uncharacteristically grim. The blood drained from my face.

Did he know something about Galina?

"The magistrate is here," he said solemnly. "He needs to ask you some questions. I need you to come downstairs with me."

I swallowed back the lump in my throat. "About Galina?"

He narrowed his eyes. "No. About Tavish."

"Then it can wait," I said, already turning back around.

"No," he corrected gently. "It can't. Tavish is dead."

Epilogue

GALINA

IT WAS dark inside the carriage.

Early morning rays of sunlight had barely even begun to stretch out along the horizon. I wondered if Davin was still sleeping. Peacefully unaware of all that awaited him when he woke up.

Of all that didn't.

My stomach twisted, and I fought another wave of nausea. Whether it was from the whiplash of going from Davin's gentle caresses to Alexei's bruising grip, or the reality of what came next, I couldn't be sure.

All of it felt like a nightmare.

Alexei adjusted his grip again, settling my hand in his lap to study the half moons he had carved with his fingernails. His thumb slid from my wrist to the bracelet and down to the charm he'd given me.

The one I wanted him to choke on.

He traced the delicate carvings of the wolf's head, his furious breaths turning to something a little steadier.

"You didn't take it off," he said, his dark eyes scanning me. "You always knew you would come back to me."

I swallowed and answered with a single shake of my head.

His touch was softer then, almost reverent. I preferred the pain.

"I missed you, *Radnaya*. We can put this behind us," he said, lacing his fingers through mine.

When I didn't respond, he squeezed until one of my bones popped. It was an effort not to wince, to show how much it hurt, but somehow, I kept my features neutral and nodded.

"Thank you, My Lord."

He was right. On some level, I had always known this would happen. Somewhere deep, deep down, I knew that things with Davin were too good to be true. That Alexei would eventually come for me. Maybe that was why I wasn't surprised to be here now.

I wanted to scream.

Instead, I focused on the cold, hard lines of the mountains, and the oppressive heat emanating from Alexei's body next to mine. Anything to distract me from Davin's soft, full lips or the way my body melded perfectly into his. Or the promises we made to each other in the dark and how I almost let myself believe that we could mean them this time.

But that was just a dream. A beautifully painful dream. And now I was headed back to the life I was always meant to have.

A perfect, dutiful Socairan Clan Wife.

PRONUNCIATION GUIDE

Davin	DAV-in (short a)
Galina	Gal-EE-nuh
Lochlann	LOCK-lan
Socair	so-CARE
Alech	ah-LEK
Chridhe	CREE-uh
Lithlinglau	LITH-lun-glow
Hagail	ha-GAYL
Masach	ma-SAUK
Mikhail	mi-KYLE
Alexei	a-LEX-ee
Isla	EYE-la
Aino	EYE-no
Avani	a-VAHN-ee

GLOSSARY

Laskipaa	Idiot
Svolach	Bastard
Svolochi	Bastards
Der'mo	Crap
Aalio	Arseling
Maliskha	Baby Girl
Radnaya	My Dear
Eejit	Idiot
Besklanovvy	Unclanned

A Message From Us

We need your help!

Did you know that authors, in particular indie authors like us, make their living on reviews? If you enjoyed this book, please take a moment to let people know on all of the major review platforms like; Amazon, Goodreads, and/or Bookbub!

(Social Media gushing is also highly encouraged!)

Remember, reviews don't have to be long. It can be as simple as whatever star rating you feel comfortable with and an: 'I loved it!' or: 'Not my cup of tea...'

Now that that's out of the way, if you want to come shenanigate with us, rant and rave about these books and others, get access to awesome giveaways, exclusive content and some pretty ridiculous live videos, come join us on Facebook at our group, Drifters and Wanderers

ElPin's Acknowledgments

As always, there are too many people to thank, and too little time to do it in.

This book was yet another labor of love, pain, sweat and major hair loss, as we wrangled it from one version to the next, to the next. After three complete rewrites, untold amounts of edits, and fighting with Davin and Galina to be the people we knew they could be, we finally have a story that we can be proud of.

We hope you all feel the same way <3

So first of all, a special thank you to Nighthawk Black wines, and Thomas S. Moore for creating the best whiskey that helped soothe our fragile author egos on nights where the words weren't coming.

We also would never have gotten to this point without our Beta Babes, our constant rocks and mini-support group. You read and reread every single terrible version of this story and you deserve an award for that.

Thank you for continuing to give DavLina a chance, even long after you hated them and this story as much as we did.

Thank you for your care-packages and words of support and the feedback we needed to make this a story we could all love again. We love you ladies more than we can ever express!

Thank you to our Alpha readers as well! Michelle, Lissa, Elyse! You ladies seriously rock!!!

To our editor and friend and superhero; Jamie, for being

constantly supportive and flexible. We don't deserve you, or your unending patience, but we are willing to literally give up our organs or firstborn children to keep you. Love you, Jamiekins.

Jesikah Sundin and Heather Renee, you are some of the best author besties that two scatter-brained co-authors could ask for. Thank you for reading and helping us refine this story, and for your constant support and cheerleading. We love you <3

A huge thank you to our Street Team and our reader group: Drifters and Wanderers. We seriously have the best readers out there. You are all so amazing and your unending patience over pushed deadlines and excitement over our projects is the fuel that keeps us going. <3

Emily, what is there but to say thank you and we love you!? We're so grateful we can call you a part of our team. Thank you for putting up with us and helping us manage our lives, books, and sanity. <3

And finally, the biggest and most important thank you goes to our families. In particular, our husbands who by some miracle haven't left us yet, despite our crazy, obsessive personalities, long hours of working on books that sometimes make us want to pull our hair out, and moderately insane bouts of talking to ourselves while we work out character dialogue. And for taking care of our beautiful children while we take on more projects than we have time or space or sanity for.

We love you, yes, both of you (don't make it weird) more than all the words in all the books in all the world.

About The Authors

Elle and Robin can usually be found on road trips around the US haunting taco-festivals and taking selfies with unsuspecting Spice Girls impersonators.

They have a combined PH.D in Faery Folklore and keep a romance advice column under a British pen-name for raccoons. They have a rare blood type made up solely of red wine and can only write books while under the influence of the full moon.

Between the two of them they've created a small army of insatiable humans and when not wrangling them into their cages, they can be seen dancing jigs and sacrificing brownie batter to the pits of their stomachs.

And somewhere between their busy schedules, they still find time to create words and put them into books.

Also By Elle & Robin

The Lochlann Treaty Series:

Winter's Captive

Spring's Rising

Summer's Rebellion

Autumn's Reign

The Lochlann Feuds Series:

Scarlet Princess

Tarnished Crown

Crimson Kingdom

Obsidian Throne

Twisted Pages Series:

Of Thorns and Beauty

Of Beasts and Vengeance

Of Glass and Ashes

Of Thieves and Shadows

Coming June 2023:

Of Songs and Silence

The World Apart Series By Robin D. Mahle:

The Fractured Empire

The Tempest Sea

The Forgotten World

The Ever Falls

Unfabled Series:

Promises and Pixie Dust